Brett Ashley Kaplan'ₛ
intertwines whale and human
highlights the need to prote
planet. Her support of whale conservation with the
proceeds of her novel will ensure the story of whales
and our shared ecosystem does not end with her book.

Regina Asmutis-Silvia,

Executive Director, Whale and Dolphin Conservation

In this richly imagined novel, Brett Ashley
Kaplan skillfully and playfully moves between points
of view, incorporating journal entries, novel excerpts,
book reviews, and nuanced environmental commentary.
Following a vivid cast of characters which includes a
young photographer documenting interracial couples,
a Guadeloupean Jewish Melville scholar, a disappeared
amateur cetologist and even Yiddish speaking whales,
this inventive novel takes us on a wild adventure from
the urban streets of New York's East Village to the
depths of the sea. Tender, confident and bold, Rare stuff
brims with vitality.

Ayelet Tsabari, author of The Art of Leaving

Rare Stuff is a beautiful, bewitching novel built on interlocking stories: a cosmopolitan photographer named Sid, grieving the death of her father, finds an unfinished manuscript and a suitcase full of clues about the long-ago disappearance of her mother. We follow Sid on a breathless search for her mother, and we dive deep into her father's unfinished adventure tale, in which Yiddish-speaking whales and a bold teenage girl set out to save the world. By the book's close, I had become friends with its characters: I wanted to jump into fast-paced conversations about life and literature with Sid, Andre, Dorothy, Aaron, and Sol, and I wanted to take part in the extraordinary multi-generational (and multi-species) community they built together. *Rare Stuff* tells the story of the very best adventure: the quest we all undertake to understand and care for our parents, our children, and the world we share together.

Jamie L. Jones, author of *Rendered Obsolete: The Afterlife of U.S. Whaling in the Petroleum Age*

Rare Stuff is a love song for being on a planet mired in senseless suffering—for maintaining the thread of humanity by weaving epiphany. The writing sings, like whale songs—haunting, lyric, crisp and taut—stretched across the page in perfect pitch. A complex space of resonant correspondences. Famished archivist, tender scholar, the Eye hears abiding fascination with history's ghosts, familial and expansive, ecological and ontological. Readers become detectives on the literary hunt for buried terma treasure in *Moby Dick*—entangled in cruel depictions, killings of sentient beings—yet engaged in history-mystery. What are we as humans seeking here? What do we find in the ocean depths of consciousness? What buried wreck, what scintillating treasure.

Heather Woods, author of *Bundling*

With inherited clues stuffed in an old suitcase, Brett Ashley Kaplan takes the readers into a painfully joyful journey of racism, survival, loss and love. Skillfully and with much sensitivity, *Rare Stuff* connects bloody history to the most burning issues of our times. The biggest achievement of this novel, with the help of Yiddish-speaking whales, is that it "gives history an optimistic twist." A hopeful twist much needed these days!

Sayed Kashua, author of *Track Changes, Second Person Singular, Let it Be Morning,* and *Dancing Arabs*

Rare Stuff
Brett Ashley Kaplan

Spuyten Duyvil
New York City

Library of Congress Cataloging-in-Publication Data

Names: Kaplan, Brett Ashley, author.
Title: Rare stuff / Brett Ashley Kaplan.
Description: New York City : Spuyten Duyvil, [2022]
Identifiers: LCCN 2022015305 | ISBN 9781956005578 (paperback)
Subjects: LCSH: Whales--Fiction. | LCGFT: Novels.
Classification: LCC PS3611.A6474 R37 2022 | DDC 813/.6--dc23/eng/20220401
LC record available at https://lccn.loc.gov/2022015305

For Ralph J. Kaplan
In memoriam

.

I
SID

Call me Sid. Under a slick oyster sky, faintly nauseated, knees woozy, I gaze into the mucky water. My mind's eye cradles a vivid sunny day, a splintery rowboat in this placid, lightly lapping water—I was ten, my father rowed deftly around the edge of the great lake with surprising grace and power, and I leaned back, letting the sun flood into my closed eyes until stars bloomed under my lids. I soaked up the bright green leaves from the thickset trees behind the beach, planting them under my eyelids; my father was miles away, muttering under his breath as he rowed, carrying on a fictional conversation from one of his novels. Some fifteen years later, on this bleak day the spindly trees cower behind the beach, farther from the water than I remembered, shrunken versions of their former selves; it's November in Chicago. A threat of snow hovers in the white sky but fails to come. I hold my father's ashes close to my chest. Before I picked them up from Spitzer & Cohen Funeral Home, I had imagined that the box would somehow be light, it's ash after all. But the simple black plastic container weighs a ton.

On the way to the water's edge, I passed boats parked on the side like beached whales with the inscription "Environmental Police." I wasn't at all sure what the environmental police would say about what I was about to do. I read the Kaddish, falteringly wrestling with the words from the small booklet provided by the funeral home. Yitgaddal veyitqaddash shmeh rabba....it's so familiar, from temple. I'm relieved no one else witnesses my execrable Hebrew accent, whatever tune I manage to sing is the wrong one. Slowly, my stomach still churning, I set the box down, peel off the wrapping, crumble the label, my father's name becomes a small fisted scrap, Aaron Zimmerman 1922-1995. I open the lid, stretch out my fingers inside. The ash, his ashes, feel strangely soft, like powdered sugar, and I resist the urge to both taste and inhale them, him. I gather ashes and place them gently, handful by handful, on the surface of the water where they meld at a snail's pace into the lichen and schmutz, watching for what seems like time without end as Lake Michigan absorbs my father, the ashes from the fire that he had chosen for his end, liquefying.

A papier maché doll with nothing but air inside, I walk sluggishly from the lake, still carrying the ash-box limply, through the tunnel with dripping off-white walls coated in colorful graffiti, back to the apartment on Aldine where I'd lived with him until graduating from college. I stare at all his endless crap. It's up to me alone to sort his stuff, clean out the apartment, and decide what to do next; dealing with all that, I yearn, for the millionth time, for a sister. And André, why the fuck had I not asked him to come? All my father's dreck, the overwhelm, threatens to bury mourning. The apartment feels so empty and yet full of imaginary humans. Pages and pages of manuscripts, some the earlier versions of his novels, subsequently published, others rough drafts that never got off the ground press in on me. I flash to an interior shot of the scores of black and white photographs of black and white faces crowding the walls of my small New York apartment. We each—dad and

I—surround ourselves with the stuff we make—a crowd forms, paper or image. We shrink, shrank.

When the emergency room doctor called, shock sprinkled down my spine, salt to wound. I plunked onto the red sofa, the corkscrew cord of the black phone curled around my ankle, a slight clovey musk rose from the worn velvet cushions, and the fuchsia light from the factory across the river turned my living room hazily, lazily neon. I picked up a glass of water, took a big gulp. But the water went down like sand. How can this be my reality? Why? This can't be happening! Maybe it's not my father, I thought, who's lying without breath alone on a small, narrow bed in an emergency room, nearly a thousand miles away, maybe they made a mistake?

In the messy apartment on Aldine, by the time I get to the bottom of the closet in my father's bedroom, I'm exhausted, in desperate need of a warm bath and a deep glass of red wine, and worn thin; like his stressed, threadbare sheets I toss in the rubbish bin. At the very back of the closet a huge suitcase sits like an overstuffed ostrich—bigger than normal as though an *Alice in Wonderland* sizing button were placed where the light pull might have been. It's the suitcase dad always used when he wanted to hide/show something to my mother. I yank on the sturdy handle on top and, with some elbow grease, pull it out. It lands with a leviathan thud as it and I tumble into the middle of the room. Each of the brass locks issues a satisfying click. I open them, an old sickly smell accosts me.

A red left high heeled shoe, only slightly worn, but beautifully, delicately wrought, stands in the case as if its wearer had only just stepped out. It stands alone amid a jumble of other stuff. Stamped on the bottom of the red shoe: 'Made in New York by Paolo Gemina,' a dark imprinted brown that you can feel as you trace the words. Size 38, left. Where was the right? Why was there only one? I get an eerie feeling from the shoe, the smell of leather too fresh for its age. I think it's trembling and then I realize that's my overheated pulse.

A photograph of a man in a fedora, sitting on a park bench, smiling broadly up at the photographer; even though he's not in military uniform a barely visible insignia of a parachute gently encircled in wings appears on his lapel. He looks familiar to me, but I can't place him; the photo is black and white, the paper heavy, but it isn't one that I printed—it's not grainy enough and taken from further away. But where had I seen him? What are all these things?

A small sculpture of a woman, reclining, on her side. She's made of bronze? or some other metal now covered in a fine, slightly speckled patina. I pick her up and her heft, like the ashes, feels heavier than I'd expected. I trace her curves, beautiful, she must have been, whoever she was. She's warm, too, as if the metal had so quickly absorbed my heat. I feel that I've also seen her somewhere, but in a different version.

A heavy glass paperweight in the shape of an egg, colorful swirls and a very tiny shell embedded in the middle. When I hold the paperweight up to the light dangling from the ceiling the swirls seem to move and shimmer. The slight colors suggest themselves rather than true colors, hints. The glass, smoother than anything I've ever touched, makes me feel as though my hand could slide right through it.

A white wax paper bag, *Café rivière de la lune* inscribed in faded letters on the outside, a smell of oil and sugar, blueberries. Inside, a key, about three inches long, with a clover leaf pattern on the handle and solid teeth. It's immensely satisfying to hold, as if the weight of it in your palm offered a balm. I sweat.

I'm about to close the suitcase and finally get into the salt bath when a small note in my father's inimitable handwriting arrests me: "Dorothy's Rare Stuff." As I read these three simple words my necklace, inherited from my mother after she left, a flat fob in the shape of a Torah with tiny doors, the handles miniscule diamonds that open to reveal Hebrew letters inscribed as if on a grain of rice, seems hot, all of a sudden, almost as though it would burn my chest and a fever would spike if I so much as fingered it.

A small scroll sticks out of the right hand of a pair of exquisite sky-blue ladies' gloves, with lentil-sized buttons dotting the wrists, the pair lying at the foot of the red shoe. I unravel it.

> *Dear Sid,*
> *The answer to what happened to your mother, if there is one, is here.*
> *Love, Dad.*

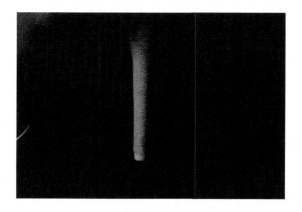

Oh my god, I must have said to the empty apartment, *oh my god.* I had been so overcome by dad's sudden death, caught in spikes of loss, and now I'm blinding furious. How could he? How could he leave me with this? I pace up and down. I want to call André, to vent. But he adores, adored, Aaron. I'm wishing André were here, to envelop me. But glad he isn't. I can't understand or explain how I long for him so acutely while pushing him away. I can only imagine his patience is wearing thin, this newest break-up is no fun. Something has to...change. I fucking cannot believe I'm supposed to sort this out.

It's evening, and cold, and I'm tired, hungry, but to take my mind off this bomb my father left me, I go out walking. Comme d'habitude, I head to Hawthorne, my favorite street in Lakeview. As a kid, I spent hours walking up and down and imagining the lives of the people in those houses shielded by big green trees, in the spring flowers more massive than my head in purple and pink filling up the street. The smell on a summer evening was fat with honeysuckle and lavender, as if floating in a delectable pond. Each garden appeared like a portal into unknown multiverses not yet chronicled. I've taken hundreds of photos here, of all those unvisited portals. I'm aiming my camera at a found still life at the base of a tree: a twig lying partially covered by a condom, when I hear my name.

Ah, Jared, hey. How are you?

Hi Sid! I'm all right. You visiting your father, I guess, he asks, innocently.

As I look up at his familiar pale white face, the powder blue framed glasses partially shielding his ice-blue eyes, I can feel his bite. The very bite that made me come, the one time we fucked. It was high school, at a party, when we were too tipsy to care about love or wrong genders. It never happened again.

Well, no, he...he... my god, I can't even say it.

Oh. Oh, man, I'm sorry. Aaron just came into the bookshop, you know, perhaps a week or so ago? He seemed, fine. Well, as fine as he ever was. He'd ordered another book about nineteenth century whaling. Grim topic, so I remembered it. Actually, he never picked it up. Would you mind collecting it for him? I'm so...

Yeah, sure, no problem.

Jared's gotten cuter since high school, stronger, and as we walk to Unabridged, he tells me about his boyfriend, a dancer who also works at the bookshop, and he tells me how sorry he is for my loss. I believe him, but it's also hard to locate that pure space of sorrow when my father left me so many reasons to be pissed. I try to pull away from that tornado. The bookshop, is, was, dad's favorite by a mile;

he'd become friendly with several of the booksellers over the years. Not only was our dog, Bart, allowed to go in with us, but, at the checkout counter, a pat on the head and a treat awaited him. Same thing at the shoe repair shop and at the pet store. Bart (who of course dad named after Bartleby), was my constant companion, until he died in his sleep on my pillow when he could barely walk. As Jared and I arrive, they're just getting ready to close up, I pick up *Melville's Other Whales,* thank Jared, and amble listlessly back to the empty apartment, slightly afraid, delaying my return by making up more still lifes along the way. I consider stopping for sushi but it, too, would taste like sand. I just cannot understand the weight of that suitcase, I do not get my father's intentions. Why? Why?

In the long overdue salty bath, I mentally scan all the stuff I found, inside, and outside of that case. A canary yellow swimsuit from when I was about nine, the elastic turned into chalk, brings back the time I learned how to swim. We were on the Cape and my father (who had schlepped his typewriter) was sequestered in our small cabin tapping away while I went on an outing with some friends, swimming, supposedly. Only I'd never been swimming before. These friends (well "friends" is probably too strong of a word) these people he'd met at Temple Sholom who'd asked, hey why don't you and your daughter come with us when we go to the Cape in the summer? Sometimes folks at the Temple sort of felt sorry for this lost writer raising a daughter on his own. No doubt rumors circulated about what had happened to his wife, and it was unsatisfactory when he told the truth: he didn't know why she never returned from a research trip to the New Bedford Historical Society.

I've often thought it must have to do with the whales, I knew so little about my mother, but I did know she became an amateur cetologist. She listened for clicks and songs and sounds and she often went out on boats, whenever she could, to chase whales, to photograph them, to hear them. She was interviewed once, about whale languages. But my father and I never received the clarity we desperately wished we could inhale like some really fine dope.

These friends, that summer on the Cape, in Orleans, had kids about my age and they were trying to be friendly. They were also the kind of people who didn't believe that children who are nine years old could possibly not swim. Aaron just never thought to arrange lessons. Before I knew what was happening the father from this other temple family simply picked me up and threw me into the pool. The deep end. I gulped and spluttered and flailed about and felt un-fishlike and ungraceful as I clawed my way desperately to the edge where the scratchy concrete felt so deliciously secure, a slight drop of blood forming on my shin where I'd grazed it on the edge. The drop turned into a small river that trailed out into the water fashioning ribbons of red dissolving into clear. I'd seen my mother swimming, graceful, long strokes, her arms perfectly arched, symmetrical. And here I was, nearly drowning.

I can never forgive that man (whatever his name was) and it took me years and years to learn how to swim and to appreciate seeing your hair float all around you in the water and to recognize how your breath changes and your arms become powerful as you practice your crawl. Eventually my legs stretched out like tadpoles as I learned a passable breaststroke. I prefer swimming in the ocean because the chlorine disagrees with my skin and makes my hair flat; but the salt feels like a balm with seaweed and fish and shells and always something captivating to look at. I must have inherited Dorothy's love of the ocean.

After the bath, I try to settle into an uneasy sleep in my now uncanny Aldine bed. I've never stayed here without my father, snoring away in the next room; I doze, dreaming that I'm painting and re-painting a door a vibrant red. Each time I add a new layer of paint the door gets darker and darker but not redder. I'm unpainting and as more and more layers thicken the heavy door, less and less paint sticks.

In the morning, I awaken groggy and overwhelmed by the chaos. Cradling a hot cup of coffee, I pad over to father's desk, peering at his beloved Corona Silent typewriter that he insisted on using, long after everyone else went digital. As if he'd dusted a moat around the writing machine, the surface of the desk just there is unsullied, sparkling even. Caught in the typewriter's teeth, the title page of a project. He had said just a few months ago, on the David Kepesh show, that he was writing something new, *American Berserk,* and that it needed a lot of work. But this is different. I pull out the lone page:

Slobgollion by Aaron Zimmerman
This story is dedicated to Dorothy,
my love.
It's private,
only for Sidney and André,
not to be broadcast.

I'm taken off guard by a fang of shock. I want to read it, really, but I cannot face it. Terrified. I shove the whole, short, manuscript into an envelope and stick it in that crazy suitcase with all the other indecipherable clues. My stomach falls as if I'm in an elevator going too fast, but I know that I can't yet handle whatever is written on those pages. Not yet. It's too soon. I have too much crap to deal with. And I'm going to need André to read it with me. I look at the envelope as if it could talk. But it stays mute and I refuse to read that fucking manuscript. Another mess from dad. Fucking thanks. Just more for me to handle.

I have to face this apartment. It seems father forgot all about housekeeping. Forgot for years. Broken shoelaces, desiccated dirty soap—how on earth could soap be dirty? But somehow this formerly white soap, lying under the kitchen sink next to the smashed carcass of a large cockroach, is filthy. In the bathroom cabinet, among hundreds of used toothbrushes, sits a lone tampon (thankfully unused), why he didn't throw it out defies all reason. The spray tops of cleaning fluid bottles. Random sticky playing cards. Boric acid in rusty containers. A ceramic cup filled to the brim with...what? salt? sugar? something crystalline that remarkably, defying gravity, doesn't fall out even though tipped over. Ancient, filthy, sponges. A thin filament of a birthday party banner. In the smaller bedroom, the one that was his as a boy, then mine, and now the one he's turned into an office, photographs in which I recognize myself over and over again, from multiple ages, wincing each time I look. Pages and pages of scraps of paper with phone numbers, information, notes—as though the only things worth saving were placed with such care in that case.

I call André. It's too much for me to deal.

I'm putting everything that isn't garbage, I tell him, into either the dishwasher or the washing machine, everything is coated in grime. It's a wonder I haven't tossed my cookies.

It's OK, he says, his voice thick, reassuring, enticing. I know you're in shock—*c'est vraiment choquant*—but you knew that Aaron's dreck would build up if you weren't there to clean for him, right? You know he lives—lived—I can't get used to the past tense—in his head, not on this planet. It's only stuff. Do you want me to come out there?

André, thank you, it's so sweet of you to think of coming. It's, honestly, it's delicious to hear your voice, as ever, and I'm sorry, like I always seem to be, sorry.

OK, so then stop being a jackass and let me get to you. I'm not teaching tomorrow...I could take the overnight sleeper train, be there in the morning.

Somehow...thanks, but.... and, I add, after trailing off, almost like an afterthought, I still love you.

*

A few days later, back home in New York, André finds me on the steps of the public library, near the left lion, where we always met when we used to go on dates to the NYPL. Standing close to him, I feel that slight buckle at the back of my knees, the soft spots all over he knows how to touch come back viscerally. I look up at him, his eyes, guarded, but present. His black hair folded into a knot. The way he spreads his palms wide when he's talking, his voice so resonant, fat. Even through this breach, it feels good to be back where we'd loved being, no matter what we're Sherlock Holmesing: obscure photography histories or biographies of Melville, James, whatever. We walk in close together, no need to say much. We breathe in the smell of polish and aged books, groove on the sense of concentration and anticipation in this reading room. Here, with its bare but graceful long aged wooden tables each with a little green glass lantern, we learn all sorts of things about the shoe designer Paolo Gemina. We take notes in our notebooks and then check in as we search. When we switch out to the digital memory machines, the blue light from the micro-fiche makes us blink and squint Magoo-style, struggling to read the articles off the harsh screen.

Aaron, André leans in and whispers to me, would have loved to be here, searching with us. A melting along my back when I feel his breath, so close.

Yes, yes, he would; but it's his zany suitcase that brought us here! What does he know that we don't know?

In a paper copy of *The Village Voice,* a small detail in a column, a photo of Gemina, his steel gray hair brushed back like Bogart's, a description of his shoe line, a brief caption. Gemina was flamboyant, a darling of the fashion world, and easy to trace through newspaper articles and many sightings in gossip columns in Milan, New York, and L.A. But after finding an article published ten years earlier the trail goes cold. It appears that he relocated back from L.A. to New York in 1985 and landed in a loft in Soho where he sparked a sort of designer's answer to a literary salon. People dropped by, showed off, got drunk, stayed over. It's quite a hub. While *The Voice* doesn't exactly print his address, enough details suggest its rough location. Heading to Prince and Mercer seems to be about as close as we can get to finding him.

We thank the librarian who'd so patiently helped us

and decide we'll avoid the sardine rush hour subway and walk downtown; we head west to Broadway, sallying by the endless stream of wholesale costume jewelry, every variety of hat and synthetic hair a person could imagine, rainbow wigs, deep purple hair, powder blue bobs. I try not to pause too often to take photos. Store fronts packed to the gills with chain after chain of fake chunky pearls. The oysters are happy, I suppose, with the rage for simulated pearls. Then past Union Square Park where dogs trot and romp, toddlers squeal, musicians play off key, and steel drums make us walk in time.

We both love Fanelli's. I figure it offers a skip, a stone rippling across a placid pond into another time zone, and I've wondered more than once if, like stepping into my darkroom, having a drink at Fanelli's isn't time travel in plain starlight. I'm excited that the red shoe has furnished us with a clue—even if neither of us has any idea where the clue might lead. Excited and fuming, a strange brew. Amid the photos on the walls of wise guys, celebrities, famous writers, we find a snapshot of Jack Johnson boasting his medal, and André describes in juicy detail the novel my father wrote featuring and reconstructing the life of this heavyweight champ. We sit at a table with checkered red and white squares, order spaghetti marinara and zinfandel and talk over all the possible angles of the shoe-clue.

So, André says, after our second glass of red, how are we going to find this character?

We decide to take another leg stretcher and see if we somehow bump into Paolo Gemina in his neighborhood.

André and I are so damn compatible, I think, as we wander around Soho, we love to walk in step, we love to wander the city. What is wrong with us together, anyway? I love being next to him, and yet, for some reason beyond my control, I have a terrible habit of breaking up with him. Why do I sabotage myself, sabotage him, all the fucking time? As we peruse, I keep catching little snippets of French here and there. This part of town is steeped in expats and tourists—or tourists visiting their expat relatives.

Régarde, chéri, des chaussures incroyables!

Mais, il est fermé, ce magasin de chaussures, on reviendra demain.

I think of Jean-Pierre Melville's film *Deux hommes dans Manhattan,* his 1959 love-letter to New York. Melville, a French-Jewish resistance fighter, kept his nom de guerre (his original name was Grumbach) after the war, out of admiration, naturally. I wish I had the moxie to do something like that, change my name to Melville. *Deux hommes dans Manhattan* reveals a deeply shadowed New York full of French ex-pats, a whole world of them, working for French newspapers or the U.N. but fully part of the city. They could switch easily between French and English, as André and I do. Sometimes our shared French comes in handy as a sort of secret language, just as he tells me his sister Marguerite and he could get away with speaking English to each other in hushed tones when they didn't want certain adults in Guadeloupe to hear.

New York's sort of France-ouest, I suppose. So many French speakers circulate on this island and the boroughs between the transplants like André from Guadeloupe, or people from the Congo, Morocco, Antigua, Senegal, Québec, and so many other places. As we wander, André says he'd always felt like a bit of a New Yorker, even before he came here, because his mother hails from Brooklyn and her sister, Thérèse, still lives there. Since arriving in the city, he hangs out with Aunt Thérèse sometimes, and catches the West Indian Day parade every year—it practically goes by her brownstone anyway. I joined them once or twice, with my camera, and took some photographs of gorgeous people in over-the-top, joy-bringing costumes. Even though I print them in black and white you can almost see the colors, they're so vibrant they can't be kept out of the image. I took a photograph of a woman—who posed so readily for me—in a scanty peacock costume all glittery and transplendent, smiling broadly at me, with André looking over my shoulder and admiring the curvaceous human peacock. I hate, absolutely hate and often refuse to have anyone snap my image.

Our feet take us back to Fanelli's and my head returns to the quest for an answer to what this red shoe might bring us. We sit right down where we'd been, wondering how we are ever going to find a character like Gemina in this vast international city.

A spike of cold air pierces our calm as a steel-haired olive-skinned man with pomaded hair, a purple cravat, and thick black sunglasses opens the door. He looks around languorously, keeps his sunglasses on, and choses a seat at the richly decorated deep mahogany and glass bar.

André, it's him!

Shhhhh. I know, Sid. Let's go.

Trying to seem neither conspicuous nor overwhelming, we casually walk up to the bar as if to order drinks. Just when I arrive at the left elbow of Paolo Gemina, André reaches his right; after asking the bartender for two glasses of wine, André says something innocuous about the cold night air to Gemina, but I can't help plunging in:

Are you? You're a dead ringer for that wonderful shoe designer, what's his name, Paolo....

Gemina, he says.

Yes, Gemina, André chimes in. We're huge fans of your work! Merde, I think, that must have sounded sycophantic to him.

Davvero? Gemina looks at us, probably trying to work out if we're shysters or not. So few people, he says mournfully, remain who know anything about real shoes. And then after, well, it's so sad, what happened to the Gemina line. She was so...pregnant with possibilities. It's been a long time.

What happened to your gorgeous shoe line? I offer, as casually as I can, I recall reading somewhere, maybe in the *Village Voice,* that you went into making shoes without taking the skins off animals—that's so...ethical!

Gemina looks at me, I see an eyebrow poking up over his sunglasses, suspicious yet happy someone's asked him: Si. You see, he says, I was becoming very interested in the possibilities afforded by other materials and at the same time I was more and more aware of other creatures on the planet and less willing to be part of their doom. Unfortunately, I think I was a little ahead of my own time—out of joint I suppose you could say—with it and the line just didn't take flight. But, it's ok. I am still here and I still have many friends.

I agree, André says, it's not as though the animals want to give up their hides in order to make sure we don't get pricked with a nail or bothered by the grit and dirt of the city.

Yes, Gemina says, turning to me with a look that lasts just a shade too long, and I felt, he goes on, too, that I was part of this very frivolous universe, the fashion world, I mean. Frivolous but so full of life, of energy. I don't feel it much now, the energy...today, today, I think I am a bit forgotten. Grey.

André and I exchange glances and even though we haven't exactly worked out a code, we know it's time.

Mr. Gemina...

Paolo, please, call me Paolo.

Yes, Paolo, I'm sorry you're feeling so grey. I wonder if this will help? I venture, tentatively, pulling the red shoe slowly out of my oversized purse, this is an authentic one of yours, yes?

As he holds the carefully wrought object Paolo's eyes grow huge, he's rendered momentarily speechless. Taking a deep breath in and then cleaning his sunglasses he gently folds them on the counter and turns to look back at his shoe.

This pair was one of my most prized creations, he tells

us. I confess I love the smell of leather, real leather, the synthetic ones do not have the same captivating aroma. I loved these shoes, and the women who wore them, they looked so glamorous!

Setting the shoe on the bar and leaning back slightly to look at me, Paolo queries: Where did you find this?

Before I can stop them a stream of hot tears flow down my cheeks and I turn sunset red, my eyes dilate slightly.

Ah? Paolo looks at André, searching for how to handle this.

I nod, not ready to speak. Si, Paolo, André says, it was her mother's shoe. I know it's weird but we found it in a suitcase….

Oh. Yes, I see. I am sorry. Looking down at his shiny black shoes. But I do happen to have the other shoe. And it's always been a mystery why I had this singular pump. It appeared, like Cinderella's lost slipper, one evening—or probably early one morning, after one of my big parties. And I never knew why it was there. Paolo checks his watch, goes to make a phone call and then returns to the bar.

I just needed to push back a rendezvous. No problem. Come with me.

André looks at me and nods consent and we all slide down from our barstools and back out into the wintry Soho air. The streets are still full of shoppers and everyone seems to be in a hurry, huddled into great coats and bundled against the cold. They're walking on a diagonal, leaning forward to ward off the wind. André and I might have passed Paolo on these streets a zillion times on one of our walks, never able to predict that this fashionable man would become the first person to spring out of that dusty suitcase. Whatever game my father is playing, it's springing to life.

We follow Paolo three blocks along Greene until he nonchalantly ducks into a side alley, taking off his sturdy padded gloves, unlocks an almost invisible door. Inside, a huge elevator appears, left over from the garment district days, with a smell of raw wood and grease and lined with slightly rusty, heavy, bars one has to close before operating. Paolo hits the 8th floor and we ride in silence. When the elevator stops, he opens the heavy latch with surprising grace and speed and steps up to his door, unlocks all three bolts, and leads us into a cavernous space.

Just a minute, let me get the lights.

As he turns on the soft lights, filling the loft with an emerald sheen, we wonder whether we've been transported into yet another time machine. The space is huge but also full of artfully arranged rare stuff. Single object shelves of varying small sizes line the walls, and as we explore we realize that many of the petite shelves hold, as if they were sculptures in a museum, a shoe, a single, beautiful, shoe. Some of them buttress shoe-sized sculptures of animals, very life-like, with teeth and claws on the wolves and tails on the whales.

Regarding one of the tiny whales, my hand involuntarily flies to my agape mouth.

A memory, blurry, surfaces as if breathing in after a long spell under water. I'm six, standing under the ninety-four-foot-long reproduction of a blue whale that hangs on the ceiling of the American Museum of Natural History. I look up and up at the great mammal, holding my mother's hand. She tells me about a trip with her mother to see the whales in the Gulf of St. Lawrence when she was a girl.

Maman, I can hear my mother saying, adores the sea and loves to bring me to the ocean to play in the waves or, sometimes to go with friends on a boat in search of amazing elongated, blue, graceful creatures like this one. Look up, little bean.

I barely remember anything of her, apart from the few scraps I could yank unwillingly from dad. When you're older, my mother told me then, I will tell you some of the amazing things I've been learning.

This memory shocks me, tumbling into my mind uninvited and so quickly. I feel sure André can see right away that something's going on.

Are you ok, Sid?

Yes, yes, it's, it's… just, this little whale reminded me of something, an involuntary memory erupted, just now.

Paolo returns, and in his hand, the other red shoe. If I put them on and click my heels together will that bring Dorothy back, just like clicking those sparkly red heels brought that other Dorothy home to Kansas? If I land at home, will I catch her at the end of the tornado? Paolo stretches out his slightly trembling hand and holds the shoe out for me; I pick it up, gingerly, as though embracing a butterfly, and pull out its partner from my purse. Lining them up, I set them down on a gilt table and we stand back to look at the miracle of the shoes reunited. The right shoe, Paolo's, was on display and so the leather is ever so slightly faded, a half-note off in hue from the left, hidden in that dark suitcase for who knows how long.

Sid, Paolo asks, have you ever wondered what it would a be a like to walk in your mama's shoes?

Silently, I slip off my sneakers, which I'm wearing with a long, grey, skirt, and place the fantastic pumps on my feet. The trace of my socks leaves wrinkle lines like the nose of a walrus as their imprint. I promenade around Paolo's amazing loft, gazing at all this rare stuff, trying to balance on the unfamiliar and slightly uneven shoes, wondering how I might ever find Dorothy.

Paolo, André says, in a small voice, guess what?

What?

These very shoes—or shoes just like them, are in one of Aaron's novels.

I amble around, feeling at once now quite tall, and very lost, disoriented, as Paolo's eyes grow wide like saucers.

Sid, hold on a minute, André ventures, let's think this through. The red shoes are in *In Love with Great Black Hope,* Aaron's novel about the boxer Jack Johnson...but what does that really signify? As far as I can tell, all it means, right now anyway, is that Aaron probably bought these shoes for his beloved as a special gift—a wedding anniversary, maybe? or a birthday? Perhaps Dorothy and Aaron came here for a party during one of their many trips to New York, looking for rare books? and then she got a headache, and they took a cab and she accidentally lost a shoe? and then a similar pair ended up in his novel. It's like Freud's 'daily residue' for novelists—the things we dream often stem from things we see the day before—the same goes for novelists so...

Here Paolo cuts him off, but gently: André, excuse me, yes, I see what you mean, but—and I say this though I do not remember Sidney's affascinante parents, so many people come and go here, Aaron must have left that one, if I do a say so myself, scarpa così bella, for Sid to find for a good reason. This is not a residue.

A small tear forming at the base of his left eye, Paolo holds both of my hands in his papery ones: Bella, please, take this beautiful object and somehow maybe she leads you to your mama. Take care of this one, André. She's a keeper, like they say over here.

I wonder then, what André is thinking? Is it something like *I wish I could keep her. I wish she would come back to me.* Or is he thinking more like *I have her. Or perhaps, I no longer know if I want to keep her, she's a handful.* I can't tell. He looks, sad, pensive, but hard to read.

Paolo, I say, your shoes are...well gorgeous is a vast understatement, they're like oracles, and I hope they can tell stories. We're so totally overjoyed that we had a chance to meet you, thank you for letting us interrupt your rendezvous, and, well, we can't thank you enough, I manage, my voice cracking. A dopo.

We saunter through the now much emptier streets, the shops shuttered, breathing and trying to make sense of the strange and wonderful world of Paolo's museum-like space, thinking and thinking what could these shoes possibly tell us? The extraordinary red heels emit an unfamiliar click-clack-click that echoes as we walk, the sounds bouncing off the buildings, their dim lights behind closed curtains. I've tied my converse laces together and slung the sneakers over my shoulder, walking with a slight swing in my step I can hear the dull thud of the canvas hitting my back as we go. My feet are freezing in those gracious pumps, but I never want to take them off, like I never remove the Torah necklace.

When we arrive at my front stoop, André kisses me gently on the cheek. Too gently. Where's the bite? I look up at him, much closer now that I'm wearing the red shoes, and probably he can see the longing starkly visible in my gaze. But we remain stuck, more than a little frightened of each other, and each afraid to give in but unable to let go. We'll get back together, I allow myself to fantasize, but in a precarious way that I think we both wish would solidify somehow. He expects me to be his anchor. And he has proven over and again that he's my anchor. I want to be sure, less of him, and more of me, of my ability to stay the course.

André, this likely will sound hollow, but I mean it in the fullest sense. Thank you. Thank you for all.

You're welcome. He remains mutely gazing down at me and I dream that he's thinking, *I love you unspeakably much, right now, as you stand there freezing in your mother's shoes, your wet eyes looking at me with that piercing stare.* But what he says: I'll see you tomorrow, Sid, get some sleep.

Mounting the steps to my apartment, the heaviest sense of exhaustion overcomes me. I plunk down in the middle of the living room, my flowy skirt parachuting out around me, toes pointing up, those incredible shoes making my feet ache and throb. As if I'd walked on hot coals. As I reach down to take them off, pick up my peppermint foot crème to give myself a foot-rub, I realize there's another difference between left and right—not just the faded leather on the right, and I wonder how I didn't feel this more strongly as I walked on them all the way from Soho back to the East Village. The sole of the right foot is slightly thickened, a mini-platform and, when I bring the shoe close to my tired and puffy eyes, I find a miniscule, almost invisible indentation.

Locating a toothpick in the kitchen bowl strewn with odds and ends, I gently push in and a tiny drawer releases from the platform of the shoe, pushed out by an invisible spring. Inside, a small piece of speckled paper, with words in dad's inimitable handwriting, very like mine, a nearly indecipherable chicken scratch:

Take this note to Mr. Oravid at the Museum of Natural History. He will know what to do.

The tiny note hits me like a giant tsunami.

This was definitely not my mother's writing because that, I know, was tidy and completely legible, as if a typewriter rather than a human hand forged it. I would recognize it from letters and postcards father showed me. I'd tucked one into my journal, once, when he wasn't looking.

My darling Aaron, the sea is so fresh and crisp here on the Gulf of St. Lawrence. Today, Maman, Michael, and I went with Captain Searles out on a tiny

vessel and we spotted three blue whales. We even saw a breach! It was marvelous and I do so wish you had been with us. All my love, D.

Aaron preserved these precious missives and I loved to read and re-read them. When I held one in my hands, I habitually pressed the card to my nose, just to catch a tiny bit of a scent. My head begins to throb, I'm so tired, everything swirls around as I flop into bed and dream of a sea voyage, my mattress transmogrifies into a ship and I float out into the wide ocean using as oars my own legs, wooden now, as the mattress-ship sails further and further away from shore. I wake up in a sweat, certain that I'm at sea, and still wearing my clothes from the night before.

André, I manage somewhat breathlessly into the phone, just as he's waking up and probably getting ready to go to CUNY, there IS a clue, an actual clue inside the shoe. I have to get off to work now, I can't be late again, but I will tell you everything later. I mean, can I, will I see you later? Please. Let's be really together, we never really broke up, did we?

His voice raspy with sleep and covered in dreams he says yes, sure, come here for dinner, ok?

See you at eight.

*

On the train up to the museum after work, I puzzle and puzzle as to why dad took this crazy labyrinthine route to give me a message. He'd said in his typically terse letter that he put everything he knew into the case. For the millionth time I wish I could talk to him; séances and attempts to communicate with the dead seem suddenly entirely reasonable in a way they never had before. I'm burning to ask, but of course, when he was alive, I asked him so many things and he almost always gave terse, evasive answers. He became loquacious only in print, or with André, or when he'd visit one of André's classes and talk to students, or David Kepesh. And now he's weirdly forthcoming while dead. But how? Again, why? But even to Kepesh, father had mentioned that mom disappeared but then clammed up—as if he wished he hadn't said anything at all about her. There's nothing for André and me to do but follow all the clues and yet it's so fucking bizarre. Frustrating as hell.

I wonder if maybe I'm still dreaming? But the subway looks real, all those New Yorkers doing their thing. The woman with her makeup bag fully unpacked on the seat next to her, holding up a mirror and, despite the jerking train, managing to get her mascara more or less where it needs to go. The pale unwashed man with a white beard reading the bible, one finger on the page, never turning to a new page just reading over and over again the same passage, his lips slightly moving. The man holding a bowling ball like a baby, a garish smiley face painted around the three finger holes. The tired mom with her twins, one on either side of her, each drumming a different beat with their pencils on the seats, like Thing One and Thing Two.

I want to photograph them all, as I often do on the train, usually asking permission, but sometimes sneakily. In the scant time since Aaron died, in the darkroom, I'm finding, weirdly, that everything, including my portraits of couples, has changed. I can't figure out why, it's illogical, like everything is since he died, but somehow the faces in the photographs become softer and maybe slightly sadder. I know it can't possibly make sense that the images transition in the face of his death but, there you have it: the stark reality that the dark room reveals perceptible transformations. As the train chugs uptown, I wonder if somehow dad's ghost weren't with me in the darkroom, he'd be invisible after all, and it's pitch black in there. I muse again why one of his few friends, Michael Gruber, a retired photographer, loans the darkroom to me. What did dad do to generate such a huge favor?

When he was alive, I was invariably disappointed at how he looked at my work. And now I feel like a shit for feeling that way. It's too needy of me. Each time he voyaged to visit us in New York, he would glance at my collection of portraits quickly, looking at my walls or thumbing through the loose prints stacked on the coffee table and making snide little comments like oh well check out those 1960s sunglasses or those two are not going to make it or well she's cute as a button...how did he get so lucky?

I never felt that he was seriously looking at the photographs or that he was truly absorbing what I'm trying to do—as André seriously seems to get it. And maybe that's because I don't fully know what the project achieves, if anything. I'm offering celebratory portraits. Yet celebratory sounds all wrong, given the histories and realities of racism that overwhelm us. I know André wishes he could trace his mother's past and her absence of history weighs on him. I'd started this series of portraits of interracial couples before I met André so it's not like I hadn't thought about interracial shtupping before then. I could see how the portraits could be misread. Misused even. André tells me he finds them engrossing. And he let me know that Aaron does too; did too. He'd let me know in no uncertain terms that he suspected that Aaron kvelled more about me—about my work, such as it is—than he was willing to let on.

When I kvetched André would say that Aaron never was the sort of parent who dishes out praise. Now that my father's physical presence evaporated, and now that I am visited regularly by a revenant in the darkroom, maybe he guides those small changes in the images?

As the train jerks and pauses in a tunnel, the lights flickering off for a moment, I catch a glimpse of a reflection in the glass—the image reminds me of an impossible path-crosser: while out trawling and photographing the East Village each day, I passed the same old man at a different time and a different place. Papery white skin, white hair, bow legged, slightly slumped and yet I ran into him at the gym on occasion. Sometimes out in Tompkins Square Park, or over at Union Square on my way to yoga, or at the juice truck as I picked up my favorite carrot ginger beet juice. It's impossible that our paths would cross every day. No rational explanation. Before my father died, I thought this gnarled man reminded me of him—they didn't exactly look alike but something in his solidity and his solitude conjured dad as if his image reflected in a foggy mirror. Now that I touched his ashes, or what I thought were his ashes, and witnessed them melting into the lake, I wondered whether this pale old man was dad's phantasma. Perpetually alone when I spotted him, I could never turn to André and ask, do you see that man? Is he real? Can you see him?

What if he metamorphosed from a pre-ghost into a regular ghost? How could I verify his reality and what statistical possibility remains that I picked out the same person in the swirl of a huge city nearly every single day without fail? I thought of trying to snap a clandestine portrait, to show it to André, who'd said he was dying to see him, yet I was certain the film would come out blank, a photo of a vampire.

Arriving at 81st Street, I sally through what I always think of as the 'secret entrance' to the Museum of Natural History, the one that offers a corridor from the train platform into the lower entrance where the first thing that greets you is a huge canoe full of rowers rowing along. The museum was a favorite spot when mom, dad, and I (and then just the two of us) would take frequent trips to New York. André and I often come here, to gaze at the strange rocks and multitudes of creatures great and small, or take in a light show in the planetarium. Now, passing through the entrance, past the canoe, beyond the huge skeleton of a wooly mammoth, past the dioramas of taxidermied animals of all varieties of tooth and claw and fur and fin, I approach one of the guards and ask, with a giant hitch in my voice, excuse me, may I please speak with Mr. Oravid?

Of course, he replies, as if that were a totally normal

question, one moment please. The guard clicks a button on his walkie-talkie and announces, Mr. Oravid, you have a visitor.

He indicates that I should take a seat.

After a few minutes a bow-legged elderly gentleman appears. I hand him the note I've unearthed, improbably embedded in the red shoe, and then step back. Snow white hair, somewhat cloudy eyes, soggy skin. I can feel the blood rushing up behind my ears and a thumping from my heart that I fear Mr. Oravid can hear, loud as a bell tower.

I...you.

Do not worry, Sid. I am not a ghost.

You can read my mind?

With a chuckle Mr. Oravid says, No, no, of course not. You recognize me because I was sent to keep an eye on you, to make sure you were ok. Sort of like a guardian angel, I suppose. But a living one—at least for now.

You were sent, by whom? I'm so confused right now, I can't even tell you.

I imagine that you are, indeed, yes, you will be confused, I'm afraid. I am not allowed to tell you who sent me, but I am allowed to reassure you that their intentions are good.

Oh, well, that's a relief! Just then I sorely wish André were here with me; I need my anchor.

Please, let me get you some coffee.

To the guard Mr. Oravid says, can you please ask Ms. Shelton to re-arrange my afternoon meetings? We will be back soon, Henry, thank you very much for keeping an eye on things. And with this, he looks up to the ceiling and then quickly back down again.

Once we settle at the Museum Café just down the street—and we happen to be sitting at the same table by the window that I remember sharing with dad when I was about 13—I'm able to look closely at him for the first time.

Sir, I begin, suddenly realizing that's too formal and blushing, may I take your photograph?

You want to see if my face registers on film I suppose?

Turning scarlet I nod, take out my camera and click a few close-up portraits, trying to capture as much detail, as many of the white beard bristles as possible. I figure André will not believe me unless I show him documentary evidence.

It's a bit circuitous, no? my father, may his memory be for a blessing, planting a note in a shoe, that was hidden in a closet that I might never have seen, the other in the pair held by its designer in a quasi-museum in a loft in Soho? Things get curiouser and curiouser. The song we always sing at Passover comes to mind...do you know it? 'And then came the butcher and slaughtered the ox, that drank the water, that quenched the fire, that burnt the stick, that beat the dog, that bit the cat, that ate the goat, that father bought for two zuzim...'

Sometimes the journey to the truth is a labyrinth rather than a freeway.

Is that updated Zen?

At this, Mr. Oravid issues a surprisingly deep laugh, like the lowest note on a cello reverberating through the café. The truth is, he says, I do not know the back story of the note and the shoe. I knew that I needed to look out for you and that you would come to me. I am one piece in what is quite a complex puzzle. My strong suspicion is that Aaron gathered the pieces but did not—could not see how to fit them together so left it for you, for you and André, to pick up the shards. I do like to think I am a piece that matters, and I do have something to show you back inside the museum. But first, I am going to deliver a verbal message that I have wanted to tell you each time I caught sight of you in the East Village, wandering around, always with your camera, always looking slightly lost even though you were on home turf. Please, Sid, take a deep breath. Are you ready?

I nod slightly.

Your father asked me to tell you that he strongly suspects your mother had no choice. She was compelled to leave when you were not quite seven for your own protection. Aaron, who I have come to know since he began researching whales at the museum's archives for *Slobgollion*, does not fully know what happened. For your survival, for her survival, for Aaron's survival, eighteen years ago, Aaron suspects, Dorothy was given no choice but to go into a sort of witness protection program. For what it's worth, and this is the hardest part of what I need to convey to you, for what it's worth, I'm afraid he has scrambled truth and fiction.

Slobgollion? You mean the manuscript? That was supposed to be for just André and me—and my mother was an amateur cetologist, not a mobster. Truth from fiction you mean he—

I don't know for sure, honestly. Aaron had intended to

publish *Slobgollion,* originally. But then he decided it was not for public consumption. Dorothy was working on whale communication techniques and language is sometimes a very delicate and world-changing thing, Sid, she was working on some stunningly important projects. Aaron feared you, everyone, would think he'd gone utterly mad if he revealed his suspicions. So he just kept quietly digging, hoping. For what it's worth, I do not think there's much cause for hope, and I do not want you to engage in a sort of false dream.

Why do I have a feeling you're not going to tell me what she was working on?

You are entirely correct. If I told you, according to Aaron's admittedly somewhat unreliable logic, that would endanger you. And, as I said, I do not have any answers, just conjectures. I am supposed to be a guardian angel not a threatening one. When you are ready, I will show you something quite interesting back at the museum.

I gulp my coffee and stand up to go. I'm so disorientated by what he's been telling me. Or, rather, not telling me. My mother uncovered something world-changing about whales? And that is why she left without trace when I was a kid? This makes zero sense.

As Mr. Oravid shuffles alongside, I adjust my normally quick pace to walk with him and try to absorb some of what he just described to me. My father had sent a message, before he died. My father knew more than he let on. As we walk, I fend off spikes of fury mixed with a stomach-sinking melancholy and look down at the hexagonal grey sidewalk pattern surrounding the museum like a moat. I'm remembering questioning my father over and over.

Dad, why don't you know?

He would repeat, mechanically, your mother went to the New Bedford Historical Society in 1977 and never came back. End of story.

But...did you look for her?

At this question dad's white face invariably transformed into a mottled beet and he reminded me too fiercely that he had tried everything, the police, private investigators, his own fevered searches, posters, missing persons ads in newspapers, everything, everything, you understand!

Then, unvaryingly, I started crying and dad reached out to comfort me.

I'm sorry, sweetie, it's just, I miss her so much, and I wish we could have found her.

After a year of searching, he threw his hands up, seemingly closed his heart to everyone but me, and read and wrote book after book. I gave up (reluctantly) my habitual prodding. But the memory of my mother grew, expanded, a cancer on my heart all these years, invisible but ever present. Burning with curiosity to know what happened to her, I thought about her constantly, but rarely spoke about her.

Especially after she evaporated, I asked dad several times to tell me the story of how they met.

Well, dad would habitually begin, shifting his weight in his reading chair, and leaning down to my normal spot on the floor, it was 1955, the summer all of Chicago was transformed by the horrible death of that kid from Chicago,

Emmett Till. Everyone was reeling, tempers flared, protests escalated, it was a heady mix of fury and hope for change. To escape it all, I went to temple—not something I usually did, but that particular Friday night I was bone tired and lonely and I wanted to hear the sweet sounds of the cantor singing. So, as I entered, I noticed a girl—oh excuse me, I suppose I should say 'woman,' right? Anyway, I noticed this redhead I had not seen before. With her pale slightly freckled skin, she looked flustered and slightly out of breath. That was it, the first time I saw her, nothing else.

But, then what! I always asked for more, and dad perpetually drew out the story, not wanting to get to the part when he actually got up the courage to talk to her. That, as it happened, was weeks later.

Well, father finally continued, things were different then—not like your generation, when anything goes!— I saw her. I was drawn to her. She seemed at once all a flutter and completely sure of herself; that combination was exceedingly compelling. She was cute, too. The cantor did calm me, and I looked at this girl, sorry, woman, often during the service, just to see what she was up to. I think she felt my eyes on her. At one point I thought I could see just a tiny trace of a blush, like a drop of blood stretching out in Lake Michigan. The next Friday I returned to Kehilath Ansche Ma'ariv and there she was! I could not believe my luck. But I was still too scared to talk to her.

So when? When did you say something? I'd asked again and again even though I'd memorized the answer.

Here we are, Mr. Oravid says, startling me out of my

reverie. Henry, can you please close the whale room just for 15 minutes? Thank you kindly.

After Henry, who doesn't seem surprised by Mr. Oravid's request, gently asks the few tourists in the great whale hall to move along and then swiftly puts up notices on the entrances that read: *Closed for inspection. Will re-open in 15 minutes*, we stand under the whale and gaze up. We don't speak, awed by the sheer size of the reproduced whale, and I remember very well now, after the memory lit up like a match at Paolo's loft-museum, standing in this exact spot with my mother. I could feel her soft hand and smell the rose-tinted hand crème she always used. She wore a silk scarf that day, a bright emerald green, and it reflected the lights from the ceiling like a Velázquez painting might have traced the glints, white seafoam forming on the crest of a wave.

Henry creeps up behind us surprisingly quietly given that he's schlepping a huge red ladder. Silently, with a nod to Mr. Oravid, he sets the ladder up and begins climbing, just to test its strength. All set, he says cheerily, as he once again leaves the room.

Go ahead, Sid, Mr. Oravid nudges, gesturing for me to climb.

With a lump in my throat and a familiar feeling of whooziness I look up at the tall ladder that leads up to the whale's mouth. For a moment I wonder if the plastic whale might speak or sing? My heart thumps and blood rushes up behind my ears as I slowly climb, remembering not to look down.

At the whale's head, a handle emerges, and I grasp it with a large exhale. I see what was invisible from the floor below: one can peer right into the whale's great mouth. A brass plaque screwed into the whale's lower jaw:

This model is based on a whale spotted by Dorothy Zimmerman in the Gulf of St. Lawrence. The whale, photographed by Michael Gruber, was estimated to be one hundred feet long and approximately twenty five years old when sighted. It is unknown whether the whale is still alive today.

I wish that Henry and Mr. Oravid had brought a stack of mattresses onto which I could land if I fell. I look down at them looking up at me and they seem to be thinking the same thing.

Go gently, Sid, Mr. Oravid says from unspeakably far away, at the bottom of the ladder, and I can see the hexagonal wood pattern in the floor that echoes the concrete pattern outside. I hold onto the handle to steady myself and read the plaque again. And then again. If I possessed as many hands as the giant squid on the ceiling in the next room, I would have been able to hang on and photograph those startling words at the same time. I content myself with memorizing them and cannot wait to get to André's apartment. I need to tell him everything, everything. How can I have been so fucking stupid to break up with him? Never again!

But first I desperately need to squelch the rising vertigo before falling without a net. I see Henry and Mr. Oravid whispering below. *Get a hold of yourself, Sid.* I mumble to myself, and then, *I forgive you for all the times you've screwed up royally.* I practice the steady breathing I'm learning in yoga, count to five, in, out, count to five again, and, finally, feeling brave enough to relinquish the life-saving handle, I focus entirely on the red ladder. *One step at a time, don't look down. One step at a time, don't look down.* I repeat the mantra to myself over and over until, finally, I faint into the giant arms of Henry, who somehow knew he'd be catching me. I dream of a slippery eel who keeps poking his head out of a lake and saying *there isn't time, I am late, late!* and then popping back below the surface of the water before I can ask him late for what?

When I wake up it seems as though many hours must have passed but I glance at my father's watch, the one I adopted when I found it during the great purge and began wearing as a ticking memorial, and only about twenty five minutes evaporated since I was at the whale's mouth. I'm resting on a sort of cot, as Mr. Oravid paces up and down, swatting at his forehead with a soaked thick white handkerchief. Sitting up, I reassure him: Hi, oh I'm really sorry to have worried you, Mr. Oravid, I'm fine. Really, honestly. Could I please have some water? And, might I ask you to call André? He should be in his office now.

About half an hour later, Henry ushers André into the small room where I'm now able to sit up in bed, holding my tea in a slightly trembling hand. According to Henry and Mr. Oravid, as they tell André, I'm apparently much improved and they think I'm recovering from a mild state of shock. They tell him that I turned white as the sheets on the cot and that they revived me using the time-honored method of hot tea spiked with brandy. I try to look at André in a way that will make him understand that his quasi-exile is truly over. I'm not sure if he can read my face or not, though.

André, André thank you so much for being here! I reach up and pull his shoulders into me. Michael Gruber, I tell him, breathing heavily, my father's friend who loans me his darkroom, he took the photo that the museum used to construct their giant whale. And more than that, my mom spotted her, the whale I mean, and was right next to him when he took the picture....and, Oh! I must be so tired! I just realized that the photo in the suitcase, of the man on the bench—that is Michael Gruber, many years ago, I didn't recognize him, he was so young then.

My heart races and calms in the same gesture and a strange surety suddenly floods me. I feel a little woozy again but I'm trying to focus on what André tells me.

Slow down, Sid. Your mom spotted the whale? And, nu?

Yes, I know, it seems utterly crazy, right? But we have to go see Michael Gruber, tomorrow, OK?

We will. Now, do you feel like you can face a taxi home?

Yes, yes, I can. Turning to the two men waiting patiently while I try to recover, I thank them, maybe a little excessively. I'm utterly embarrassed that I fainted like one of those 19th Century heroines whose intricate lives my father so often read:

I do appreciate your looking out for me, Mr. Oravid—although I confess, I was a little freaked out when I kept seeing you cross my path. I remember very clearly, I was standing outside a groovy shoe store, lusting after some lime green high heeled shoes that were totally out of range and, in the glass of the store window, I saw your reflection just behind me, glancing in my direction and then passing along Avenue A. Your slightly green reflection passed through mine, yes, exactly like a ghost. I always told André I wished I could see if you would come out on a grainy print in the darkroom; I was indeed afraid the prints would be blank, you're right about that. But thank you, I understand now that you were making sure I was OK.

After lots of hugging and fussing Henry and Mr. Oravid help us into a cab as if they are loading Fabergé eggs.

I lean on André in the back of the taxi all the way down Fifth Avenue and east on 14th. We're too stunned to speak so we just watch the city fly by.

*

In the morning, Saturday, I pull out the suitcase of Dorothy's Rare Stuff again and we gaze at the photograph: a man on a park bench, sitting, smiling, looking up at someone he knows very well—probably not a lover, no gleam in the eye, just adoration, spiced with a hint of putting up with a lot of stuff. The insignia is almost missable, merely a small metallic pin on the lapel. But clearly, he thought it mattered enough to wear it proudly.

André there he is, Michael Gruber.

I reach for my coat and try to slip on my shoes at the

same time. André quietly dons his jacket and hunts up his boots, following me out of the apartment and down the stairs. It's chilly but not brutal and the light feels filtered through the white sky as the city wakes up.

You know, I say as we walk west across 10th Street, passing the park on our left, when I first saw that image, the man on the bench, he looked so familiar, but I couldn't place him. Uncanny. Dad must have—might have—snapped this—and do you recognize the park? It's right here, Tompkins Square Park! This could have been the same bench I photographed you on that very first time we met. What are the chances? I hold his arm tightly then and we walk very closely together, in time with each other's rhythms. I long for the reunion we'll have in my loft-bed later.

Everything seems to interconnect. Maybe, yes. When we return from visiting M. Gruber, let's compare benches.

Are you teasing me? Sometimes I'm unsure when he's joking and when he's soberly serious.

Oui.

Michael Gruber lives in the West Village in a small one-bedroom basement apartment near where 11th Street improbably intersects 4th Street. As we walk, I'm telling André that Gruber is one of the few people in the middle of the city graced with a fragrant garden and when I was a child and dad and I would come to New York, Michael's garden reminded me of something out of an English novel. Roses, with a million new and tantalizing smells, a crusty, splintery table in the middle of the small space with a few spindly chairs scattered around like shells on a sandy patch. One felt as though the roses might intertwine with one's limbs turning one into a citified nymph of some sort; but it wasn't an unpleasant sensation, you just felt the fullness of the natural world out there in that small garden. Michael isn't English but he likes to 'take tea,' as he calls it, and so he would bring tea and cookies outside. Michael was a paratrooper in World War II with my dad and dad's early novel, *The Eagle's Nest* is based on their shared experiences. When I mention this book, André, who's been contemplating writing a sort of biography of dad, tells me:

This is my least favorite of Aaron's books and I can't quite put my finger on why; it certainly echoes his time as a paratrooper on the frontlines when the Unites States airborne divisions first reached Berchtesgaden, but it feels, I don't know...forced.

Instead of broaching the topic foremost on my mind, of what's going on with us, André never fully replied to me, when I'd begged us to be properly together again, as we cross Seventh Avenue I describe a conversation dad and I had when I was about twelve, why? I'd asked him. But, distracted, as usual, and not focusing on what I was telling him, that I'd learned that day in school about WWII, he replied, looking up from *The Wings of the Dove*, why what?

Why did the Nazis kill almost all of Europe's Jews?

At this question, the entirety of his attention turned to me. He took off his glasses, I tell André—a sure sign that father was ready to focus, and crinkled his brow so that it looked like two parallel wave lines in synch, scrunching at the same time.

Well, honey, the truth is no one knows for sure. Historians have been arguing about this ever since the war ended. Some people—the intentionalists—believe Hitler and the Nazi movers and shakers had a clear idea that they wanted to liquidate all of Europe's Jews; other people—the functionalists—feel strongly that the Nazi genocide emerged as a structural outcome of the war, because it was more convenient to kill the slave laborers once they were exhausted and nearly dead anyway.

Well, what do you think, dad?

The truth is, I don't know. Neither makes sense to me—I mean, both make sense, but I can't fully understand either position as the whole thing is so beyond, so outside of everything we'd been working towards in terms of Jewish assimilation and acceptance into the European fabric.

Even as a child, I appreciated the fact that my father never 'talked down' to me.

So, if the Jews of Europe were fully part of Europe—part of, as you say, the fabric, then why?

My father sighed and let out a long, slow breath. Right. Good question, he replied. Hate is very, very old. Nearly every day—about 200 per year—species go extinct. We don't care for our planet as we should. And humans do not care for other humans as we should.

Is that why you read so much?

He froze at this, his shoulders stiffened as if it were as cold as the spring of '45, and a flash of anger flew across his bold features. Then he softened, a statue turning into a teddy bear. Yes, Sid, I suppose so. Reading is much easier than dealing with people.

And the books never leave, you can open them again and again and their words, their promises, keep.

The tinkle of Michael Gruber's doorbell yanks us back to the present, on 11th Street. But it's a hollow bell and my shoulders slump as I realize Michael isn't home. I'm crestfallen as we begin trekking east again, as if Michael were some sort of lifeline that I needed to hang onto, desperately.

Just outside the slim entrance to Smalls Jazz Club, we see a handsome elderly gentleman, his arms pulled long by several grocery bags stretched to bursting.

Sid! Michael exclaims, setting down his bags and starfishing his arms out to enfold me. I catch a smell, cloves, and suddenly feel that it's my father holding me. After an extended embrace he pulls back and looks at me, takes my hands in both of his and I feel his warm, firm grip.

What luck to bump into you two. We're just near my place, can you? Would you be able to come over for tea—I just procured a wonderful apricot tart.

We laugh and tell him we'd just left his front gate.

After Michael unlocks the gate, and sets down the bags, he holds my shoulders so he can look me fully in the eyes again and then his face clouds as he says abruptly but sweetly, you look alarmingly pale, we will take tea. Alas, it is too cold to sit in the garden, but we can squeeze in here.

As we settle at the table, Michael fusses in the kitchen and brings out a green tray with slices of apricot tart and steaming tea with milk in a proper milk jug and white sugar in a gleaming bowl topped with a tiny silver spoon.

Sid, I miss your father so much, Michael says with a sigh

as he sets the tray down. We didn't get to see each other so very often, in the last few years, each of us feeling the molasses speed that unfortunately accompanies ageing, but we did correspond via (albeit short) letters and the odd phone call here and there. I loved him, you know? Like a brother, like a brother I never had.

I can't help it. More unannounced tears—I wonder if the well will ever run dry so surprisingly many have bubbled up since my father died. André puts his arm around me and squeezes; I look up at him and our eyes tumble into each other. Breathing more slowly, I reach into my satchel and hand Michael his portrait. As soon as I explain the suitcase full of Dorothy's rare stuff, the blue gloves with the letter, the shoes, Paolo, the visit to the museum, Mr. Oravid and Henry, the voyage up the great ladder into the whale's mouth, Michael, who'd started taking notes with a tiny pencil in a small golden notebook he fished out of his breast pocket, becomes very pensive.

No wonder you are pale, my dear girl. You've had quite a shock. Well, I did wonder how Aaron would choose to tell you what he found, or rather, the zany story he was concocting because the truth...

You mean he—

No, he did not know what happened to your lovely mother. But he had, well, he had made some progress, he found out parts of the puzzle, but he was never able to fit them together, or rather, what he fit them into would seem like madness, even though he never gave up trying, never gave up until—

But, now I'm crying all over again, damnit, but he told me he stopped searching after a year.

Yes, I know. He wanted you to move on, to be endlessly free of trying to solve a probably unsolvable mystery. He wanted you to feel that there was nothing else to be done so you could have a childhood, a life, as they say.

But, I would have, I would have tried.

I know. I know. I argued with him about this but there was really nothing I could do—nothing, except, of course, help you in any way I could—

The darkroom.

Indeed. Now, remind me, what exactly, and please be very precise, did you find with this photograph?

We describe all over again each item in the suitcase. After a taut silence, a long sip of tea, a bit of flaky tart, and a delicate scratching of his chin, Michael concludes:

Well, it sounds as though your father got closer than he let on.

Closer?

Yes. We know that Dorothy continued her interest in whales. And we know that she focused on the intersections between sound and language, music and sense, whale song was particularly intriguing to her. She was totally amazed by that wonderful composition where Hovhaness incorporated whale song into an orchestral piece. As you know, I went with her on a magical whale watching adventure off the coast of St. Lawrence, I was crushing on Captain Searles—

I put up a hand as a hard brake on the flood of revelations. The truth I had been searching for nearly all my life might be much closer and much curiouser than I could ever have imagined.

*

I'm working on a series of prints today, and experimenting with a new, high-contrast paper. But I can't stop thinking about these endless forks of truth that unfold through myriad possible multiverses. It feels right, somehow, that I saw the last flicker of my father in the darkroom because being here furnishes a damp portal out of the city, in the intense quiet of its moist cinder block walls, you step out of the current of time completely, floating as if gravity-less. Working with black and white film tumbles me back into the past, falling into a warm bath of many faces, ghosts, some. Occasionally my mother's face flickers underwater and then resolves into the visage of a living woman. Sometimes, wondering what all these chemicals might do to my body, I breathe in and hold my breath for a minute just to see if I can chart the poison as it parachutes my lungs. The pungent smell of the developing fluid coats my teeth in something metallic yet comforting. I watch with tense expectation as damp faces emerge through the water, undrowning; people come to life when they dry out, as if I give them mouth-to-mouth resuscitation. I want to pull my father from that lake the way I pull his photograph up from the developing bath. And then I want to shake him into telling me what the fuck he's thinking, putting André and me through this wild goose chase.

I'm arguing with a ghost. I've installed a clothesline inside the dark room with old-fashioned wooden clothes pegs to hang up the prints. Pushing the photos to extra-grainy, multiple little dots appear, each a shrunken pointillist painting. I heighten the contrast even though these subjects' contrasting skin tones do that but I try to force that effect stronger and more beautiful at the same time. Rarely, I place stuff on top of the paper—translucent objects such as pieces of thick glass, a shell, a pendant, or bits of plastic to create strange shapes, a floating kaleidoscope. I'm going to incorporate that translucent thick glass paperweight dad left for me—for us—as a clue. Now and again these experiments forge unexpected special effects but generally it just looks like I screwed up. I make so many mistakes. What else can I do? The darkroom is on the West Side, on 23rd Street in a cranky old building surrounded by floral supply stores. Each time I go there, I imagine wearing a trench coat with nothing under it, a fedora jauntily cocked on my head. Like some imaginary me out of a J-P Melville film.

I would love to see that, André would say, reaching out to see what's under my coat. He's so attentive. Too attentive. He makes me feel stifled, and yet that's incredibly stupid. I love it when he touches me, and he knows just how. But I constantly disappoint him, somehow, and that makes me pull back. It's as though I'm always afraid of screwing up, so I screw it up ahead of time, so that I don't have to worry that I will ruin this delicate thing we've built.

After work, as the sun sets—I love the phrase *coucher de soleil*, the sun goes to bed, making the winter light soft and slightly cantaloupe tinged, André and I meet at the edge of Tomkins Square Park for a little flânerie, to try to sort out the emotional jumble of Michael's hints. I keep facing up to it, only to turn away. Exactly as happens with my love. As we walk, my camera strap tangles in my long scarf and I feel a bit slapstick, like a Monty Python character. We spy a woman with hot pink hot pants and matching hot pink Doc Martens, wearing a pink coat. This intriguing figure perches on a bench, never-minding the cold, on the edge of the park. There has to be a story there, and we know it will never be told to us; snapping a photo of this woman bleaches out her story at the exact same moment I capture a glimpse of it. The grainy black and white image of this stranger who will metamorphose into an anonymous portrait will destroy all that ravishing hot pink captured by flash, but a strong sense of her wonderful oddness, her difference, her self-fashioning into a playful, unscripted mode will remain. Was there a moment, I wonder aloud to André, feeling the frosty metal of my camera against my cheek as I frame the image, when this woman thought, *Yes, that's it! All hot pink! My life has been incomplete until now.* Or was it a dare from a friend? Or just bit by bit she kept adding on to the original idea so that she could swim every day in a magical, portable sunset? Forgetting the fine details of all the people and things I drink in with my camera frightens me. Maybe irrationally panics me. Who can remember everything? When I describe these intense fears of forgetting, André recounts a Borges short story about a man who died because he could not forget.

It was so painful, he tells me, this abundance of memory. Imagine storing the shape of every cloud you'd ever seen in your head?

I speculate, as we head in the direction of the river, that a trace of my father will emerge through the chemicals in the darkroom, in the print of this hot pink lady in the park. She looks lonely, and yet all her own, just like Aaron. Taking André's hand: It's as though pieces of him, a fleeting expression, a gesture, a solitariness, a pair of baggy trousers—reflects in strangers.

We see a couple approaching and, just as I'm about to hand them my come to my studio card, I realize that I'd already taken their portrait—I recognize them from my wall. They greet us warmly, each reaching out their hands to enfold ours, gestural carbon copies each to each. One of the women cocks her head in the direction of the bench.

Yes, she's quite something, André says, as if by way of reply.

Hey, thanks for sending that portrait of us—it's hanging over the fireplace. We just love it. I think the portrait made us appreciate each other even more.

—.

Oh, I'm so sorry, I didn't know that would make you cry…you ok?

Jeez, I'm leaking all over the place. My father died, quite suddenly, and André and I, I mean, I'm…

I feel you, it's rough. Hang in there, OK?

Thanks. And, listen, I will let you know if I have any news about the photobook, ok?

No worries, the woman rests her hand comfortably on her swollen middle.

Mazel tov! Please do come back to my studio with the baby, I would love to take her? His? portrait, well, all of you together, will you?

We'd love to.

I wipe my stinging eyes. André pulls me in close, his hot chocolatey breath making warm tracks down behind my ear and down my back. We head east again; I'm feeling slightly deflated, and I tell him I'm giving up on portraits for the day. Some sort of longing tugs at me—the woman's softness, her self-assurance, the weight of her hand nestling into her belly.

We return to my apartment to unpack the suitcase all over again. André's being incredibly patient as the suitcase begins to take on the character of a third wheel in our relationship. Patient but just barely. André's lips are tight as he tells me he's going to grade some papers in a café. As soon as I hear the door click closed behind him, that sinking in my stomach again and the loneliness floods in, mocked by all the images of mostly smiling couples lining my walls. I unspool all their lives from their images, conjuring worlds for them so much smoother than mine, filled with more surety than I can ever dream.

The achingly smooth figure is my companion now. As I stare at the sculpture, something tickles at the back of my mind, a pine needle scratching.

I have seen this before, definitely but where? When I was a kid, my father often took me to museums when we traveled the world in search of rare books: New York, Chicago, Montréal, London, Washington, Paris, Vienna, Amsterdam, they've begun to blur together in my mind's eye. We played a game, name the artist! he'd command, and then would glance around a gallery and pretty much get them all right. I loved it when he screwed up, and he always seemed really irritated. He hated being wrong and he would generally walk off in a huff.

Each time André and I gambol around a museum, I try to truly see the images, to read them deeply. And, much like my anxiety about forgetting the minute details of fascinating faces I glimpse in the city, the nameless hot pink lady, I get upset by how much I forget, even after looking, sketching, sometimes photographing canvases or sculptures. Magic spills out of the stillness of gazing intently for a sustained time at a painting. Our favorite museum in New York is the Frick. We gravitate to the old, lost world the museum invites you to enter—rich, velvet couches line the rooms, and the pieces stretch out before your eyes so you can genuinely see them. And, in some cases they offer the uncanny illusion that they can see you, too. El Greco painted St. Jerome so that his eyes follow you wheresoever you go. We look up at him, fix his gaze, and then circle the room—trying not to fall over anything—attempting to catch him looking away. But he never does. It's a painterly trick we can't fathom but it thrills us. But I shrink into the deflation that I hadn't seen that sculpture at the Frick, and my apartment feels heavy with emptiness, those people looking down at me from the walls are no help.

Staring at the small sculpture resting comfortably on her side in that peculiar suitcase, a flash of sunlight bounces off her metallic skin, I begin to scroll mentally through every museum we'd ever spent time in. Was it at the National Gallery of Art's East Wing? I remember going there with my father soon after it opened. The giant Calder mobile on the ceiling holds a particular fascination for me as it catches the light while it sways and swirls and over the years, I took hundreds of pictures of it at different times of day with azure light turning to auburn. When in a good mood, father treated me to an ice cream at the café between the buildings, and I sat beside the cooling fountain that ran right through the wall. I could never understand how a fountain could be embedded in a thick wall and as I licked my chocolate ice cream cone, I felt the double cold on my shoulder from the fountain and on my tongue. But it wasn't there that I'd seen the sculpture.

Closing my eyes and allowing the reclining woman to crawl inside my head, I breathe in and out and try to fill in the surroundings of the sculpture in my mind's eye, willing the background into fragile existence. Finally, I see, as if painted in swift brush strokes behind the naked lady, the white, white cold marble, the houndstooth patterned, buffed hardwood floor. I can channel the hushed atmosphere, the ancient-mansiony texture of the place and I realize quite firmly that she's at the Kunst Galerie on Ninety Eighth and Fifth.

I find André at the café and he looks relieved to have an excuse to procrastinate grading those essays.

Aaron and I took a trip to New York when I was eleven, I tell André, as we head to the subway, and attempted to go to the then newly opened Galerie. He cultivated a particular interest in this museum housed in a converted mansion designed by the same architect who crafted the New York Public Library because he was just beginning what would become prolonged research into *The Cracked Vase*. He was trying to find out everything he could about Nazi-looted art, which the Kunst Galerie specialized in exhibiting. We'd entered the museum and were about to get tickets when the guard asked, Miss, how old are you? When I told him he silently pointed to the sign: No one under twelve allowed in the museum or the café.

Crestfallen, I'd felt the injustice of this blanket rejection and vowed to be the sort of person who'd frequent this and other museums. My father didn't bother arguing, which I wish he would have, just once, stuck up for me; he just turned on his heel, me trotting along behind, struggling to catch up, and left. As we turned the corner back to the Park, I'd paused for a minute to press my face up to the glass of Café Mendelssohn, beholding the sparkling room, the mirrors reflecting at various angles the well-dressed diners enjoying their lattés and sachertorte in this mini-Vienna on the park. As I pulled my disappointed little face away, ten fingerprints smeared the pane, and I paused to paint the schmutz into a Rorschach test. It became a point of pride later, after I moved to New York, to frequent the

Kunst Galerie and to enjoy Café Mendelssohn whenever I could. André and I spent a beautiful afternoon there, some time ago, with mamie.

The Kunst Galerie became a pivotal space for Aaron, and, while writing *The Cracked Vase*, he'd peruse the museum and pace, muttering bits of the novel under his breath so people often thought he was talking to himself. Consuming the museum's small archival room, he researched the provenances of looted objects, often found after lengthy searches and secured only when extensive legal battles were won.

Now André and I stroll into the main hall and I pull the replica sculpture out of my satchel and we stand there, in the cavernous white marble space, gazing at the eight-foot long reclining nude, exactly the same as the mini one I'd started carrying around instead of the one red shoe. She's so smooth, this giant stone woman, and you want to touch her, to trace her curve lines all the way around her hips. She's enormous and yet totally relaxed in her marble body. It was as though the tiny version I held took a hint from Lewis Carroll and swallowed an *Eat Me* pill, growing massively bigger. I rip my coat off strangely briskly, I'm suddenly sweaty and clammy, and tip my head up to André, he's standing there tracing each curve of the woman with his racy brown eyes in a way that makes me squirm, and then we read the shiny brass plaque:

Betta Goldheim, "Lucy," 1923. This remarkable sculpture was unearthed amid the tunnels below Cairinhall,

Reichsmarschall Hermann Göring's holiday retreat in Bavaria. The anonymous donor finally received her rightful property after a protracted legal battle in 1983. The donor's father, an amateur art collector, purchased the massive nude in Vienna in 1924 from the sculptor herself. It was among the prize possessions of their family and held pride of place in the courtyard of their villa on Rosenweg. Like many other valuable objects, it was taken by the Nazis with a crane when the family was deported to Nisko and then to Theresienstadt. The generous donor bequeathed it to the Kunst Galerie for all the world to see, and to remember.

It's *The Cracked Vase,* right? I ask André, putting my coat back on, is she still alive? The donor? Or her children?

The huge hall swirls and it's as if we were standing still and the museum floats around us, underwater.

Finding the ground, retracing our steps to the front desk André calmly asks to speak to one of the curators, and I marvel that he can be so chill; after some static on the walkie talkies we're directed to wait at Café Mendelssohn. As we face each other under the gilt mirrors and over-the-top chandeliers, I turn to the glass and see, as if she were standing there in the blazing, sun, my eleven year old self, staring in, longing. In therapy I'd learned to reach out and hug that kid, trotting along to match strides with her father, growing up motherless. But it's all so cheesy. I look away from her, that eleven year old.

Sitting at one of the very tables I lusted after, André and I turn over and over again where this giant clue might lead.

His upper lip forms a slight moustache from his cappuccino and I want to lick it off, but a tall man in an impeccable suit strides confidently over to our table, sits down, and raises his arm imperiously for the waiter. Ein latte, bitte.

Zo, he begins in a thick accent—Austrian? German? You vant to know more about de sculptur-e (he says "sculpture" as if it had three syllables).

Yes, and I take out the mini replica of the sculpture, rubbing its smooth surface with my sweaty palms, hand it to him across the table, as if I were offering him a genie's lamp. The waiter places the latte right next to the reclining woman without batting an eyelash and the tall man sips his drink gingerly, waiting for me to explain.

My father, may his memory be a blessing, left this sculpture in—well among his belongings and we would like to know how it connects to the more than life-size model here at the Kunst Galerie. Also, Herr? I am sorry, I don't think you told us your name? My father, the novelist Aaron Zimmermann, wrote a book about looted objects entitled *The Cracked Vase,* and we wondered if there was some connection there? We know that he researched the Kunst Galerie's vast collection of looted and then gratefully returned rare objects.

The man sets his latte down, his attention now fully on us.

Ah, I see. My name is Hans Becker. I must meet with another curator all the way downtown.

Becker glances at his heavy gold watch, and then looks back at us. But, please, do come with me. I have been retaining an important missive for you, from one of our generous patrons.

André and I look at each other. Blinking. We've been scripted, we're in one of dad's books, surely, yet another person hails us as if he jumped out of the suitcase, breathing.

We follow Hans up the graceful white marble winding steps and just at the place where the banister curves around to the left, we enter a small door to the right that I'd never noticed before, almost a hidden door which Hans opens deftly with a small key that he pulls down from under his beautiful suit sleeve and which seems to be bracleted to his wrist. We stand in an office with blinding white walls and a very simple, elegant, sturdy wooden desk. Hans sits down, opens the drawer, and hands me an envelope. It is square, light blue, and on the outside, the words: *For Sidney Zimmerman.*

I gulp.

You don't have to open it now, André offers, running his fingertips along the top of my arm.

But I sit down right there on the spotless floor of the hidden office in the Kunst Galerie and carefully, so as not to make a jagged rip, open the envelope.

The handwriting is from another century, a careful script from the era when people took the time to learn how to write in school, in fountain pen, with the telltale blobs and fatter sections of some letters than others, a stray dot on the edges here and there, a handsome chaos that looks intentional yet urgent. I feel a shock run down my spine, looking at it, and, also, fury, at my father. Did he forge this letter?

Dear Sidney,

You do not know me, and I am not sure if you ever will. I am afraid that if you are reading this, it means Aaron is no longer with us. I will be very old by the time you read this, if I am still here. Please, let me explain.

My name is Greta Eltman. I was born in 1910 in Vienna. My father, like your father, loved to read and to think and to imagine. He was a banker by trade but his real passion was art and when he could, he collected. He was very fussy about which pieces he chose to acquire. But, little by little, he amassed a beautiful, carefully curated collection of art works that we proudly displayed in and around our villa on Rosenweg. Before the war came to Vienna and the crowds of Austrians greeted Hitler as he marched toward the Heldenplatz at the Anschluss, before then, in 1937, my father knew we had to flee. He took some of his treasures, he gave some away to dear friends for safe-keeping, and the rest were simply stolen by the Nazis. There was no way we could have taken Betta Goldheim's amazing reclining nude—she was as big as a baby whale.

We were not able to transport much on the boat with us to New York. And we were lucky to get out. We watched those gloating Austrians greet the Nazis with their arms aloft, their faces lifted in triumph, we watched it from New York, via the newsreels in the cinemas. Slowly, we built a life here. My father had several connections in the banking world, and my mother made herself busy settling my sisters and me into our new lives. I became a New Yorker.

Many, many years later I received a letter from Chicago, from your father. He was researching you know, his Cracked Vase, and he wished to speak to people who had gone through long and often painful lawsuits to try to regain some of their lost art objects. He found out about our family because there was an article in The Forward about us. Since he traveled to New York often, for his researches into rare books, he came to my house one morning and I offered him tea and we began to talk. And talk. It must have been quite dark by the time Aaron left that first day. But he returned again and again. We became good friends. He came back several times and I like to think those conversations helped him with his work.

One day, I decided to give him a gift. The small-scale model of the large sculpture that is now in the Kunst Galerie. The sculptress, Betta, had given the model to my father and we managed to pack that in with our rare objects as we fled. My father reasoned that he could use it to regain the larger than life final version. And he was right, the model proved to be an important piece of the lawsuit.

At first, as he held the smooth model in his hands, Aaron said he could not accept such a gift but I teased him that this was only the shrunken version, not the real thing. He took it very carefully home. I did not see him after that for some time—I think he had finished the book and was on to new subjects, the one about the young boy in London, I believe? That one also has a rare object in it, not unrelated to our collection. Aaron sent me a first edition of The Cracked Vase, inscribed with these words: "To my dear Greta, inspiration, generous friend, brave survivor of the worst. Warmly, Aaron."

Then, many years later, he arrived at my door without an appointment. "Greta, I do not think I am very well." You know how your father never minced words, ja? "I would like you to help my daughter, Sid. But not yet, not while I am still here. Just, after..." Then I could see a small tear just below his left eye. He trusted me, and I was very grateful.

I do not know how I can help you, Sid, or why he wanted to wait until "after" but I have done exactly as he promised and written this letter to you, and entrusted it to Hans at the Kunst Galerie until the time was ripe for you to read it. Come and see me anytime, I hope I am still here when you arrive.

Warmly, Greta

At some point while I read the letter, Hans must have slipped quietly out of the room. André reaches down now, to pull me up—I've slumped rag doll style on the floor.

It's a lot, I know, hon, he says, do you want to head home or? but I get the feeling he intuits the answer before I utter it: Let's go straight to Greta's—who knows how much time we have left.

We walk down Fifth Avenue, on the street side, not the park side, past the Guggenheim, past the Met, all the while discussing this strange new turn. The brown, bare trees edging over the stone wall from the park seem to egg us on. The winter birds still talking. I ask the air around us at least twelve times in those twenty something blocks, Why, dad, why? Why all these complicated clues? You're driving me crazy! As usual, he doesn't answer. This posthumous game he must be enjoying playing with us is making me uneasy. Where will it all lead? My father flabbergasts me from beyond his grave, or rather from all the way out in Lake Michigan. What if I hadn't found the suitcase in the first place? Then what? Or what if I had but we remained unable to follow the clues to their conclusions? And do they ever conclude? Father could never have told us what he suspected so he just threw all the rare stuff he'd dug up into that case and left it for us, this rubik's cube of multicolored questions, no real answers.

We reach the stately old townhouse where, Hans had told us, Greta Eltman had lived since her family arrived in New York before the worst, in 1937. We don't have an appointment, of course, any more than father did when he told Greta he was not well, or when they began talking for hours that stretched to years. André rings the doorbell and it tinkles like one of those bells to call people to dinner in *Upstairs Downstairs*. Then silence. We stand staring at the thickly painted great red door, the door that I had dreamed on Aldine, with the cherubic brass knob in the very center and just when we we were about to give up, the portal opens a crack and an elderly lady, who could not have been more than five feet tall, peers out, a small white dog hiding behind her heels. Yes, hello? she says, can I help you?

The woman opens the door, steps out onto the street, the little dog on a thin reed of a leash. I am just about to walk Bruno, she tells us.

But before we say anything, Greta's features soften, and she smiles broadly, Zidney, André, I recognize you from a beautiful black and white photo Aaron gave me. Zo, you've read my letter? walk with me.

Bruno hews closely to her, as if he's afraid of us, but as soon as Greta reaches out to take my arm, as if we'd known each other our whole lives, as if she were mamie, the little dog, his eyes ringed in light pink, looks up and pisses on a tree.

Circling the block and landing back at Greta's house, I wonder if her parents reproduced their villa in Vienna here in the city. Everything looks as though it tumbled into the present from another time. Another portal, like the darkroom, like Fanelli's. Seeing us looking around, our jaws agape, Greta, as if reading our minds says:

Ja, it is very much like home here. We tried to bring the

world we missed so much just a little bit here. But we have some new world things—look! And she proudly points us toward a pair of Frank Lloyd Wright chairs. Oak, clean lines, that deep forest green he liked to use. We settle in the chairs while Greta insists on bringing tea.

Once she returns with a tray laden with tea and cakes and lumps of sugar, and once she pours out tea for all of us, she finally sinks back onto the couch opposite us.

Zo, you've found Lucy.

I extract the mini-Lucy from my satchel and hand it gently to Greta. Honestly, we have no idea what to make of this, any of this. Do you?

Ah, yes, it has been some weeks since I have been to visit Lucy. I do go, you know, even at my advanced age, to the Kunst Galerie. Hans and the other curators are so generous to me when I go there, they insist on fussing over me and serving me Linzertorte and espresso. You see, Betta, the sculptress became great friends of my parents. She never told the whole story to them but now, with the benefit of all those years to think, I wonder if that Lucy she so lovingly sculpted were not, how shall I say? A little more than her friend?

Yes, André agrees, I wondered the same thing. I confess, I suppose it's a bit sexist, well I thought the sculptor was a man, the body seemed so lovingly rendered, as if he shaped her as he might touch her.

I'm embarrassed to feel a faint trace of a blush heating my cheek as he says this, and I suddenly wish we had just climbed the ladder of my loft so he could demonstrate what he meant.

Yes, I interject, clearing my throat and focusing on the present, I think André is right, it does seem to have been made by a lover. Did she, did they, I mean, survive the war?

We don't know for sure, Greta says, taking a sip of tea, they went into hiding, changed their names so they would not sound so Jewish, and then, well, no one knows. We did look, from here, after the war and found nothing. We can only hope.

We all stare down at our shoes.

Your father, Greta, at last rousing us all from our mournful reflections, continues, is full of strange ways? No? He was sure I could help you but I do not know what you need.

It seems you are always helping him. You helped him with his book, you gave him this beautiful sculpture—and, I don't know, either, how you can help us, or, we can help you?

Ah, but your father did help me. My children, wonderful as they are, have moved on with their lives and I rattle around this gracious house, quite alone. I loved it when Aaron, who was a bit like a son to me, came to visit. We talked and talked and he encouraged me to tell him every detail of our lives in Vienna. For his book, you know. It was bittersweet, yes, because memory sometimes comes too strong and then I remember we can never go back. Even though our world is entirely shattered, it's almost as though it's there, encased in glass, but inaccessible, as if that whole world were underwater and I couldn't swim. I can see it though, our old world, through the thick glass, I just will never arrive there again. But I do so love, did so love, to talk with Aaron about things, he's so intelligent. And Sid, he spoke so much about you, he was very proud, he kvelled about your photographs, but you know that, of course. And André, he felt you were becoming his son. I read the obituary, you wrote this, Zid? Very beautiful. But why was there not a funeral?

At this the skin around my ears turns slightly pink and I can almost feel the heat rising up from under my collar, as if in a cartoon. I worry it might be visible to Greta and André.

André wrote the obituary, actually, I say. He's working on a sort of literary biography of my father. It will be the first. Greta, he seemed so very alone. It's only after he's gone that we're finding out all sorts of things—you—for example, my father never told me about you. And also Paolo, Mr. Oravid…. It's too late now, I think, for a funeral, but maybe, well what do you think? A memorial service?

You see! I *can* help you! Ja—we will arrange a memorial service, right here. And maybe Esther can come from Québec City.

You know my grandmother?

But of course, my dear, we talked for hours, your father and I, and I know that your poor mother, Dorothy, has been missing for quite some time and that Esther, who I so enjoyed meeting, lives still in Québec City, in the colorful house of your childhood summers, and that she, like Aaron, like you, have never stopped longing for Dorothy. And hoping, maybe a little?

The salty tears drip right into my sweet tea and Greta rises creakily to hold me, much as mamie would have.

Over the weekend, André stays at my place. I love having him back here, I love how he feels, and how he always knows where to put his hands, his soft mouth, how he traces every line as if he were drawing me, or writing on me. He listens. But I'm also terrified when we're back together, each time. I'm bound to screw it up so I feel feet on egg-shelly. On Saturday morning, he saunters out to pick up pain au chocolat, and when he returns he takes me on the living room floor, the sun blindingly coating the room. The beach inside in November. When I come the sun enters my eyes, so bright it's black.

After, as we gulp down big drinks of coffee and tuck into the pain au chocolat, still slightly warm, dribbles of chocolate coat our mouths. I sense that he's suspicious of this togetherness at the same time he craves it. We're tightrope walkers, treading gently along this narrow path we've created for ourselves. I try to hope I can unfuck it this time. But I can't trust the sensitive surety. I can't know, ever, and that thought fills me with dread. Fear of forgetting, afraid of staying.

As I take another bite and look at André a bit forlornly, I'm thinking about what Greta said, that I've been missing Dorothy for so long that maybe I am no longer really able to feel the ache? There's only a dull spot inside, rubbed flat from persistent handling, where my longing used to be. I feel, sometimes, utterly numb. Stuck. But somehow finding that suitcase, finding those shoes, the whale, these are like a match being struck on all that numbness, something breaks through and I'm finding, if not exactly an island of hope—it's much too late for that, isn't it?—then unquenchable curiosity at least. Today we're going to crack that envelope and read my father's manuscript.

André indulges me as I pull out the curious suitcase, open it up, and stare at its contents. Tucking the envelope under my arm I pull the key out of its sack. It's heavy and so satisfying to hold. It looks as though it would fit into a writing desk of some sort, the kind of thing Greta, or mamie would have...

Wait—André—the key, mamie, I think, has a rosewood writing desk with a key like this one? Could she? And this grotty bag, it's the café near her...

With a thin flake of dough trembling on his enticing lip André tells me that the only way to find out is to go to the great house. You've told me, he says, that it keeps pulling you back in reality, in dreams, in memory, a neodymium magnet you haven't the power to resist. And I adore your grandmother—remember? She asked expressly, when she was here, that we come and visit her.

And, I say, tu me manques mamie, and need to tell her, in person, about everything.

We decide to leave just before Thanksgiving, so we won't have to miss work.

I'll pick you up, André says, generously, right after my class on Wednesday, ok? At 4? Can you go to the travel agent next to Shlovsky and get our tickets?

Bien sûre. Are we ready, now, for this? I'm terrified.

André pulls me down next to him on the sofa, the thick padded packet in his big hand.

II Slobgollion
By Aaron Zimmerman

I have seen them riding seaward on the waves
Combing the white hair of waves blown back
When the wind blows the water white and black.

We have lingered in the chambers of the sea
By sea-girls wreathed with seaweed red and brown
Till human voices wake us, and we drown.

   T.S. Eliot,

      The Love Song of Alfred J. Prufrock

Solange refused to pry out and thrust away the miniscule grains of hope she held, stuck as if deep into the very flesh of her palms. But it's true, her mother, Helen Amaral, had been missing for quite some time. And now her father, Ishmael, had been gone for a year. Solange lived with her grandmother during junior year of high school. And on the day the whale came, Solange went missing too.

The Amaral home, an architectural wonder full of surprises, is favored with bedrooms and main rooms all facing Cape Cod Bay. When the inhabitants of the house open their windows they can see, hear, and inhale the sea. The house is situated gracefully in the seaside town of Orleans, in Barnstable County, on Cape Cod's elbow. The air in this town is salty, the streets are salty, and there's a fine layer of rust on all the metal. Cape Cod Bay stretches out on one side, and the angry Atlantic reaches out seemingly infinitely on the other. When they travel away from the sea, Sol has trouble sleeping without the sound of the waves landing on the shore, circling back, hitting the sand again. She loves the endlessness of that sound.

Because of her father's work as a marine biologist and the President of the National Cetological Society, instead of a basement, an aquarium rises out of the ground below the house on stilts. Stingrays, Hamlet Fish, Blueface Angelfish, Clown Triggerfish, Moorish Idol, Lionfish, copious others. So many gorgeous, colorful fish who do not always get along, but generally reach a kind of detente. If you were to stroll downstairs, all of your preconceived notions of basements as havens for skeletons and ghosts would be exploded. The Amaral basement, because it had no walls, wasn't a basement, and was light, and full of color. The aquarium stretched from floor to ceiling, and at night NASA designed sun-lights illuminated it.

Solange loved to stargaze and so she would turn the lights off and look through the water at the sky, charting the subsequent blurring and refracting. A little narrow pathway arrayed around the outside of the aquarium so they could observe all the colorful fish. A skinny, bright red ladder stretched, like a seam falling straight down from top to bottom, in case they felt compelled to climb in.

Ishmael worked with a team of skilled engineers to reinforce the ground below the tank and install the huge aquarium. They were drilling and sawing for some time to get everything set up. The glass pieces arrived on an enormous flat-bed truck and a dedicated team assembled the tank right below the house, between the thick stilts. Ishmael always joked that they needed to be careful, who knew what would come up out of that much water.

Going down to visit the fish was always Solange's quiet, peaceful space. Along with her grandmother's painting studio, this became one of the few places where she did not feel overwhelmed. She often descended to the watery world below and dreamed, eyes open, sometimes absorbing the feel of the sea below her eyelids.

One day, as she stared into the aquarium—she was concocting a story about one of the fish, the one she nicknamed Macbeth because of his bright red color, a very strange thing happened. As she stared into the tank the bottom began to dissolve. Smooth grey-blue skin crept up through the floor of the tank. Then, with the sunlight shining full on and reflecting off the water, causing her to blink rapidly, the visage of a whale appeared. The crack of the mouth came first, followed by the slight trace of the baleen as the mouth opened slightly. It took a good minute for the eyes to appear as a formidable, gorgeous, gigantic blue whale swam into the aquarium, without spilling any water, or breaking any glass.

As the whale sang his voice rippled and bent, as though he were singing through a viola. As he sang the sounds seemed to linger in the air, held up, as it were by salt. He begged Solange and her dog, Maisie, who'd trotted behind her down the stairs, politely, to hop on his back. Sol slipped a little, getting on, but then found that if she gripped gently with hands, feet, and knees, she could manage to hang on tolerably well. Because Maisie was unable to straddle the cold, slippery skin as Sol could, the dog sat upright and Sol hugged her. The whale swam with the teenager and canine on his back effortlessly through the floor of the basement and into the sea.

Naturally, the forty-foot diameter aquarium is much smaller than a roughly one-hundred-foot-long blue whale. It's also true that the concrete floor of the tank, triple reinforced with rebar, could not be breached by a whale and then seal up again as Sol witnessed when she glanced back at her home on her way down and down. It's just as true that it could not have happened, as it is true that it did.

Once Solange settled on the whale's back, and figured out how not to slip into the sea as they traveled rapidly along, the blue whale sang in his willowy, yet steel tinged, way, "Hello Solange," and before he could sing more, she yearned to interrupt him, to explain that she preferred to be addressed as "Sol."

"Ah, Sol, then, my name is Marvin. You may be wondering why I am taking you into the sea. Please, do not be afraid, take a deep breath and I will explain."

"But—." And her words evaporated into a bubble as the whale plunged below the water again. But, she had been wondering, how did Marvin know that she was about to ask him to call her Sol? And why did she suddenly feel a welcome flood of warmth, despite the brisk saltwater, right after the thought 'I am freezing' formed in her consciousness?

"Yes," Marvin continued singing, "I'm sure you have lots of questions. I'm so sorry but you won't be able to talk easily until we get to the Congress. Humans are very limited in that way."

Sol was sure Marvin could discern that she was nodding but she did not know how he would be privy to this knowledge. The whale's eyes were about 20 feet in front of where she was sitting, wishing he'd installed a handle so she could hang on a little better, and his eyes, surprisingly small for his size, and just over the striped part of his mouth, looked out sideways.

As they cruised along, Sol recognized several kinds of fish but also experienced the thrill of observing new and unusual ones. The water swirled around her, sometimes a hazy lavender, at other moments, as the sun and the clouds tangoed and transmogrified above, mud-toned, turquoise, or grass-green. A school of bonito swam by, smacking their fish lips audibly under water. A large school of dolphin cruised alongside for a beat or two, playing an elaborate game. Sol enjoyed watching the bubbles float up to the surface as she exhaled, and she was getting comfortable, sight-seeing and absorbing all those shapes of green and brown seaweed on the way to wherever Marvin was taking her. Then she saw it: the unmistakable straight up and down triangular fin, but flat and attached perpendicularly. Light grey stripes on pale grey skin.

A Tiger Shark.

Ever Ishmael's daughter, Solange knew all the details: a handful of sharks eat humans every year, while humans kill millions of them for delicacies like "shark fin soup" (she would never dream of eating that). She knew not to be scared; and yet she was enormously frightened. Before she could alert Marvin, she heard him turn to the shark and say something. She could have sworn she heard the word "essen." And then perhaps..."nisht...tzu" bubbled out. Indeed, she had correctly grasped the words, and they rolled around her tongue. Marvin must have sang, "Zi ist nisht tzu essen!"

"Ja, ja," the shark, to Sol's amazement, replied, "Ich vays. Aditi unz a zogt as mir mussen nicht essen di mentschen vos is gekumen in dem yam. Mir vays."

"Marvin," she thought, "why are you speaking Yiddish with that shark?"

"Oh, that? Sometimes when we whales have a hard time understanding shark-tongue we revert to using human language to communicate amongst ourselves. Oh, and don't worry, he won't eat you."

She nodded again, letting out a large stream of fat bubbles, to show that she comprehended that Marvin told the shark not to eat her and that the shark replied that Aditi (who is that, she wondered?) told them not to eat the humans who were in the ocean (whatever that meant).

Marvin seemed to get very excited when he knew she understood and he asked, "You speak Yiddish?"

And then she thought: "No but my Nana sometimes speaks Yiddish and so I picked up a little, I guess."

Sol felt surprisingly relaxed, all of a sudden, knowing the sharks were harmless and she recalled then Nana's quiet, beautiful paintings that would habitually help her calm down after the stresses of high school. She would often float into the studio where Nana painted and where she stored her canvases and just gaze at them, much as she tended to look out to sea. Sol felt that Nana's paintings perpetually changed the more she looked. The tableaux remind her of sand-sculptures soaked in water. Only with Nana's paintings one does not need to move them to experience their motion, they seem always rocking. Sol prefers the abstract ones, how they evoke water, even when that was not Nana's express intention. Sometimes Nana lays down a color and then adds other colors above it, but one can still perceive the original shades shining through, translucent, like layers of thin multi-colored silk. Some time ago, she recalls now, floating under water on Marvin's back, feeling dreamy, and wondering why she wasn't more shocked, afraid, it seemed normal to be riding this graceful whale and she remembered staring at the paintings. In Nana's studio, Sol's legs had stretched straight out in front of her, while Maisie framed her face with her paws, resting her chin flat on the floor. Nana came in quietly and sat down next to them.

"Vos ton ir zen, ziskeyt?" *what are you seeing, sweetheart?* she asked, gently stroking Sol's hair.

"I see layers and layers of colors. It looks like when the water changes color and there's a dividing line between the turquoise and the deep blue, like an archeological dig where you can see the different aspects of the earth as you go deeper—as I saw in a PBS documentary. Your paintings are so beautiful, Nana."

"And you are a sweetheart."

Solange gazed out on the horizon as if Nana's painting had come to life, turned to salt water, and she saw the now peaceful looking shark's tail as he swam out to a group of other sharks. They appeared to her just as a bunch of boys on the playground— precisely like kids from her old school- hanging around, chatting, sometimes playfully cuffing each other. Not much difference, really.

"We're almost there," Marvin sang, "hang on tight, OK?"

Marvin then took a sharp turn and plunged down and down. "We are going to the Whale Congress," he explained carefully, "there may be a lot of information that might be hard for you to digest right away. And for that, I am sorry."

Marvin leveled out and turned his great neck as best he could to her, "I know this is a lot for you to take in, but please, I will need you to focus completely and listen with all your might to everything Aditi tells you."

Marvin turned briskly to the right, as if entering an underwater cave. But this space, which seemed to Solange bigger than space itself, was no cave. An emerald green, calming light flooded in from above and Sol witnessed hundreds of whales all pointing towards the center as if waiting for something. In this moment she knew what awe meant. Marvin sang out to Sol to disembark, which she did. Gazing out and absorbing, trying to absorb, the infinite magnitude of the ocean, Sol felt, treading water next to Maisie, infinitesimally small. Each whale's face betrayed a different expression. Blue whales, Minke whales, right whales, humpbacks, in all sorts of shades of blue, grey, speckled brown, some with a multitude of barnacles stuck to them, others smooth as soft butter. It appeared as though the aquarium Ishmael had built were re-sized to an order of magnitude approaching a billion.

As she treaded water, Sol could not fully grasp the size of the whale in the middle. This must be

Aditi. And she made the blue whale on the ceiling of the Natural History Museum in New York appear as small as a squid. How Sol marveled at her voice! Aditi sang in a tremendously low, rich bass emanating from the very center of the earth, as if she were expounding from below the ocean's floor. Ishmael had explained to Sol that whale song can be 188 decibels but she could not have conceived fully, until Aditi sang and Sol felt the reverberations through her ribs, how that depth of sound could be experienced.

At first, Aditi emitted a song lower than the cello's C string, but then the song morphed into words. If Sol strained her ears she could hear... English.

"Whale Congress commences!"

All the other whales shifted their bodies up until resting on just their stomachs, they appeared to be standing at attention. Stiff with anticipation. Aditi closed her cloudy eyes, and as she did, each whale dropped their tail back down with an impressive thump. The water rippled and pushed out from the circle and Aditi opened her eyes once more. Bobbing up and down from the combined tail smacks, Sol imagined a helicopter hovering overhead, its occupants treated to an incredible sight. Enormous bodies of these splendid, sensitive, ill-understood animals, all facing a small human (and canine) alternately treading water or resting with her hand on the back of a blue whale. If Sol paced from one side of her house to the other, that would be approximately fifty feet. She would need to pace that twice to approach the length of Marvin, or Aditi. And all of these gigantic animals focused on her. She felt that they wanted something from her but she could not imagine what that could be.

Sol longed for her father to send her a sign. A year had evaporated since she'd last seen him and she greatly feared she would lose forever the sensation of his bristly chin spiked with sharp black and white hairs and his unique smell, the smell of soap and cloves. It was fading. She could no longer breathe in and smell him, as she would have done, hopping up to him whilst he sat in his reading chair. She struggled to remember the sound of his voice—the exact pitch when he would high five her after work (his vain attempt to seem cool and prepared to deal with a teenager) and ask, "how's it going?" He would then scratch Maisie just where she liked it, behind her ears. Sol felt a prickle along her spine as she wished beyond all hope that Ishmael had befriended these talking whales. He'd been researching whales in Alaska when he failed to return. Nana engaged every possible means to find him. Nothing.

Sol now heard an enormous sound, like a many times amplified shofar on Rosh Hashanah, echoing out all around her.

"We have invited you here today to seek your help with a most crucial mission."

Sol very much wanted to speak, to tell this immense blue whale that she was just a teenager, that she had no idea how to do much of anything other than read books, stare in wonder at Nana's paintings, or at the aquarium, or the stars, dream, and hang out with Maisie.

A burst of sunlight catalyzed a great shimmering on the whale's back as Aditi sang, "I know you feel you are a mere youth and why would we ask you...The truth is, you are the only human who can carry out the mission."

Sol struggled to absorb the implications of the vast blue whale's music, and she began to think that perhaps she was dreaming. Ever since she could remember, she'd experienced vivid dreams full of sea creatures and underwater escapades, so it didn't seem unreasonable that she was still warm in her bed with Maisie snoring on her pillow. She stared at the immense array of whales and pinched herself awake. As she did this, she realized that she tasted salt, so she must not be dreaming. She must be awake, below the surface of the sea, yet somehow breathing comfortably, with her hand holding her up by touching the hollow on the back of a blue whale, a whale who felt like an old friend, a whale named Marvin, all while listening to another humongous lady whale with a voice like Darth Vader telling her that she, skinny Solange from Sea Horse High, was going to somehow save the world.

"No Solange, you are not dreaming," the great whale continued, "I am afraid this is very real. And very urgent."

"OK," she finally mustered the courage to say, and as she spoke, a beautiful, lilting whale song poured out of her throat, much to her surprise: "yes, this is an awful lot for me to take in," Sol sang, "I'm feeling overwhelmed. And yes, I was wondering if I were dreaming. Also, you haven't told me what I'm supposed to do. And I want my father. Now. Please."

The whales all looked at each other then, but did not reply. They seemed to be engaged in intense, but utterly, utterly silent dialogue. In unison, the whales at the center of the congress turned together and regarded the human in their midst. Sol mused that Ishmael, were he with her, would likely be scribbling furiously in an underwater notebook, observing this curious whale behavior with the utmost exactitude.

Aditi had a lot of explaining to do, yet she would not—or perhaps could not—answer Solange's question about her father. Aditi told the wide-eyed teenager that whales rely on an energy source, virya, that helps them direct sonic waves across vast distances.

"All the whales of the planet," Aditi sang, "converse using the methods we have developed over centuries of engineering. The human energy corporation, Airavab, based in Boston's Hancock Tower, desperately wants to steal our energy. Their director, Drake Barents, plans to destroy the remaining whales of the world so that his corporation can instrumentalize our virya to enable him to grow even richer."

Solange felt certain that she'd heard of Airavab, but her father had never mentioned an energy company that had anything to do with cetaceans.

"We work with Akira, a double agent who navigates the interface between the whale universe and Airavab. He pretends to be Barents' right-hand man, but really, he's giving us information and supplying the humans who live with us with necessary nutrients."

All the whales were statuelike, listening to Aditi. Solange swam up to take a big breath and catch a ray of sun, even though she could breathe underwater, she was getting nervous about not having any actual air, and then she ducked down again, switching sides to hang on to Marvin with her left arm as her right began to ache and throb as if in tune with the undulations of the sea. She paused to wonder how she could breathe so well under water but somehow it felt more inconsequential than one might imagine. Her goggle-free eyes neither stung nor smarted and she concluded that if the fish and whales can see perfectly clearly underwater without goggles then she could, too. The light shifted as the whales took turns heading up for air, casting long shadows below the surface.

Solange determined that if she wasn't dreaming, she must be tripping. But that wasn't possible, either. Where was her father? And why wouldn't these whales tell her?

Aditi sang on: "Scientists at the National Cetological Society, including your father, who of course first connected us with Akira, have discovered that we've been trying to communicate with humans. We sent messages that said things like 'save the humans' and 'save the planet' but then something got lost in translation and we heard reports back from the surface that bumper stickers popped up on your cars (thankfully no longer fueled by whale oil) that said 'save the whales.' Barents is well aware that if we are successful his plans to control the other animals, acquire vast sums of money at the cost of the planet, and keep charging ahead with mass consumption despite what all the scientists say, will disintegrate."

"So," asked Sol, "how have you been trying to spread sensitivity? And, am I here because of my supposedly special sensitivities? And, how can I possibly be warm, without a wetsuit or anything other than my jeans and sweatshirt on? How am I breathing?"

"As far as the whales are concerned," Aditi's shofar sounds, which had paused briefly to listen to Sol's questions, continued, "our messages have been crystal clear—we send them every day. It may be that it was a little bit of a mistake to use Yiddish as the human language for our transmissions but at the time that we started sending the messages in 1905 there were millions of Yiddish speakers on the planet and we had no way of knowing that they would be almost eradicated. I.G. Eizenbet came to live with us for a while—Marvin's mother remembers this, she was a tiny whale at the time—around 1900 and taught us Yiddish. We taught Eizenbet rudimentary whalese. We do not understand the attempted eradication of the world's Yiddish speakers any more than we understand the attempted genocide of cetaceans. We chose Yiddish because it was an international language with a widely distributed press; we tried to infiltrate some of the Yiddish language novels with our messages. So far we have not been able to trace any record of human comprehension."

"But, how would you know if we humans had been able to hear your messages?"

"Well, more of you would be sensitive and fewer of you would be violent and you would actually take care of our planet. We found out later that records of whale song were being disseminated on the surface. And even when a human composer incorporated whalesong into a symphony, still no one seemed to be listening."

"OK, so how am I supposed to help? And where is my father?"

"We need you to convince Drake Barents—we have determined that he will listen to you."

"I'm noticing that you don't answer me when I ask about my father."

"—."

"I see."

"Marvin," Aditi sang, shimmying around, away from Sol, as though she couldn't look at her just then, "please show Sol and Maisie to their room."

A bit like an obedient automated car, Marvin rapidly swooshed over and teenager and dog climbed on, going only a little distance away from the congress. Sol fought back iron reams of anger at this lovely whale. Why wouldn't she tell her about her father? She must know, right? And why wouldn't she explain how she could breathe? But she needed to concentrate on what Aditi had said, not what she omitted. And now they were at their room.

Sol struggled to believe what she witnessed when she and Maisie scooted off Marvin's back and began swimming. Several rooms made of thick, slightly bumpy glass shimmered below the water. The light from the gentle summer sun filtered through the sea and turned the glass a magical turquoise-greenish color. As the water moved, the light shifted so waves of color washed over the walls, painting them with the shadows of shapes of fish, starfish, sea-horses, an underwater carousel of shape shifters.

They entered and found ample air, and fresh water rippling gently in a petite tank by the corner of the clear glass room. It was warm with moist air as you might find in a Victorian greenhouse nestled inside a verdant park. Sol took a breath in and held it, just to see if she could really breathe. Unbelievable, she thought, am I now a prisoner in the most beautiful place on earth? She was afraid, unknowing, but also somehow weirdly calm, as if the rocking ocean were a crib.

Marvin hovered outside the glass room; Sol and Maisie could hear him loud and clear through the thick walls.

"Long ago we whales figured out how to use cavitation and sonic engineering to shape sand into glass. You see we had to protect certain people from Airavab..."

"Cat?" Sol asked, scratching her head, now slightly itchy, caked in drying salt.

"Cavitation is a method of turning sound waves into force—it's how shrimp capture their dinners. But, well, we possess whale-sized sonar and we shape the sand from the sea floor into glass walls so that we can fill rooms with air for our human protectees to breathe, underwater. We had to make rooms low down enough that they cannot be seen by passing boats or the occasional helicopter but high enough that the pressure would be ok for you."

"Protectees? Marvin, I am so, so tired and you are not really making sense."

"I am sorry, Sol, go ahead and rest now. I promise you Aditi and I will explain more, although probably not everything, tomorrow. Sleep."

"I hate to ask you this because I know there is plenty of krill around here for you to munch on but I am starving...and Maisie probably is too."

"Oh yes! So sorry, my mom told me to bring you to her before you go to bed! Come back out of your house, and hop back on, Sol and Maisie, we'll be there in a minute!"

Marvin whooshed them over to a lovely green cave, very spacious with stalagmites and stalactites growing up from the floor and hanging on from the ceiling.

"Ma!" Marvin called, and a smiling blue swam out to meet them. Sol had the clearest feeling that if the whale had arms she would've hugged her, smothered her with whale love. The whale swam over and greeted them warmly:

"Sol, I've heard so much about you! Marvin was keeping me from you! Marvin, nu? what am I, chopped liver? But I got to see you at the congress. You must be starving, sweetie, come over here. And I have something for you, too, Maisie, welcome back."

Welcome back? Sol wondered at this. Maisie had already met Marvin's mom? Go figure, she thought, shaking her hair and watching it flow out all around her, buoyant in the salt water. Sol remembered a day some months ago when she returned home from school and Maisie was inexplicably wet; Sol assumed she'd just fallen into the aquarium and then gotten herself out again, climbing the ladder like a pro, shaking off most of the water but leaving some telltale wet spots on her fur. But now she knew Maisie must have been here. If only the dog could speak!

They swam over to a small glass compartment and inside: peanut butter. Sol felt a slight surge of disappointment, not being a huge peanut butter fan; but she was nonetheless happy to see that jar. Marvin's mom invited her to reach into the compartment, which she explained, Akira kept stocked for just such occasions, and take the peanut butter back to her house. And then she showed Maisie a dog bone, which elicited much tail wagging.

Our place. Sol thought, lying on the surprisingly comfortable glass bed. The ocean was so calming and yet busier than grand central. Colors Sol had never seen before swam by, combinations of golds and purples and reds. Eels and fish and enormous strands of snakelike seaweed sallied on by.

Sol's head swirled prodigiously and she failed to quiet it. She knew she had to contemplate for a long time and quite deeply before accepting Aditi's mission. Deep breaths, she repeated to herself, deep breaths. Aditi told her that she was chosen because of her sensitivity and because of her father—that she was, oh you know, the perfect human to get the whales' messages across. So, what was she supposed to say to Aditi's heavy question? "Like, no, I don't want to save the planet?"

Why would this Drake Barents listen to her? Sol inhaled and exhaled slowly several times, as Helen, before she evaporated from her life, had taught her to do, and, lying back on her new bed, looked up at the stars refracted through the glass ceiling. Maisie came in for a cuddle. The universe was so big, so very, very old, so full of questions. She gazed at the stars huge and hotter than anyone could fathom.

"The whales developed over the millennia," Ishmael had conveyed to her repeatedly, and now lying on the glass bed underwater Sol could almost hear his voice, now nearly singing like a whale, "a very complex navigational system that relied on a combination of echolocation and stargazing. We humans mistakenly think that whales swim up to the surface every twenty minutes or so only for air. But they pop up to check out the location of the sun, the stars, to read the clouds for a weather report, and eventually, after thousands and thousands of years, to see what threatening looking boats might be lurking about, men (and they were all men) balanced on their rocking vessels with huge harpoons in their meaty hands ready to kill."

Sol imagined Aditi, a color blue that she had never seen before, not even in many of the whaledreams she'd dreamed when her father would tell her bedtime stories, not even the color of any sky she had ever seen nor any of Nana's paintings concocted, star gazing just as she was, in that moment of indecision. Aditi was a blue that shifted as she breathed, that got darker when she was frustrated with humans and their infuriating refusal to listen, that seemed to glow lighter when she looked into Sol's eyes and began to hope.

How weird. An oxygenated glass room in the ocean, that's my place for now. I already miss Nana. I had been missing mom for so long that I extra miss her now, as I munch on peanut butter and seaweed before drifting off to a rocking slumber.

Sol dreamt that an angel fish came right up to her face and puckered its lips and began eating small animals out of the tangled, salty, mess of her hair while singing an enormously loud, deep whale song. Then she dreamed of a blue rabbit, bigger than a whale, swimming quickly through the ocean and escaping her grasp as she reached out, to catch it, drowning.

She awoke to a bright day, a whale face outside her room, bigger than she could fathom. Stretching and then swimming out, Sol gazed into Aditi's eye and she could tell that the whale held her tongue, waiting for Sol's answer:

"Aditi I've thought everything through and I am ready to accept the mission you have set out for me—although I feel like maybe that's a totally crazy thing to do."

Aditi swam to the surface for a great expulsion of air and a whoosh as her blowhole made what must have been a stunning display above the surface of the water. From below, Sol saw the white sea foam crashing down and spraying out as if she were swimming under a giant waterfall. Then Aditi began singing in her deep, unbelievably thick and rich voice, and Sol envisioned a dark chocolate mousse with dark chocolate drops. As the great whale sang, Sol imagined that she was catching words, but this was a new language, only for cetaceans.

"Aditi," Sol ultimately ventured after the undulating song that unfurled like long lost gravitational waves came to a slow stop, "what are you singing about?"

Aditi sighed and turned her great body sideways so she could look Sol directly in the eye. "I am letting the whales of the oceans all over the world know there is a glimmer of hope."

"Oh, no pressure then."

"You cannot know how much this means to us, Solange. We've been communicating with humans, inviting you very clearly to come and talk with us, for so long. No one came. Eventually, about seventy years after we learned Yiddish, a whale communication aficionado and marine biologist came to stay with us—she had a very impressive, if rudimentary whalese under her belt and she spoke Yiddish so she helped us—or a few of us, anyway, learn English."

"What happened to her?"

"We don't know. We will talk about that no further."

"OK." Arguing with Aditi seemed like a bad idea so Sol just listened. But her mother was a whale communication aficionado who disappeared when Sol was ten. So she hung on these words of Aditi's but also knew there was no way to get the great whale to budge or to say more. She had other things on her mind, and, while she'd pretty much given up ever finding her mother, she felt sure the whales knew exactly where Ishmael was hiding.

"You may understand our frustration better if you knew more of our history. You see, our oil, the oil we make in our flesh to keep us warm, wended its way through human engines..."

"But," Sol gently cut in, singing out, "I wasn't around for any of that. I mean, my father did tell me—repeatedly, and with enormous indignation, fury, even—about the horrible age of whaling but by the time my generation came around, whales had become venerated, everyone I know has a 'save the whales' sticker. Well, ok maybe not everyone, but, like, lots of people."

"I know, dear one, the genocide happened long before your time, but we cannot forget so easily and so very few of us blue whales remain. I've given birth to six babies—the last one twenty-three feet long! We are regenerating, and we do see that some humans are helping—your father, of course, and now you, and, naturally the indispensable Akira. But we need our message to be heard, and part of that is letting humans know about the sins of the past. Burying the pain will not heal us or, frankly, you."

"You're right, Aditi, and you were saying there are other ways? I'm sorry I interrupted you."

"My dear," she sang as she shimmied closer to Sol, "yes, there are other ways to be. If you humans could only open your hearts to the interconnectivity that is all around you then perhaps we can help you save this delectable planet. Humans fail to realize that our natural balancing act in the oceans helps you!"

"So, what about my father, Aditi, did he—I mean does he—try to fully understand you?"

"Yes, Solange, he does—he tries very hard and has been one of the humans who has come closest to full comprehension. But, I am afraid, at great cost to you and Nana."

"Cost?"

"Sol," Aditi resumed, looking much more re-laxed, "your father, Ishmael, has indeed figured out our Yiddish transmissions. And because of that, Airavab put out a call for him to be assassinated, and then we immediately brought him into the sea for his own protection, a year ago."

Sol felt a little dizzy just then and wondered brief-ly what would happen if she fainted under water.

"Where is my father? I—I demand..." But she let her words float off into ineffectual little bubbles. It was ridiculous to demand anything from a crea-ture who weighed approximately one hundred and seventy tons. Sol had already calculated that Aditi was roughly three thousand times more massive than she. Yet curiously, if Sol was, in round num-bers, five feet tall, and Aditi one hundred feet long, the whale was merely twenty times longer than the human teenager. Aditi looked to be about fif-teen feet high and tenish wide—this would make her volume some fifteen thousand cubic feet where-as Sol's volume would be something like two cubic feet. Ratios, Sol figured, would look sort of like this: 1:3000 (weight), 1:20 (length), 1:6000 (volume). When someone so massive is so close one feels over-whelmed in the biggest way imaginable. Sol swore, then, never, ever to end up on Aditi's bad side, and she tried to mask her fury that Aditi seemed to be hiding her father.

"Yes, Sol, you're right," Aditi continued, her musical tones softening, "you can—you should demand to see your father. He will, I very much hope and trust, return to us soon but he's currently engaged in a crucial mission. And yes, you are quite right, not all humans are so insensible to the needs of the planet. But honestly, it is galling to watch from our watery world as the humans destroy the dry land and warm the ocean so much as to threaten its very survival. We are trying to change all that and it is simply maddening not to be heard. But enough of my frustration! We need to tell you about your mission. And, Solange, please hear that we do, all of us whales, we do recognize fully that what we are about to request is a ton-weight to launch on a teenager. Yet human teenagers, much as are whales, and, for that matter, dogs, are very often underrated. Are you comfortable?"

Treading water next to Marvin, and sometimes scrambling up onto his blue back, the faint taste of salt on her lips, magically warmed by whale sonar, breathing easily, yes, Sol was very comfortable.

"Yes, Aditi, I am ready," she sang out.

"We need you to get into Airavab headquarters and convince Drake Barents, through rational argument alone, without violence, that his greed is a temporary stepping stone that will ultimately ruin the future for his children, for all the planet's children, and, if there is still a habitable planet then, his—everyone's—grand-children. You must convince him to stop his mad quest for our virya."

"But, why would he listen to me?"

"Because you are the future, because of your youth, your innocence, your surety, your special dog, these will all melt his heart. He will hear you."

"My special dog?"

"Yes, I refer to your dog, Maisie. As you may know—did your father tell you?—whales descended from wolves. We have been communicating with Maisie ever since you adopted her..."

"Seriously? You talk to Maisie? I mean sometimes I thought she was listening to the sea...I guess she was listening to you, then?"

"Yes. Now, Sol, here is Akira. I will let him brief you as I must attend to a matter of some urgency in the area of Boston."

Sol turned to see a man with long black hair flowing out behind him swimming up to her and Maisie. She couldn't help noticing that Maisie wagged her tail rather vigorously when she saw him. Akira seemed to be one of those people who could juggle burning swords while doing the crossword puzzle and making dinner. He explained that had managed to set up the first meeting with the dreaded Drake Barents on the pretext that new information about how to attain virya had surfaced. In consultation with Aditi, he set the meeting up under the false name "Lotus Nistaraka." Akira, of course, had the challenge of needing to both plan to be in Airavab's offices in Boston at the time of the meeting, in case anything went wrong, and pretend he didn't know Sol at all.

The Airavab office in Boston crowned The Hancock Tower. Despite wanting to keep it as a tourist attraction, the city could not decline the vast sum Barents offered to buy the entire edifice. There were protests at Boston Common when the deal was announced but nothing could be done: Airavab already owned the formidable tower.

Barents wished to have unobstructed views of the back bay, and this was simply the best spot. Sometimes he ventured up to Provincetown so he could gawk at whale watchers heading out to observe the whales frolicking alongside the boats as the tourists took pictures.

"Click away," Barents would mutter while emitting a nasty chuckle, "these may be the last leviathans you see!"

From the outside, The Hancock Tower looked the same as it had since it opened in 1976. But Barents completely redid the inside. He made it almost entirely, absolutely blindingly, white. White floors, white walls, white ceilings, white elevators with pale blue buttons, white lights.

Panting, from having rushed to the base of the

tower, Sol and Maisie stood blinking in the lobby, catching their breaths. An enormous guard came over to them, peered down as if looking down a ladder, and asked, abruptly, "Can I help you?"

"Yes, thank you, I am Lotus Nistaraka," Sol managed to say, while suppressing a tremble in her reedy voice, "and I have an appointment with Mr. dre—with Mr. Drake Barents."

"Hold, please." The guard, with an eyebrow archly raised the only sign of his surprise at seeing a dog in the impeccable building, went to call up on a white phone, and then returned, "Right this way, take the elevator to the 60th floor."

Maisie looked up at Sol and they walked over to the elevator. On the way up, Sol's lunch of peanut butter folded into seaweed rolled around like one of Maisie's balls in her stomach and she practiced the calming breathing Helen had so lovingly taught her.

The elevator opened into a room with breathtaking views, all around. They squinted in the brightness and toured the room with their eyes. Then they stopped. Wearing a white suit with white shoes, Barents sat at an enormous glass desk. He did not get up when the elevator doors opened. In fact, he barely looked up from the ledger in which he scribbled.

"Hello," Barents finally said, after leaving them standing there for what seemed like an endless amount of time. "I am enormously busy, please tell me why you wanted to see me and what you have to offer regarding virya."

So much for just getting to know him, winning his confidence, Sol thought, this guy is high pressure.

"Hello, how are you? It is nice to get to meet with you, sir." Sol could not figure out how she was keeping her lunch down.

Looking up from his ledger, something seemed to catch Barents when he heard Sol speak. And then he saw her. He softened for an instant, and it looked as though the ice-man might even shed a salty tear. But his face quickly hardened, his whiter than white cheeks losing the slight flush Sol had just barely caught there. "I said, I am very busy," he repeated.

"OK, then, sir, I will cut to the chase. The U.S. Navy is storing virya inside Area 38, right there on the Cape Cod National Seashore."

III
ANDRÉ

In the morning I take the A train from West 4th to 125th and walk up to CUNY's North Academic Center, picking up coffee and a creamy profiterole from my usual truck en route. It's a crisp day, the coffee warms my hands as I head to my Melville class. My students, some not much younger than me, might be tired, in need of Thanksgiving break. But they always surprise me. I'm remembering that when Aaron had been a special visitor to class in September, he'd proudly paraded for them an antiquarian copy of *Moby-Dick*, the rare edition held them all spellbound—the thickness of the pages, the agglomeration of more than a century of hands feeling them, the dank smell of the 1851 dark red leather cover. My students peppered Aaron with questions—some of them had read a couple of his books—and he took his time answering them all, fully. He had a capacious way of talking, using his hands to illustrate his points, his white mop of hair bouncing over his pink-white face as he paced around the classroom picking out the counterintuitive detail to share: that Melville deserted one ship and mutinied on another. That he was briefly jailed. That *Moby-Dick* was originally called, simply, *The Whale*. Aaron asked them what that change meant and they engaged in a robust discussion which flabbergasted me because sometimes the kids can be a little reticent with visitors. But Aaron had a way of pulling people out that contrasted sharply with his otherwise solitary, odd-duck, bookish way of navigating the terrifying emotional geographies of the world.

I chuck my coffee cup, lick the cream off my fingers and hope I don't have chocolate on my lips as I open the classroom door. Even after teaching for four years, I still get a little flutter in the pit of my stomach before each session. Impostor syndrome.

For today's class we're discussing one of the most intriguing, frustrating, and miraculous short stories, "Bartleby the Scrivener." I don't know if they will love it, but they should be able to see, because we've already read "Billy Budd" and parts of *Moby-Dick*, how different are Melville's subjects and tones, like jazz to classical, one student says. Yes. We begin talking about the narrator and I ask them to pin the descriptors. He's safe, prudent, methodical, and peaceful.

So, would you say Melville intimates that we can trust his narrator?

General agreement, lots of nodding, yes.

Are there any times when we might question him? How does he treat Bartleby?

Well, a pale white youth with bright blue hair pipes up:

The narrator does admit his own expectations for utter obedience, like Bartleby was a slave or something. He says he has an 'expectancy of instant compliance' and he's totally floored when Bartleby doesn't.

Doesn't what?

Doesn't comply. I counted twenty-one times that Bartleby says some variation of 'I prefer not to.' That's a lot of non-compliance.

Yes! Indeed! Now why do you think, all of you, that Bartleby doesn't want to comply?

As I ask the class this question, mutiny swells in me. Maybe I, too, should prefer not to comply with Sid's crazy world, with her ups and downs, maybe I should just tell her I prefer not to?

So, he worked in the dead-letter office, right? Another student, wearing a bright red wig with two thick braids scrolling down his back, says, tentatively. Maybe he was dead all along, like the narrator tells us, 'Dead letters, does it not sound like dead men?' Maybe Bartleby is, like, a ghost?

Interesting. What do other people think of this suggestion?

I feel, a boy with shiny skin and neon bottle bottom glasses, offers, like he's rebelling against the money-grubbing wall-street world. They are in this office, right?, hemmed in by two walls—Melville turns the walls into metaphors for the stifling nature of capitalism, I think.

Lots of nodding and general agreement.

Super. Let's turn now to how Melville describes his characters. I'd like us to compare how he introduces Bartleby to how he introduces Starbuck, OK? So, Bartleby is first 'pallidly neat, pitiably respectable, incurably forlorn. It was Bartleby.' Now, let's look at Melville's description of Starbuck...oh, right, of course, you don't all have *Moby-Dick* with you. That's ok, I have mine.

We know! They chant this, almost in unison, I like to think, lovingly, indulgently, but maybe also mockingly.

Well, I pretty much always have a copy. It may not be the 1851 edition Mr. Zimmerman exhibited, but still. Anyway, here goes, I won't read the whole description, you can look at it later, at home, I know you're all, ahem, just dying to re-read it, here goes: 'The chief mate of the Pequod was Starbuck, a native of Nantucket, and a Quaker by descent. He was a long, earnest man, and though born on an icy coast, seemed well adapted to endure hot latitudes, his flesh being hard as twice-baked biscuit. Transported to the Indies, his live blood would not spoil like bottled ale.' I'll skip ahead a bit here, just one more sentence: 'Looking into his eyes, you seemed to see there the yet lingering images of those thousand-fold perils he had calmly confronted through life.'

As I stop reading this I pause, standing before the class, still as a cottonwood tree, grudgingly accepting that I will never prefer not to be within sight of Sid's thousand-fold imperiled eyes. She's an unlikely anchor, I grant you. But I'm at home wherever she is, and I have an uncanny sense that

I'm similarly a moveable home for her. I recall bell hooks: "Then home is no longer just one place. It is locations. Home is that place which enables and promotes varied and everchanging perspectives, a place where one discovers new ways of seeing reality..." Yes, I hate to admit it, but she's my home. These years together, mostly together, and this suitcase, this fragment of a weird text from Aaron, this might just break us open enough to bind us. Maybe. The utter precarity of love. The whole class stares at me. Blinking. The utter precarity of trust. A beat too long flies by, a kaleidoscope of indigo butterflies.

Sorry, (throat clearing), so, tell me, what's going on in this description? How far back or perhaps more aptly, how far into the blood does Melville go in introducing this thin, yet solid character?

After class I'm in my office, clamoring to pause my obsessive thoughts about the clues Aaron left us, stop already with all that, and work on my damn book, well two books. Once I finish the book that will be shaped from the grey clay of my dissertation, I'm planning to write the first monograph on Aaron; I'd already begun gathering reviews and interviews. There's no monograph on his work, yet, and I had figured I'd have an excellent chance of incorporating long interviews with Aaron into the project. I worry slightly that it's Machiavellian of me to calculate like this. I wish I'd talked to him more, I couldn't know he would die···it was so sudden. And how am I to handle this weird, private, fragment he'd left us? Since he asked us not to share it do I need to exclude *Slobgollion?* Sid had remained mute after we'd read it···I will need to ask her in Québec what she makes of it all. As far as I can tell, Aaron protected himself from the cold truth by constructing a fiction around Dorothy. How long would that have kept him afloat? I totally understand why Sid couldn't articulate how she must have—might have felt reading that. The manuscript muzzled her.

The collection of book reviews I'd already gathered fits into a manila folder, and I pull one out:

The Eagle's Nest
Aaron Zimmerman
Buzzhouse Press
Reviewed by Saul Weiss
Commentary 15 July 1970

Aaron Zimmerman's largely autobiographical debut novel, *The Eagle's Nest,* tells the story of two American soldiers, Isaac Israel (clearly modeled on Mr. Zimmerman), a Jewish American paratrooper, and Mike Goodall, a black paratrooper, both trained in Alabama to jump from planes. The novel is set in the stunning holiday retreat in the Bavarian Alps where Hitler vacationed so often in the company of Eva Braun, entertained dignitaries from around the world including Prince Edward and his scandale of a wife, the divorcée Wallis Simpson. This holiday retreat turned out to be quite a surprise for the airborne divisions, but this novel does not stay with their perspectives and emotions. Zimmerman's novel has a magical element to it—and it may be that fine line between the real within the fiction makes the novel falter.

During basic training, missing home, missing decent grub, Isaac and Mike befriend a German American who, though recently naturalized as a proud US Citizen, was drawn to the Hitlerjugend as a boy but emigrated after that with his anti-Nazi family to Hollywood. The friend, Wulf, tall, handsome, blue eyed, and mischievous, becomes invaluable to the airborne division because of his translation skills. Isaac hails from Brooklyn and speaks some Yiddish so understands an awful lot of what they hear over the radio they infiltrate; Wulf translates everything at lightning speed as if he were a translation machine. Isaac, Mike, and the other paratroopers arrive in Salzburg during one of the coldest springs known to humankind as an unusually heavy snow blankets the surrounding mountains, lending them even more majesty and gravitas. From Salzburg they travel in a convoy of jeeps up the winding mountain roads and into the town of Berchtesgaden. Mike and Isaac had no idea, before they landed, how incredibly beautiful they would find this Nazi homeland. They knew in an abstract way that Hitler selected for his holiday retreat a very unusual and delicate part of the world and they'd even seen the *Life Magazine* full-page glossy spread of the compound glowing with the magisterial mountains looming behind. But none of that prepared them for the breathtaking beauty they beheld as they climbed up the mountain.

This is where the novel shines—Zimmerman carefully walks the tightrope between understanding the pull of Nazism, giving that pull and the majesty of their holiday nest its full due while also demonstrating the horror, the horror! below the surface.

In reality, Aaron Zimmerman and a friend of his, who like the character was a black paratrooper, had been part of a small division of men who would not be particularly useful with a gun and as a consequence were charged with finding and cataloguing anything that might have been looted from ordinary families before they were deported to their deaths. Zimmerman, who is a librarian, made use of his then nascent librarian skills and his friend, Michael Gruber, who later became a photographer, was tasked with taking photographs of wrenched objects. Zimmerman describes in the fictional version in great detail some of the rare stuff that was looted: priceless paintings, sculptures of all sizes, jewelry wrought with love and care by the finest craftspeople in Europe.

One day, in *The Eagle's Nest,* Wulf, Mike and Isaac go on a recognizance mission in the tunnels carved into the mountains below the Eagle's Nest when they happen upon a small boy hiding there. They begin to talk with him, at first Wulf translating but then all of them speaking German or—in Isaac's case a weird mix of Yiddish and English that seemed to work. Over the weeks stationed in this beautiful place packed with evil, Wulf, Mike and Isaac bring the boy food and supplies and, for some reason, they decide not to tell their commanding officer who they have discovered. They make a silent pact to keep mum. As the novel progresses it becomes less and less clear whether or not the boy is real. He starts to take on weird attributes that Zimmerman never explains and by the end you just simply don't know where the line between the gruesome reality of war and the fantastical story of this kid, who might have been the son of a Czech worker who helped build the colossal stone perch, was actually there within the fiction or became a metaphor for all the forgotten victims of the war—the Slavic workers, many of whom died of exhaustion or fatal accidents during the construction of the megalomaniacal house atop a giant mountain. The Eagle's Nest came to represent the epic reach of Hitler's power, the unstoppable greed of the great dictator, reaching ever further and with more madness for what he wanted, very much like *Moby-Dick's* Captain Ahab had done. At all costs, without regard for human life or the delicate balance of the ecosystem of the mountain that Hitler hollowed out in order to plunge an extravagant elevator straight through it, the dictator drove ahead with his plans.

Zimmerman's debut novel demonstrates a new, and

promising voice in American literature. But the arc of the story is not quite as well defined as it could be, and there is something grating about the reader's inability to determine fantasy from reality within the novel. Still, he has used his experience during the war to demonstrate larger themes about looted objects and forgotten victims.

Filing the review back into its place, and gazing down at the street from my office window, I remember that when Aaron described, either in person or in his novels, as he often did, and at great length, moments of history, moments he'd read in the paper, he always worked to interconnect things for his readers, for Sid, even when she was a child. He wanted her to know that while all of these discrete moments held their own stories there was a kind of through line between discriminations that touched each other. Not that all traumas equate. Far from it. But we'd be foolish to make everything too discrete—that would be far too tidy for the chaos of the universe, the planet. And I'm finding something very similar, thinking through what C. L. R. James argues, about the connections between Ahab and Hitler.

A strange interplay develops in my mind's eye, as I continue the mysterious process of alchemizing my dissertation into a book (a process that seems will never end), between Sid's black and white photographs of black and white people and what Melville was doing with black and white and brown folks in his magisterial book. When I researched at the C. L. R. James archive, I found a bunch of rare stuff he'd written about the racial make up of the *Pequod*—unusual, James said, for a novel penned in 1851 to have a strong black man from Africa, Daggoo, along with a South Sea Islander, Queequeg, and even Pip, from Alabama who James said would be "hailed as the greatest hero of all." Melville's whole book arced toward Ahab's quest of the enormous white whale and yet the crew was this incredible mix of people—men—with all kinds of stories. Just like your photos, as I'd told Sid, are supposed to be about race, or about celebrating the breakdown of old racist ideas, they are really about love. Just like *Moby-Dick* is supposed to be this great quest, it's truly about conveying the problems with the whole racist slave owning world Melville was from. I look down at the page, I've doodled an image of a spiral. I stretch it into a sketch of one of Sid's portraits.

I held her from behind, I recall, inhaling, scratching over the sketch, and feeling hungry, some time ago, I'm not sure precisely how long, resting my chin on the top of her head, breathing in her magnetic concoction, and gazing at the vast collection of photos wallpapering her cramped apartment. Soaking in all the different poses: the pale-eyed, pale-skinned man with his arm slung over a dark brown man, his delicious dark eyes staring straight at the camera, straight at Sid. The man on the left's eyes looking at his lover, gushing; or, the couple sitting next to each other, but with a foot or so between them, Sid's red couch reflecting back at them, both sitting bolt upright, concrete pillars with rebar for spines, their pinkie fingers just slightly reaching for each other. Nothing knitted the couples together, I thought, they were just so many different people on the same wall. Sid managed to take a theme and deconstruct it in the very same moment—the couples possessed the one outward similarity of color difference and then so few similarities within that difference. As I looked at Sid's walls, I always imagined my parents there. My father would likely have been regarding my mother with stupid fawn eyes and she would have been composed, looking directly at the camera, as unafraid of it as she was of dying. They would have fit right in. The landscape of mixed races.

Sid perhaps inadvertently offers proof with this experimental collection, I told her, that other factors and not merely skin tone should determine difference. Her graceful images reminded me of something from *Moby-Dick*. Flipping through the pages of the dog-eared copy I keep at Sid's house, I read out to her a juicy moment when Melville reflects on whiteness:

"But not yet have we solved the incantation of

this whiteness, and learned why it appeals with such power to the soul....Is it that by its indefiniteness it shadows forth the heartless voids and immensities of the universe, and thus stabs us from behind with the thought of annihilation, when beholding the white depths of the milky way? Or is it, that as in essence whiteness is not much a color as the visible absence of color, and at the same time the concrete of all colors..."

Sid looked up at me, whispering to me in a way that made my spine go soft that she loves it when I read aloud, that she finds my voice, rich, slightly accented, spicy, ringing in the air like the aftertaste of a lemon dipped in cayenne.

A lemon dipped in cayenne, I asked her. Expliquez-moi ça. But, I replied that, when all your amazing photos are lined up together, it's the white people who disappear and the black people who stand out, it's almost as though you've rendered Melville's words in images and concretized the idea of whiteness as absence, as threat of annihilation, as endpoint.

I'm hoping, I told her, that you can publish at least a sampling of these stunning portraits. *While the portraits are about race,* I imagine writing in an introduction to the smash hit photo book, *they also launch an argument for de-prioritizing the very category they set out to document. What emerges,* I figure I'd write in the glossy coffee table edition, *when the images all vibrate next to each other, like light waves on different frequencies, is that the similarities and differences between the couples should be aligned along new categories: 'relaxed,' 'happy,' 'anxious,' 'tense,' 'nervous,' 'in love,' 'exhausted.' If you look at the images again with these categories as your guiding lenses, then family resemblances start to pop up. But those resemblances are entirely separate from the outward similarity of their interracial love, even though that similarity is the raison d'être for the whole collection.* As soon as I started saying all this to Sid, she cocked her head sideways: It isn't working is it, this collection? If that's what you want to say, why don't you just say it?

No, I replied, reaching out to trace the half-moon curve of her collar bone lightly, that's not what I mean, I mean it *is* working...it just may not be working in the way you thought it would.

I was complimenting her and yet she thought I undercut the project she worked, and continues to work on, with such determination, persistence, intensity. The impossibility of ever communicating to/with people you love.

Love, I continued, rubbing the tense muscle behind her neck, what I'm trying to say is that the project works because these couples have such clear personalities, they blaze through due to your brilliant framing of them.

She looked up at me with those amazing eyes of hers, and I melted into them. Again. And again.

In my office, I fiddle with a pencil, doodle an idle image of a tree. I should head home. I've been dragging my feet on transforming the dissertation and maybe this dreaming of a literary biography of Aaron is a distraction? Or a way to stay closer to Sid? It's a strange system, I always think, that a dissertation is supposed to be something that can be changed into a book but can't yet be a book. It's like writing an embryo. Pushing the Aaron folders away, and pulling an all too familiar sheaf of papers close, I stare at all the extensive comments from my committee—and they don't all agree, and I am constantly in the agonizing process of re-shaping what I've already written into a new form, as if the words were clay and scrambling to form a large sculpture out of an older, smaller one. The words spin, another endless kaleidoscope.

I keenly wish I could pick up the phone, call Aaron and see which of the multiple directions my committee offered he would advocate. But I'm here in the empty office where I was the night he died when the door flung open, electrically, as if its hinges would uncoil from the blast. Sid stood there, shaking, framed by the doorway, the fluorescent lights of the hallway behind her spreading an incandescent halo over her long, shiny hair, her eyes unrecognizable, red. So lovely on better days, her eyes were swollen as a balloon, her shoulders utterly deflated.

He's dead.

What? Who? Sid, love, what···

My father. I was in the darkroom, I saw his face underwater, just for a flicker, and when I got home, they called, the emergency room···

That night she was a red-eyed ghost of herself, and I loved her all the more for it. She's not beautiful in any normal sense of the word, but she exerts a kind of power, pretends not to know it. A compact person, closed in on herself, white, but off-white, with long, dark hair and an uneven face, she walks quickly as though she knows where she's heading, even when she doesn't. She can't hide anything, her amazing cerulean-jade eyes are legible, even when she wishes they weren't. Chilled by a floating mirage of Aaron in the developing chemicals, Sid knew, before she got the call. How we know in the marrow of our bones even when we push knowledge away. This must be what Aaron was feeling, writing the fragment of a novel where Dorothy is protected by Yiddish speaking whales. How he had to push the fact of her disappearance away, shove it into a fantastical form.

After Aaron died Sid had insisted on going to Chicago alone, to scatter his ashes. Alone. Making order out of Aaron's tumultuous apartment was no small feat, and, I should have been there to help her. I should have been with her the whole time. But she's stubborn and she just had to go without me.

But...why? She never gave me a good reason, being temporarily broken up never stopped us from doing everything together before. But when she said she needed to face all that alone, I supposed she knew her heart better than I did. Mais, expliquez-moi ça.

The night Aaron died, when she came right here to my office, I reached out to enfold her. Paused. And she took a step and pushed into me, for all the world like she'd never left.

It's evening now, and I've not gotten much done. To distract myself, I open up the file I'm keeping of reviews of *Moby-Dick* from 1851. "Who would have looked for philosophy in whales, or for poetry in blubber?" (*John Bull*). I love that one so much. But other reviewers found the novel "interminable," "provoking," "a perfect failure," one of them wished "both him and his whales at the bottom of an unfathomable sea" (*Literary Gazette*). But another favorite: *Moby-Dick* "appears to be a sort of hermaphrodite craft—half fact and half fiction" (*Evening Traveller*). I wonder if that's what Aaron is doing in his weird book, half fact, half fiction a sort of hermaphrodite, too. Between the world of grief and the salty sea. Another reviewer had coined the term "whalishness" (*Weekly News and Chronicle*) and, as I walk back to the train, I begin to imagine this whalishness taking Aaron over, that fact/fiction border always such a struggle for him.

The streets are loamy and dank, the chill crawls

through my coat and under my skin. As the train chugs downtown, I wonder, again, why I'm willing to risk this Thanksgiving voyage with Sid, so soon after we precariously get back together. It seems inevitable that we will fall in love all over again (not that we ever fell out, exactly) and sink into each other, as we keep doing, over and over again only to fall out. The fallout each time the same but somehow different. Each time we break up we never really separate, we sort of, how shall I say this, pause. Yes, we pause rather than break. We speak via phone and see each other often during each pause. But now I hope that, back together, Sid can stay the course. The suitcase, somehow, will make her stay, as if its original intention were inverted. I reason with her, internally, knowing that I won't dare to speak this aloud, that if she could only keep steady, a gently rowing rowboat, and stop struggling as if she were Houdini in a straight jacket self-tied under water, then maybe this time it will work out. And maybe we will find out something tangible about Dorothy and then perhaps Sid can discover some kind of peace. I can't explain why, and I don't know what a therapist would say, but somehow, as if Aaron and Dorothy were on a ghostly see-saw, it's as though the combination of Aaron passing away and the suitcase offering strange hope for some news of Dorothy, somehow in that shifting balance there will be an opening for me. The endless optimism.

When I arrive at Sid's place she opens her door, but doesn't immediately let me in, as if she's deciding something. But she looks up at me and I see a trace of black lace bra emerging by her collar bone. I step in, she steps back. Her front door leads right into the kitchen. Not very promising. But then, an inner room, swallowed in darkness, and with a noir view out onto the garbage shoot, the alley, and into the thick glass windows of neighbors we can see but will likely never get to know. That's where her bed, our bed, is, propped up on a loft to make room for a small desk below, where Sid sits sometimes with a magnifying glass, poring over prints. When you push on to the living room you're rewarded with intense sunshine in the day. On evenings like this one, if you crane your neck and look east, a breathtaking view over the East River into Williamsburg and the huge Domino Sugar Factory beyond leaving sweet pink footprints on the surface of the sparkling water. Sid makes us grilled cheese and we stare distractedly out the window at the neon lights making their way across the East River. Pink fairies doing a jig on the light waves.

We fuck, as we had earlier in the day, then, on the floor, in the blazing sun, now, in the dark, in her loft; but it's a bit like sleeping with a statue. Sid hasn't, despite what she says, come back to me. Not fully. Or not yet. After, holding her, I drift into a weird dream: an aquarium filled with all the items in the suitcase, floating, the red shoe, the sculpture, the photograph, the heavy paperweight, the dream-soggy key, all light as feathers and swimming around like brightly colored fish.

*

On Wednesday, I pick her up in front of Shlovsky Moving Pictures just a hair past four. It's very old-fashioned, rare, to pick her up that way, like a proper date. She's waiting for me at the entrance of the building, a large duffel bag at her feet and a light blue woolen hat on her head. She nestles into her grey corduroy coat lined with faux fur, her extra-long Doctor Who multicolored scarf wraps around her neck. She wastes no time with small talk when she plunks down next to me in the back of the cab, kissing me gently on the cheek after she hauls her bag into the trunk, slamming it shut hard, comme d'habitude.

In the cab, resting one hand on my thigh and gesticulating with the other, Sid tells me that when she first beheld it in the suitcase, that red shoe flooded her with memories—she'd watched the 1948 film *The Red Shoes* more than once and read the Hans Christian Anderson story, repeatedly. Quite unlike the film, the fairytale version is not really about dancing, but more about the compulsions inherent in any quest. The girl in the fairytale, Karen, wears the red shoes on the day of her mother's funeral. Sid's longing for her lost mother cuts me to the quick, always, as I would never be able to search for my mother. Because they never found Dorothy, no funeral or memorial for Sid and Aaron offered closure, and I know that's unspeakably hard for Sid. The dead live on, yes, Faulkner, you're right, "The past is never dead. It's not even past." As the cab bumps over potholes, honks, and we hear the driver cursing the traffic, I replay my mother's funeral for Sid: my father, sister, aunt, and I, I tell her, were among many mourners when she slipped away too quickly from liver cancer when I was not quite 13. All the spaces of Pointe-a-Pitre filled for my father with memories of his beloved. Metamorphosing into a gorgeous ghost my mother imbued the sand, the air, and the sea with his memories of her. Still, now, everywhere my father looks, he sees her, reaches out, misses her. Not that our parents always got along swimmingly. Marguerite and I remember plenty of fights when we were supposed to be asleep and not listening, as we were, crouching below the banister at the top of the stairs. We heard them as they first talked in tense tones and then full out yelled. But even through all the fighting—in their own mix of English and French, a recipe only they seemed to know how to emulsify—we knew that they loved each other and loved us.

I sorely wish, Sid, that you could have gotten

to know my mother, Charlotte, for she would have adored you.

Well, actually, I think but do not say, Charlotte would probably have given you a stern talking to for all your indecision regarding me.

Mother was not to be messed with, I say, hoping Sid will get the hint, she was warm in all senses of the word, and would hold your hand any chance she got; she always seemed to understand what Marguerite and I were going through, as if she could read our minds. Don't get me wrong; she was warm, yet stern. She would never let us slack—we were held to high standards in all ways.

She taught English at the high school, I remind Sid, annoyed that she'd forgotten what my mother was so passionate about. As if she hadn't listened when I'd told her, years ago; but in the same breath of annoyance I relent, realizing how rarely I speak of my mother. And yet, I want Sid to know my family, even as we're en route to her grandmother, I want her to hear me this time. Like our parents, I say, we mix up our languages at home, so Marguerite and I often speak as much English as French—my father, of course, is fluent in English, the international language of physics. He'd been at a physics conference hosted by NYU in 1960 when a cousin in Crown Heights invited him to her house for dinner. Charlotte, still living in her family's brownstone just up the street, just happened to be among the diners.

Oh, Sid says as we cross the Williamsburg bridge, gaze back at the skyline, the grey water lapping up the edge of the island, I didn't realize your parents met on a sort of blind date. In the interstices between light and dark the lights of the buildings kissing the sky.

Yes, I reply, the view from here is gorgeous, non? my father is too shy ever to ask anyone out on his own, so he needed a nudge. His cousin just somehow knew that they'd click—my father dreamed of someone like her, amiable but also structured. He didn't know it, but he longed to be with a woman who wouldn't let his gushy romanticism go unchecked—but a woman who would also, at the same time, nurture it. They began dating long distance, my father taking every opportunity to come to New York and my mother grabbing all excuses to visit her extended family in Guadeloupe.

Mother's funeral in Pointe-a-Pitre, I tell Sid as we sit in chock-a-block traffic on the BQE, was crowded with people who genuinely seemed to care for her. Marguerite and I stood in black, next to our father, at the gracious old edifice with the curly wrought iron balconies where we always gathered for town hall events. We strove to stay composed as we welled up with tears. Students and colleagues from the high school, our friends and family, my Aunt Thérèse, who still lives in the same brownstone in Brooklyn where she and my mother grew up, so many people from the community, my father's colleagues at the Université. All those people tried to reassure us but I remember just wanting to kick them all, hard. The impossibility of sharing someone else's grief. The limits of empathy.

Just like you, love, were furious at that doctor calling from Chicago to tell you about Aaron. Nothing can ever fill the hole left by mother leaving us so fast.

The bangles, Sid says, gently, they're from Charlotte.

Yes, I reply, my breath soft now, knowing she's fully with me, she gets it. It's important to me to keep the three gold bangles my mother was graced with at her birth in Brooklyn and which she wore proudly until her last day in the hospital, when she turned to me and said, André, hurry up, come in close, put your ear to my mouth, I don't have much time left, love. Please, take these, and here she struggled to pull them over her withered hand, take these and keep them safe until you have a baby. Let her wear them and remember me. I took them, kept them for ages in my breast pocket, just over my heart.

Looking out the window as the traffic begins to ease and we approach the LaGuardia exit, I'm feeling how emigrating to New York took me away from my distraught and mourning father and then opened up portals to new worlds I never would have known, but the sensation of the sea, the salt smell of the place sticks. Sid and I both felt guilty, leaving our grieving fathers, a strong pull to be away took over. I need to bring you there, Sid, I want to say, you should see what it's like, what it feels like. I want you to sleep with me as a woman not a statue in the house I lived in until coming to New York. But now, instead, I think but do not say, I'm going with you to visit your grandmother. Our see-saw always lands on your side. Will that ever shift? Or am I just to keep on giving? The question mark persists.

Our taxi arrives at the airport, and we check our bags and enter the departure lounge. We sit at the bar by the window, gaze out at the lights on the planes, each window illuminated like a small light bulb. Sid reminds me that in Anderson's "Red Shoes," a wealthy lady, spotting Karen at the funeral, takes her in, but burns the red shoes all up. The child then acquires a cursed pair of beet red shoes that force her to dance and dance and dance until the executioner takes pity on her and cuts off her feet. Sid takes the one red shoe, the one with the secret drawer, that Paolo found for us, out of her oversized purse (I confess I think it a little odd that she's still carrying the shoe in her purse but I decide it's prudent not to say anything critical to a mourner, and I guess it's better than the sculpture, which she'd schlepped for a while) and inhales deeply the leathery smell. My mother, very proper all the time, would have been dismayed. But, holding the shoe at arm's length next to one of the dangling glass lights over the bar to see better, Sid muses in a dreamy voice:

It's beautiful and so very, very finely wrought. Did my parents dance together while mom wore these shoes? But then, father went back to Paolo, maybe to a party?, and dropped the shoe with the note? Why did Aaron not show me this suitcase—I have so many questions. And I ache for dad to answer me, or show me a sign. But there's nothing from him.

I don't notice anyone looking askance at this striking woman holding a shoe at a bar. The barman is looking down, drying some wine glasses carefully with a white towel, removing water spots, and everyone else waits for a plane, whiling the time away by reading *The Times* or a novel.

You know, I say, taking her hand, that's probably for the best? Or would you prefer to be talking to people on the flip side?

We board the plane in the dark and watch from the small window as the city shrinks smaller and smaller, the buildings eventually looking like cutouts in a winter store-front, as we get higher, stars begin popping out of the winter sky like flashlights coming on in a dark forest from afar.

Sid, I query, as we settle in to our seats, how did Aaron know you would find Dorothy's Rare Stuff, and the manuscript?

He knew.

Does he know where she is, then?

—. She turns to gaze out the small egg-shaped dark window.

Your father always had great faith in you. I wager he thought you could figure it out if he put all the clues in one place. Probably, as Michael was saying, he died after trying and failing to find her but he saw a glimmer of hope in passing down his collection to you, and maybe, to me, too.

He loved you, André, in his funny way, you know? I think he always hoped we would, well, I would⋯

Oui.

*

When we arrive at Esther's great house at midnight, a little bleary, she waits for us with a snack of runny, wonderfully stinky brie and crackers coupled with a bottle of dark red port. The key, the café, Sid begins to burble out but Esther insists we wait till morning to discuss it all. Waving her hand as if to erase all thoughts of the clues, Esther gushes.

André, I am so thrilled to see you again! It's been too long since I visited you in New York and it's a terrible thing that you've never yet been to my house. It's Sid's house, too, you know? She spent all her childhood's summers here. Tomorrow you will get the full tour—Sid, shall we take him to the attic?

Ooooh oui, mamie ça serait merveilleux, on va lui montrer des choses rares.

But Sid tucks her chin oddly down as she says this.

You must be exhausted, you two, sleep and then, yes, in the morning I will take you to the *La rivière de la lune* for breakfast, and maybe later, the attic.

Esther looks unchanged since I'd met her in New York. She's a sturdy person. Short, slightly stooped over (who wouldn't be, at her age) with a shock of white curly hair that she attempts (fails) to tame into a bun. Beneath the creases and paperyness of her pale skin her peacock blue eyes are crystal clear; there's obviously a whole lot going on in her head. She's the sort of person you want to talk to and listen to for hours, and I can see why Sid loved coming here every summer, especially after Dorothy...

I elect to sleep in the blue room and Sid choses the green room. I imagine Sid bathed in a field of emerald green light cast by the glass lampshades in that bedroom, and I feel as though I'm swimming in the blue room, like I'm home, on the island. From the outside at this time of night the house might have been a collection of jewels under the sea— each brightly colored room next to the other. From the inside, through Esther's artfully arranged glass lamps, the color of the room you're in bounces back at you. Naturally, I long for Sid, sleeping alone in all that delectable green light. But we're somehow being respectful, we think, sleeping apart (although I imagine Esther is quite a bit more modern than we're allowing).

Lying in the blue bed, feeling how lovely it must be to be close to your grandmother, I never knew mine. And it seems Esther has, or is willing to adopt me. My grandparents, on both sides, are abstract, since they died when I was too small to remember them and I only have sense-memories of them. A smell, an inhalation, a feeling of warmth. The privilege of knowing where you come from. The agony of not. From my father I've inherited the long series of expulsions, conversions, and clandestine lives of his Jewish-Caribbean ancestors, going back hundreds of years but converted at some point to Christianity and then emerging back into an embrace of their never forgotten Jewishness, all those Shabbats behind thick curtains, unseen. The shame of converting, the uncertain joy of returning. My mother, from West Indian New York, aka, Crown Heights, doesn't know much about her family generations back, she doesn't know from where exactly her great-grandparents were plucked or much about their lives. Cutting sugar cane, probably. How could she know? Those stories are blocked, unknowable. My father spent his whole life on the island; people got used to them, my parents, they were not so unusual, an interracial couple, and life was likely easier for them in Guadeloupe than it would have been in New York or Chicago in the 1960s. I came out looking much more like my father than my mother—but with a little twist; my sister takes after my mother, carbon copy. Almost. She's got her own twist.

But now I, like my mother before me, am a New Yorker. The city pulls me in but I feel so precarious there and, like everyone else who reads literature for a paycheck, I want a full time, tenure track job. I want to be free of endless uncertainty, the annual contracting that leaves my stomach in knots. I check all the job announcements I can find and apply to a few jobs but never get anywhere: too many 19th/20th century American Literature scholars out there, I guess. I'm not sure how long I'll keep trying and I don't always tell Sid when I mail in an application. I'm getting really sick of not having more firmness but I console myself by remembering that certainty, as Nietzsche, or, Derrida, would tell us, is an allusion. How does Nietzsche put it? "Truth is a mobile army of metaphors, metonyms, anthropomorphisms..." But still. I want Sid to be sure. Sure of me, sure of wanting me like I want her, now. I want truth to have solidity.

I hadn't mentioned the professorship at the University of Chicago that'd caught my eye; I mailed my application right before Aaron died and I could almost see it nestling up to one of Sid's photographs in the dark recesses of the mail box between our houses, on the corner of 7th Street and Second Avenue. It did not feel right to bring it up with her while she was in mourning. Mailboxes always figure for me as portals, transport devices, and not in the least ordinary. I'd always imagined that, in the unlikely event I actually get that job Sid and I, if we could only get back together in a more permanent way, would hang out with Aaron once we'd relocated to Hyde Park. I'd have finished my first book by then, and would be working on the literary biography of Aaron. We would take the leisurely bike ride north, all along the lake, past the Magnificent Mile, to his apartment and spend copious afternoons walking around Lakeview, stopping by Unabridged, getting more coffee, and talking and talking. I never had a chance to tell Aaron about my nascent biography. And now it's too late. The lateness, the impossibility of speaking with Aaron. I'd also visualized Sid and I meeting him at the Rare Book Room and whispering over 18th and 19th century books by Melville, about cetaceans, early Henry James editions, laughing together about "whalishness," hermaphroditic borders between truth and fiction. I cannot fathom that Aaron isn't here. That I can never call him or see him again.

I turn over, fluff the pillow again, try sleeping on

my side. But I'm unsettled. After Sid had broken up with me in early October, she'd had the audacity to tell me she still loved me. I don't get her. We'd been together, albeit with some offs and ons, for four years, and she broke up with me, feeling "stifled" (how?) and somehow "unfree." But we struggle, balance, or rather struggle to balance proximity and distance, absorption and space. The always impossible concoction between too close and too far. Every time we get back together she tells me she's hemmed in, as if I bruise her delicate self; but each time we break up again she complains that she misses me and finds my absence hurts, heavy as a Beluga whale pressing on her chest. She has breathing problems—can't breathe with me far, can't breathe with me too close. Expliquez-moi ça!

She'd told me that she'd come to feel as though each break-up were re-written on some scroll in invisible ink. As if she could read the script, illuminated with a lit match and then she'd know what to do. As if I have no say in the matter. As if I won't get sick of this game. This separation amplified her *douleur*, her father died so suddenly. Maybe that's why we're back together. But I won't be used as a prop. I just fucking won't. It's as if, she'd said, a man-sized crack opened in the sidewalk at her feet at knowing Aaron would never be reading in his chair again, at having to tell me he's gone. As if I don't have a me-sized fissure in the ground at my feet, dealing with her and all her mishigas. As if I'm not mourning Aaron's passing intensely, too.

Aaron and I became awkward but close friends and Sid seemed surprised, when we used to visit him, at his wide volubility in the company of her boyfriend. He trusted me, for some reason, not unfounded, almost right away, unfolded around me, somehow, and asked me all about Guadeloupe and even broke out his French. Channeling my mother, I feel I can understand what Aaron's sudden end means for Sid—or at least I think I can. And I'm already keenly missing his acerbic wit, his ability to quote and dig out bits of prose as if he's merely checking the weather. I'm even missing Aaron's bad jokes and quips. I'm hoping she sorely wishes she had said yes when I proposed. Fuck, that feels foolish now, as we, together again, sleep in separate rooms at her mamie's house.

I give up, sit up in bed, inhale the country air. The memory of Sid, Aaron, and I poring over a huge book, sticks to me like a barnacle. Aaron's sudden departure spirals me down and down as if he were augmenting the gravity below my footsteps, I think, as, lying down again and tossing and turning in mamie's blue room, getting sleepy but unable to rest, Aaron, like me, reveled in digging through rare editions, finding notes tucked into them or pencil marks in the margins, reading around as much as reading the actual text. As a relatively young man, with *The Life Raft* (1975), he began achieving modest success as a fiction writer. He'd written two books before Dorothy disappeared and then, after the Jack Johnson book, which he'd already started researching, his work took ever more fantastical turns and he became less and less connected to reality. Over the years he was graced with a few well-placed reviews, yet his novels never sold much. He still couldn't (and wouldn't have, even if that had been possible) given up his day job as an archivist at the Rare Book Room in the University of Chicago Library. It always struck me as stark, the contrast between his ordinary, bookish life, and his (often, not always) fantastical creations. Aaron's novels are so varied, he loves to experiment with form, to pay homage to the literary heroes he devoted so much of his time, sitting nestled in his reading chair, perusing. Our shared admiration for Melville wove Aaron and I together, and I loved it when we would go to the library and gaze at the rare books, especially the 1930 Rockwell Kent illustrated edition of *The Whale* that Aaron acquired on one of his many trips to New York to scour antiquarian bookshops and estate sales. A few years ago, scrunched together in the Rare Book Room, Aaron, Sid and I pored over the slightly musky smelling, heavy volume and she whispered, Oooh I love how Kent shaded in the background with fine lines so that the night is darker than black, and the moon creeps in like a small white coating of snow.

Aaron relayed to us amazing details about the illustrator. How Kent was fond of saying, "I want to paint the rhythm of eternity." How he was a mystic. How he lived in Greenland. How he met there Leni Riefenstahl. We mined the language for nuggets to bring out like delicate truffles when we were hungry.

Psst, André, Aaron whispered, gesturing for me to lean into the big book, and read Melville over his shoulder: "Gnawed within and scorched without, with the infixed, unrelenting fangs of some incurable idea" or, look, here, "The White Whale swam before him as the monomaniac incarnation of all those malicious agencies"..I'm constructing a villain, Aaron confessed to me, somewhat conspiratorially, like he didn't want Sid to hear him, who, like Ahab, is gnawed within and scorched without, who's possessed by vengeance, driven to genocidal urges due to an unfathomable loss.

I realize with a mild shock that that villain must be Drake Barents in *Slobgollion*. He hadn't told me which text got the gnawed, scorched fellow.

Aaron had become another father to me, I muse, hoping to drift off to sleep, so like my father, always grieving for his lost love, but so unlike him. Somehow Aaron could pull on you, draw you out. Listen—even when he seemed a million miles away. We'd see him maybe two or three times a year, but each time felt weighty, not to be trifled with.

And that day he'd come to my class, we'd talked for hours afterwards, on a long ramble around the village while Sid was working in the darkroom. All fall I'd been phoning him regularly for writing help. And I feel like I'm drowning, just knowing he isn't there. How could we know that his sudden departure would open up a portal to the burning question of what happened to Dorothy?

*

I arise to the sparkling blue of the walls, the thick coverlet on the warm bed, the bright azure winter sky. It's Thanksgiving Day but that doesn't matter north of the border. The sun fills the great house in the morning and each room, looking out towards the garden, floods with placid light. Esther gently raps on the door with her pliable pale hand with Sid poking her puffy morning eyes right behind her.

Come in, I say, I'm just waking here, I couldn't get to sleep—thinking about Aaron, and all···and it looks to be a beautiful day.

Oui, oui, ma chère André, il fait beau! Viens avec nous au café!

As we bundle into the old Citroën she asks her granddaughter, You have the paper bag? I hope? It's a passkey. And she winks at me.

Oui, mamie. Il est ici, dans ma poche. We drive

for just a few minutes and then see the petite, gilded sign, *La rivière de la lune* the script matching the paper bag perfectly. We enter, and as I request a spot for three, a gentleman at another table catches my eye—he looks, well, he looks as though he were looking for us. Roughly Esther's generation, a checkered suit with a scarlet cravat that beautifully sets off his pale brown skin, he appears to be from 1949 rather than 1995. The waitress brings us our menus and, gazing over the top of mine so I can see him, I see that he's looking over the top of his newspaper all the better to fix his eyes on us. It isn't an entirely a pleasant sensation; he appears harmless if curious.

Tu le connais? Sid asks, but before Esther can reply, the gentleman suddenly stands right in front of us.

Sid, André, she says, much to our surprise, this is William.

Nice to meet you both, he exclaims, extending a weathered but sturdy hand to each of us, I have been waiting for you.

Please, Esther offers, sweeping her arm over the one remaining empty chair, join us.

Your father, William begins, taking a deep breath, and wasting no time. But before he can go on Sid interjects, You know my father? Oh, of course! He mentioned you in the interview, on the David Kepesh show!

Yes, quite. I saw that interview, too. His last. Oh. I'm so sorry, Sidney.

Go on, Sid says, please.

Aaron consulted me during research for his novel about Jack Johnson, who is, well more accurately, was, my father's dear friend. As you must know Aaron was very thorough in his research and we spent hours and hours in his apartment on Aldine or right here at the café reminiscing about Jack. Aaron told me all about you, Sid, about how proud he was of you, about your transformative antiracist art projects, about your dedication to your craft, about your mother, lost for so long, oh yes, we talked quite a bit. Your father was, how shall I say this....quite a character! But once I grew accustomed to his slightly odd ways I also grew quite fond of him.

So was I, I say.

Aaron's book about Jack Johnson is my second favorite Zimmerman book. It has a wonderful texture, and is very accurate on the details of the boxer—or it seems accurate. I never fact-check. But it has this emotional distance, something with which Aaron definitely struggled.

The waiter brings coffee and steaming croissants, Sid plies William with questions:

William, what was Jack Johnson really like? I mean, André and I read *In Love with Great Black Hope* so we have a picture painted by my father in our minds' eyes, but was the Galveston Giant actually like that? What did you think of dad's novel? I only read it once, and as I said to André some time ago, dad's novels somehow make me lonely so I never pored over them as a literary scholar might.

I like the book very well, and I'm just an art lover, not a scholar. It did seem that Aaron focused more on Lucy than on Jack himself, but that's ok, you know? It was a wonderful thing to see all those long talks your father and I enjoyed rendered but transformed by his vivid imagination. He sent me a signed copy.

Did other people interview you about Jack?

You know, that's an interesting thing...no, even though my father was, especially in the final years, very close with the boxer. Very close.

I suppose, I say, that by the time he retired up here he was sort of forgotten, right? Trust good ol' Aaron to sculpt a life out of a forgotten, but very important figure. So, William, what do you do?

I run a very small art book press, Luzzatto, named after one of my favorite, yet fairly little known, Italian artists.

That must be fascinating.

Indeed! It is. Sometimes it's touch and go, and there's a thin margin for error but overall, I love it. I especially love bringing out younger or forgotten artists.

I look at Sid, but she's clearly thinking about that

heavy valise just then, and not taking, or choosing not to take, William's hint. She pulls the paper bag out of her pocket and hands it to William who picks it up and, placing it close to his nostrils, inhales deeply. He pulls out the key and holds it, weighs it with his palm.

Ah, this takes me back! You must have found the suitcase? I feel as though all those items Aaron told me about were here, as if they could spring out of the case and bring him back along with them.

At this I almost imagine I can see Sid's chin hitting the floor of La rivière de la lune.

How do you know about the suitcase? William looks to Esther and then to me and finally fixes his wizened gaze on Sid, takes both of her hands in his and looks straight into those surprisingly labyrinthine eyes of hers: Your father put everything he could figure out about your dear mama into that case. And he told me to encourage you to follow every clue. I am here to tell you to hope! But I'm also terrified to tell you that because I worry that he's concocted some sort of false hope. I don't know. But I am here to help in any way I can.

At this Sid blinks.

Hope?

So, she says, the fragment he left us, William, do you know about this, too? This crazy fiction of people, maybe including my mother encased in a glass room below the sea, living with whales who speak Yiddish? God, it sounds insane just to say it.

No, I know nothing about a manuscript. Aaron just asked me to be ready, after he was gone, to be there for you.

William hands the key to mamie and we bid him farewell, huddle into the old Citroën as the bright day chills, the clouds invade, and the diffuse white sky threatens snow. In the car I recall the review of *Black Hope*.

THE VILLAGE VOICE, 19 OCTOBER, 1983

IN LOVE WITH GREAT BLACK HOPE
BY AARON ZIMMERMAN
CARVER, ROTH & KINBOTE, $6.95; 224 PAGES
REVIEWED BY CAROLA SPRINGER

AARON ZIMMERMAN'S THIRD NOVEL, IN LOVE
WITH GREAT BLACK HOPE, YET AGAIN A DEPARTURE
FROM HIS FIRST, THE EAGLE'S NEST WHICH DEPART-
ED FROM HIS SECOND, THE LIFE RAFT, WAS SPARKED
BY HIS BOYHOOD WANDERINGS AROUND LAKEVIEW,
CHICAGO WHERE HE OFTEN FOUND HIMSELF AT
THE IMPOSING GRAVE OF JACK JOHNSON, FORMER
HEAVYWEIGHT CHAMPION OF THE WORLD, BURIED
AT GRACELAND CEMETERY IN 1946. ZIMMERMAN
TOLD ME ABOUT HIS ENDURING FASCINATION WITH
JACK JOHNSON AND RELAYED THAT HE READ WITH
GREAT INTEREST EVERYTHING HE COULD ABOUT THE
BOXER. HE ALSO SPENT HOURS AND HOURS INTER-
VIEWING FRIENDS, FAMILY MEMBERS, AND ACQUAIN-
TANCES OF THE GREAT FIGHTER, ESPECIALLY WIL-
LIAM BENEDICT. BUT ZIMMERMAN IS VERY CLEAR AT
THE OUTSET: "THIS IS A WORK OF FICTION BASED
LOOSELY ON THE LIFE OF THE GALVESTON GIANT."
ZIMMERMAN CONFESSED THAT HE LOVED THE IDEA
OF THIS BURLY MAN FIGHTING AGAINST THE ODDS
AND MAINTAINING THE HEAVYWEIGHT CHAMPION OF
THE WORLD STATUS BRAVELY IN 1908 WHILE DATING

AND MARRYING HOT WHITE WOMEN. ZIMMERMAN, EVER CAREFUL TO INCLUDE DETAILED HISTORICAL CONTEXTUALIZATIONS IN HIS NOVELS, DESCRIBES THE PARTICULARS OF THE RIOTS THAT ROCKED THE NATION IN 1910 WHEN JOHNSON WON AGAINST JAMES JEFFRIES, THE WHITE BOXER WHO CAME OUT OF RETIREMENT IN ORDER TO BE THE "GREAT WHITE HOPE." JEFFRIES WOULD SUPPOSEDLY DEFINITIVELY PROVE THAT WHITE PEOPLE ARE STRONGER, BUT HE WAS SOUNDLY BEATEN BY JOHNSON, THE SUPERIOR PUGILIST. IN CHANGING THE TITLE FROM WHITE HOPE TO BLACK HOPE, ZIMMERMAN, A JEWISH-AMERICAN WRITER, IMPLICITLY SHIFTS THE CONSCIOUSNESS FROM WHITE TO BLACK. THE VERY CONCEPT OF THE "GREAT WHITE HOPE," AFTER ALL, IMPLIES A WHITE SUPREMACY THAT MAY WELL HAVE MADE ZIMMER-MAN UNCOMFORTABLE.

WHILE ZIMMERMAN IS NOT A HOLOCAUST SUR-VIVOR, THIS INTRIGUING, SATISFYING NOVEL ABOUT JOHNSON NONETHELESS RESONATES WITH THE JEWISH EMIGRÉ FILMMAKER MICHAEL ROEMER'S CHOICE TO MAKE THE STUNNING FILM NOTHING BUT A MAN IN 1964. ROEMER NOTES SPECIFICALLY THAT IT WAS HIS ALIENATING AND TERRIFYING EXPERI-ENCE IN NAZI GERMANY THAT LED HIM TO DESCRIBE IN SUCH EMPATHIC DETAIL BLACK LIFE IN THE SOUTH ON THE CUSP OF THE CIVIL RIGHTS MOVEMENT.

IN ADDITION TO AN EMPATHIC BLACK PERSPEC-TIVE, ZIMMERMAN ALSO TAKES ANOTHER RISK IN THIS

NOVEL BY WRITING FROM THE POINT OF VIEW OF A FICTIONAL AMALGAM OF JOHNSON'S WHITE WIVES WHO HE NAMES "LUCY." ZIMMERMAN PORTRAYS LUCY THROUGH A THIRD PERSON OMNISCIENT NARRATOR AND, AS A WOMAN I HAVE TO ADMIT HE DOES A SURPRISINGLY CONVINCING JOB OF CROSSING THE GENDER DIVIDE, SOMETHING FEW MALE WRITERS DARE TO ATTEMPT. LUCY FALLS HEAD OVER HEELS FOR THE DASHING BOXER AND BECOMES TOTALLY SWEPT UP INTO HIS SIMULTANEOUSLY GLAMOROUS AND HELLISH LIFE. THROUGH LUCY'S POINT OF VIEW ZIMMERMAN SHOWS US THE SCINTILLATING WORLD OF CAFÉ DE CHAMPION, THE NIGHTCLUB THE "GALVESTON GIANT" OPENED IN HARLEM AND WHICH WAS ABUZZ WITH MUSIC, DANCE, AND LARGE, SPORTING LIFE BEFORE HE SOLD IT. THE CAFÉ THEN BECAME THE FABLED COTTON CLUB. BUT THE GIANT, ALWAYS RESTLESS, COULD NEVER SETTLE INTO ONE VENTURE, OR ONE WOMAN. IN A PARTICULARLY MOVING SCENE, ZIMMERMAN RELATES HOW LUCY FOUND A PAIR OF INTENSELY GORGEOUS RED HIGH HEELED SHOES, ALL WRAPPED UP IN A BERGDORF GOODMAN BOX WITH A BIG BOW AND WITH A CARD: "FOR MY LOVE, SUSIE, KISSES, JACK." A PALE, TERRIFIED LUCY CONFRONTS THE GREAT BOXER ONLY TO HAVE HIM DISSOLVE IN TEARS AND APOLOGIZE FOR HIS ENDLESS INFIDELITIES.

AT THE END OF ZIMMERMAN'S NOVEL, LUCY AND JOHNSON SETTLE IN QUÉBEC WHERE THEY LIVE

OUT THEIR LIVES IN AN UNEASY BUT RELATIVELY STABLE PEACE. ZIMMERMAN GRANTED JOHNSON MORE HOPE THAN HE HAD IN REALITY AND THE FICTIONAL BOXER NEVER WENT TO JAIL FOR TRANSPORTING A WOMAN ACROSS STATE LINES FOR THE SUPPOSEDLY IMMORAL PURPOSE OF CROSS-RACIAL LOVE AS THE ACTUAL JOHNSON DID. THE HISTORICAL PERSONAGE, AFTER SERVING TIME (AND FIGHTING IN) THE FEDERAL PRISON IN LEAVENWORTH, KS, ENDED UP PERFORMING IN VAUDEVILLE ACTS AND DYING AT THE AGE OF 68, DEBASED AND NEARLY FORGOTTEN.

BY REWRITING THE STORY WITH SO MANY PERSPECTIVAL SHIFTS AND CHANGES FROM THE HISTORICAL RECORD, ZIMMERMAN AT ONCE CONVEYS THE PROFOUND MELANCHOLIA THAT ACCOMPANIED ALL INTER-RACIAL RELATIONSHIPS IN THE EARLY PART OF THE 20TH CENTURY AND OFFERS SOME HOPE. AS I FELT WITH HIS FIRST TWO NOVELS, THE EAGLE'S NEST (1970) AND LIFE RAFT (1975) HE'S BOTH AMBITIOUS AND IMBUED WITH A GREAT EYE FOR HISTORICAL DETAIL, OR FOR DETAILS IN GENERAL—BUT SOMETIMES HIS CHARACTERS REMAIN SLIGHTLY FLAT. LUCY FEELS FULLY FLESHED OUT AND WE ARE RIGHT THERE WITH HER THROUGH ALL THE PATHOS OF HER HUSBAND'S ENDLESS CHEATING. SHE RESONATES WITH LOSS ON AN EPIC SCALE, BUT THE BOXER HIMSELF, FOR ALL HIS HUGENESS, REMAINS SOMEWHAT SMALL.

"Let's go visit Felix," Esther startles us by suggesting as we find ourselves heading out to the Beth Israel cemetery to see her great love, felled by a heart attack in 1976, luckily for him before his daughter became a missing person. Sid only retained a blurry memory of her maternal grandfather—she was six and in Chicago when, sitting comfortably by the fire Felix nodded off, never to awaken. Esther was busy cooking in the kitchen, she tells us, she'd come into the drawing room to kiss him and say, Felix, and then, repeat, because his hearing was not so good by the end⋯ Felix, honey, dinner!

Annoyed at first that he wasn't getting up to join her at the table in the kitchen where the two of them ate their suppers as they chatted about the news, about their aches and pains, about the weather, about the past, about their daughter, son-in-law, and granddaughter, she soon realized he was uncommonly still. She called an ambulance but it was too late, nothing would have saved him. The emergency team assured her that it would not have mattered if she had found him earlier. Aaron, Dorothy, and Sid arrived the next day and the funeral took place soon after that.

Esther was tough, so, at the age of 69 she learned how to drive (Sid and I found her driving slightly scary but passable), figured out how to pay the bills and care for the garden and the great house, took over everything Felix had always done. But below her tough hide, we could see, she was mourning, always mourning his loss. Just like my father will always mourn and pine for my mother, just as Aaron, until the end, ached for Dorothy. The three of them, Esther, Felix and Dorothy, made a small family, and robust as Esther always tried to be, Felix found her tender spots and she leaned on him even though she would like to pretend she didn't.

Her husband's resting place lay beneath a simple, but graceful black stone: "Felix D'Espinosa, 1905–1976. Mari aimant d'Esther, cher père de Dorothy Zimmerman, grand-père de Sidney." Sid had never been to visit her grandfather here and, taking in the carefully arranged flowers, preserved in the crisp Canadian winter, the gently placed memorial stones, asks, mamie, how often do you visit grandpa?

Oh, you know, every day. I miss him, Sid, il me manque.

I remember telling Sid, after she'd scattered Aaron's ashes, You're worn thin. You're raggedy. Please, let me take care of you, just a little. Even if you don't want to admit it, tu me manques.

And she told me that she'd always thought it was strange that in English it's the 'I' who misses the 'you' but in French it's the 'you' who misses the 'I.' I could see that Sid was wishing there were some way to visit Aaron. It had been so quick, her torpedoing his ashes into the lake, and it seemed to be what he wanted, but now there was no going back, there'd never be a memorial stone. The endless irreversibility of time. The stickiness of loss.

We can visit him, love, at the lake, even though he doesn't have a tombstone, ok? I say, putting my arm around her cold shoulders. She looks up at me, quiet.

Esther continues, I usually like to visit with my Felix, you know, so I can tell him what's going on in the world, take a walk beneath these glorious flowing trees, I have some other friends here, too. That's what happens when you're 88, n'est-ce pas? In the summer time the flowers wilt so fast but now I don't need to bring him a fresh batch every day, they last a little while.

Turning to face the headstone, Esther addresses him, Felix, hey Felix, Sidney is here, and this is her···well I think her boyfriend, anyway, look, Felix it's the handsome, whippet-smart, and adorable, André. Esther turns to look up and wink at me playfully as she says this, and then, after cupping her ear and leaning into the gravestone adds, Felix wants to know when you two are going to tie the knot?

Sid doesn't respond to this but I think I see a trace of pink land on her left cheek.

We amble around the cemetery and Esther sometimes nods hello to her friends, underground.

Sid and I wish we could read all those beautiful Hebrew letters—well, she can pick them out and sort of pronounce them, but not very well. I know Esther is being sweet, and playful; but I'm getting sicker and sicker of all the confusion between us. Just while I start to feel like I can't stand it anymore, I also know that I can, that I will, that I am waiting but I begin to sense my wait will be short. I can't, won't mutiny. We're back to together but in that way that leaves a filament thin layer of frost between us, chilling the sheets. I don't want to be walking on tenterhooks perpetually.

Suddenly, I see a grave with a familiar name: Azevedo. Sid, I cry out, pulling her away from a monumental plinth she is struggling to read, look!

Yes, Esther says then, pensively, André, it's such a beautiful Sephardic name, yours, and Azevedos (not all Sephardim, of course) are everywhere—all those expulsions, burnings, and diasporas. I remember you told me once that your father's family arrived in Guadeloupe from Brazil in the 17th century?

It's a bit fuzzy, fuzzier than it should be, n'est-ce pas?, my sense of this history, but from what my father told me it sounds like they did arrive from Brazil, were welcomed, got settled in—they were fishmongers, I think? and then, when the Jews were inevitably kicked out again a few years later they managed to use the suppleness of the Azevedo name to their advantage: they converted to Christianity and stayed that way until my grandfather decided to reclaim the Jewishness the family had never really lost. I've been to visit him at the cemetery there, on the edge of town, the Jewish section right next to the Creole section. But my parents chose not to push religion on us. Marguerite's become something of a Christian lately, she goes to a Moravian church in Point-a-Pitre, and she's started praying regularly, I believe.

I can only imagine, Esther says, the longing that must come with so much not-knowing. I have a little of that, and also, a little gemischt history on Felix's, but not quite as gemischt as yours. My father, may his memory be always for a blessing, was a Rabbi and my mother a kid-maker, bookkeeper, house cleaner, chef, and in-house comedienne. They swept into Montréal in the great wave of Jewish immigration from the Pale in 1900. I grew up speaking Yiddish at home and French in school and by the time I met Felix on a cold winter day in 1930 ice skating on a frozen lake—a day not unlike this one, the weather keeps over the centuries rolling along mostly the same—I was already headstrong (as Dorothy would be) and determined not to take all the crap (excuse me for saying so, but he really did dish out crap) my mother took from my father. Felix's parents were an Ashkenazi-Sephardic salad—his mother, also from the Pale, but his father from Portugal. Perhaps because Felix D'Espinosa had been so shy, Esther said dreamily, perhaps because there was nothing he could do when I looked at him with what he always affectionately called my liquid brown eyes but sigh, Felix agreed to everything I said and no one ever doubted who wore the pants in our family. So, in 1937, seven years after our marriage, a girl was born, and we decided to name her Dorothy, meaning 'gift of God.' Not that we were religious, just happy to see her.

I echo gift internally and think but don't say I'm too much of an underground romantic to bother with external romanticism in the form of something as stately as a church, though.

If I were ever to go anywhere near institutionalized religion, I say, it would be to a synagogue. We lit candles on Fridays, that sort of thing, but it isn't as though I know anything about Judaism, really...

Too bad Aaron isn't here anymore, Esther says wistfully, he was not religious either, but, well, you know, he read everything and was sort of like a walking Encyclopedia Judaica. I don't know that he knew much about the rich and complex history of Caribbean Jews but I wouldn't be surprised if he did. And, I especially wouldn't be surprised if he'd started researching all about that history, oh, around four years ago. Felix knew a thing or two, as well, and he would have adored you.

Esther surprises me by standing on her toes to pull me down so that she can kiss my cheek.

Shall we return home? she queries. It's chilly, non?

Hoping to avoid a somewhat frightening ride, I offer to drive us back to the great house and we all sit silently in the car and then, as we bundle back inside Esther asks me if I'd like to see this famous attic. We pull off our coats and boots in the somber entryway and climb the stairs.

All along the stairs Esther has placed photos, nearly one for each step, in a straight diagonal line so that each image is about the same height above its corresponding step as the next one. She must have measured carefully. Some are from Sid's portrait collection, some are family, Felix, and a scholar, must be Felix's father, faded, the white beard covering his pale, studious skin, his eyes downcast, hands holding a heavy book, a rounded cloth hat on his head.

The landing at the top of the stairs lined with heavy trunks, various tchotchkes perched on top, small sentinels to a capacious area.

To the left, the surprisingly large, yellow bathroom contains a giant portal carved into its ceiling. I had seen the entryway in the morning and wondered why it was so oddly located almost above the bathtub. Esther, ever unexpectedly strong, picks up a long wooden stick with a metal hook on the end, a small version of Captain Hook's hand. She places the hook exactly in the right spot and asks me to help her pull down. As we do, a ladder emerges from the ceiling. I unclasp the lock and heave the sturdy steel ladder all the way down, checking it for stability as it parks on the bathroom floor.

So, Sid, you want to go up first?

I'm astonished to see how pale her pale skin has become. No, no, André, you go ahead. It's amazing up there—full of surprises. But I can't handle it right now. I'm going to take a walk and take some photos, if that's ok, while you go up?

Sid mentioned this attic many times when she described the great house so I didn't quite understand at first her reticence. She'd portrayed it as an utterly magical holding place for all things past. I wanted her to explore with me and I squash a burgeoning onion of disappointment as it balloons in my gut.

Over the years her grandparents stored a myriad of lost objects up there, so I don't know exactly what I am about to find. I ascend the ladder, struggle to locate the light switch as eerie filament thin cobweb hairs graze the back of my hand; as my eyes adjust to the dim light, rare objects pop out of the darkness. Glass vases, small sculptures, folded clothes, everything a tumble, some of the stuff frozen there, in storage, but as I amble around a slow realization emerges: the attic is a shrine to Dorothy.

Her dollhouse remains in a corner, intact, with

its carefully arranged, slightly cobwebby inhabitants; over there, a teddy bear, over-sized, one yellow eye slightly askew; and, at the back of the attic, by the window, a large box full of photographs. Dorothy as a three-year-old, smiling, one hand holding her mother's hand, the other holding Felix's. Dorothy as a teenager, a tight-waisted full flowing flowery skirt, smoking a cigarette and leaning back at a jaunty angle. Dorothy and Aaron on their wedding day, she in a simple white dress, Aaron looking black-haired (his hair was a snowy owl white by the time I met him) and dapper in a grey three-piece suit. I hold this one, carefully. Sid will need to see this.

Next to the photographs a thick envelope sits on top of a small table. I pick it up, dust it off. The postmark is dated September 10, 1977. It's addressed to Dorothy, but it has never been opened.

I tuck the envelope in the back of my jeans, allow the wedding photo to float like a drunken seagull down to the floor, and slowly climb back out of the attic, close up that portal to a world excruciating for Sid. I shove the envelope into my suitcase. When I find Esther downstairs in the sitting room, she seems to know how I might be feeling so she gives me a firm hug and asks me to light a fire. Sid comes back from her walk, pink and slightly chilled, and after some time the fire roars and we all sit on the couch opposite and gaze into the flames, dreaming while awake.

Sid, love, Esther finally says, I was extremely upset, shocked, really to get that call from you, when Aaron left us so suddenly. And I am relieved, grateful, to Greta, that there will be a memorial service.

Sid begins explaining that it was Halloween night, she has to rehearse Aaron's ending over and over. The way repetition makes impossible realities real.

As you probably know, mamie, she says, taking her grandmother's hand, the West Village celebrates beautiful drag queens in big, bright costumes and elaborate, vivid make-up, and André and I usually go—I take my camera—to be among the glory of the Christopher Street Parade erupting euphorically on the other side of town. But I felt low that day, and just couldn't muster the energy to walk all the way across to the West Village, with all the swirl and swish of dresses and the crowd pressed around me.

As she says this, Pound's *faces in the crowd: Petals on a wet, black bough* pounds in my head and I wonder if maybe this atypical reluctance to join the spectators at the parade was a premonition that a creeping metamorphosis would take Aaron away.

After that doctor called, Sid goes on, I gazed out the window. It was so beautiful out there, even though, even though I was in shock, she says. I think I still am. I fainted, did André tell you? At the museum, under the great whale. But that night, with the voice of the doctor still ringing in my ears, the evening sky spread out over the construction across the street and the sun was setting to the right while its colors reflected in windows and mirrors all around in pinks and turquoises. I think I took some photos, just to capture that moment. I didn't want to forget. Even though the neighborhood is in the process of changing, you'll need to come back and visit us again, mamie, it's still so magical, especially that time of day, and gazing out over the area I've wandered and captured on film always calms me. I remembered then that dad (was it a premonition?) wrote to me some time ago, you know, one of his many dry, terse, letters.

Oui, Esther says, your father was a master at the terse letter! I still have a stack of them in the attic! All together, they form a sort of absurdist patchwork.

Yes, oh, yes, that's so true. Sid's laughing as she says this, the skin by the side of her eyes crinkling slightly. Dad's letter...don't you think it strange? Sid, when I die, I want to be cremated.

Strange, Esther says, yes, very. I would think Aaron would be opposed to this and prefer, like Felix, to sink into the earth. And let me guess... he hadn't supplied the name of a funeral home or anything that would help with the practical details.

Sid nodded and went on reminiscing, after staring out the window, she says, until all the sunlight faded and electric lights sparkled like luminescent fish leaping out of the buildings, I finally found the energy to take the train up to CUNY. I knew I had to get to André that night.

Yeah, I think, you had to get to me. But you still weren't sure, were you, that you wanted to be with me. What can I do to make you sure? To make me sure?

So, Esther prods her, what else is on your mind, ketzele?

It must have been, I'm afraid, right at the very moment he passed away that his face flickered over a portrait of a different man in the darkroom. The image emulsified into someone else so fast, but I saw him.

Esther and I each have hold of one of Sid's smooth hands.

But, let me tell you, before finding that incredible suitcase, well—and actually, now, after stumbling on it—I had, I have, well, we have, a lot to deal with. Dad's books, coated in thick layers of crud, still seem golden to me. I just can't see a way to part with them, any more than I can imagine letting go of the apartment. I began thinking about that last night, here in your green room. The apartment gets thicker every year as though one could trace its rings on an ever-widening tree. All dad's books covered in his strange multicolored, multi-year commentary. For some reason when we got here last night the apartment settled on top of me—maybe it's that when I would come here, to your lovely house each summer, I'd always come from there. I love that place—even though, well, it's seen better days.

You don't need to worry about that right now, ziskeit, there is time. How did Eliot have it? "And time yet for a hundred indecisions/ And for a hundred visions and revisions," something like that. You're so young, Sid, there will be time for all. Aaron loved you, you know, even if he didn't always show it.

Prufrock! I pip up, and yes, mamie-Esther's absolutely right. I think, really, he didn't know how to show it.

Then how, I'm wondering, did Aaron somehow show me—and not his daughter? It's as though his endless mourning for Dorothy placed a layer of cling film around Sid, smothering her, but also keeping her from him⋯or maybe keeping him from her. He'd recognized a co-mourner in me, I suppose, and I was new and unwrapped.

I knew, Sid says, very quietly, I couldn't live with those crumbly ashes, their accusatory chalky faces staring at me, and I knew that dad would want to spread out into the lake. I knew that I had to do it for him.

We all gaze at the fire again.

You know, Sid says, breaking the silence, I'm haunted by the lake, the ashes. Could they re-forge into my father and would he rise up from the water and walk home through that dripping, creepy tunnel to confront me with his drowning? When I got to the lake, with the ashes, its edge was wholly altered compared to what I remembered. As if I held a landscape-sized photo from the past over the present, when I stood there despite the grey November sky, I saw us, in the past, when I was a child. Dad was right there with me, then, as, oddly, now, but he may as well have been miles away, in another world, muttering under his breath as he rowed, carrying on a fictional conversation from one of his novels.

Oh Sid, love, maybe we should go to bed?, or rather, I added, to our beds? I trace the arc of her elbow with my index finger.

Yes, yes, soon. I just want to tell you both one more thing. It was quite remarkable, in a quiet way. As I sat on the sun-soaked floor of our apartment on Aldine, unable to do any more sorting, another photo pressed against the present, erasing it, as a fire in summer, just like this one, came crowding into my inner eye. Do you remember, mamie, when I was little, after a hot, salty bath, I would descend the stairs sleepily, settling near the fire, right here, legs tucked under me?

As she says this I imagine a kid-Sid sitting like

a stone Buddha gazing at the orange flames licking the wood as a hungry wolf might devour its prey.

You would always come in, Sid goes on, turning to her grandmother, when I sat here, I'd be waiting for you. I would hand you a thick wooden brush, hoping for the pleasure I knew would come if I could only stay calm, and you'd slowly brush out my hair as it warmed by the fire. I would say:

My back is melting, mamie, and the melting comes through my head and down to my feet.

And you would say: You'll melt, sleepy one, up-stairs, into bed. And, with my hair, gently brushed I would make my sleepwalking way into one of the bedrooms and my still moist hair would meld into the soft pillow as if sinking back into a warm bath. Do you remember? And somehow, that sinking sen-sation, it was so comforting and yet it came back to me like a bodily memory right after I scattered dad's ashes, as if, as if...I were sinking into the lake with him.

*

Morning, and I go to the green room to rouse her. André, Sid says, looking up at me, and I can't quite tell what her look means. But she stands up, reaches out to me and as I envelope her I inhale her slight coconuty hair and have a little trouble keeping things calm. She has no idea, I imagine, what it's like to be so close but to be unable to go further. She rests her hand gently on the small of my back.

Sid, come here, I say, moving her hand away, running my fingers down her arm and nudging her over to the sofa in the corner, away from the bed. Sit next to me. I know you're hurting, losing Aaron... it's so much harder than anyone who hasn't been through it can understand... I know how you feel. And you're not the only one mourning, you know?

I know. And you do know, how I feel, don't you?

I try. We're on the couch, and I pull her in closer to me and then, feeling her stiffen, let go and stand up, a little abruptly, bashing my knee on the end table.

Well, I'd better go help Esther make coffee, see you downstairs?

I look down at her before heading out and she's so small, curled into herself like a slinky, as if she were one of her own portrait subjects but without the other figure in the scene. I'm thinking that we have to find out what happened to Dorothy, Sid will never rest until she knows, she'll never be able to be as giving as I need her to be unless we can find.... something from that unexploded landmine of a suitcase Aaron left for us. Something in that envelope I stole from the attic. But what if we already know?

I'm tired, Sid, tired of this see-saw.

I know. I know. Please, can you just stay? Can you wait for me to come? Those eyes. How can I put my foot down? But I'm not going to stay on this rollercoaster ride this girl puts me through, that's for damn sure. And yet, I feel I have no choice everything hinges on unpacking these weird meanings. That's when I decide firmly I am going to hide the envelope I'd found. Mamie will never know it's gone.

But what I say is:

Sid, do you remember when we went to the NYPL to find a record of that obscure early American photographer who had defied all odds by capturing an image of a pair of lovers, a zaftig, beautiful white woman embraced by a tall, handsome black man wearing a beret? We'd dug and dug through the archives and you'd said that you loved my ability to follow all the zany things you come up with. You know I would never have let the fact that you're being somewhat nutty deflect me, I just prepare to help you with her quest. That's what I do all day anyway: search. Search for meanings in literary texts, in the quirky writing of my students, in crusty old papers in archives. You let me know you appreciate the fact that I look closely and listen closely and I absorb—or try to, anyway—your photographs with what you call an unmatched intensity.

What made you think of that, just now?

I was just thinking of your photographs, of the book you'll make. Maybe that portrait of Dorothy and Aaron on their wedding day, the one I found in the attic reminded me. Here, I brought it down for you.

I pick the portrait up from my nightstand and hand it to her before going down. She stares at it as if its ghosts would sail out of the surface of the image.

We share breakfast with Esther and then, to capture the light, sally out over to the St. Lawrence River, stopping along the way for a spot of lunch, and then ambling along the bank, Sid taking photos as we go. While we're on the bank of the river, it's cold, but we pause to gaze out for a moment.

You haven't said anything about *Slobgollion*. What do you make of it?

It's madness, utter madness. But you're the bi-ographer⋯what do you make of it?

Honestly? I don't know.

Me neither.

And Sid, the key, are you afraid?

She just nods meekly.

We return to the great house in the early eve-ning, and Esther is waiting for us, her brows knit together as she greets us. Mamie, Sid asks, kissing her, what do you think of all that William said?

My daughter, you know, is...or maybe was? a very determined, headstrong girl—and then a very headstrong person. No force on this earth could have kept her away from her little girl. So, hope is not a bad idea. I know Aaron was trying...always trying to find her...and I do think he located a few clues, but I suppose he just couldn't know, none of us could, can know how to put them all together.

We cluster into Esther's sweet-smelling kitchen and Sid and I start chopping mushrooms and aubergine while Esther puts on some aromatic brown rice.

Esther pauses to sweep her arm over the whole multicolored house.

She told us that she and Felix moved to Québec when Dorothy was a baby so that Felix could accept a post as Professor of Archaeology at Laval. They would not have dreamed of a house like this, she wanted us to know, a little embarrassed at its scope, but a colleague retired and decided to move to the States to be with his daughter so he sort of passed the house along to them, and, she continued, turning to Sid:

This is where your mother learned how to walk! She was moody, as a girl, and sometimes, a real pain. But she had her heart and her head in the right place and she was determined. No matter what she did, she was determined. A little lost, maybe, but strong all the same.

As she says this, it looks as though some sort of peace has found her or perhaps she found it?

After dinner Sid tells Esther she is ready. She pulls the key out of its strange encasement and fits it into the delicate writing desk in the green room, where Esther enjoyed handwriting letters to many correspondents over the last half century or so. Opening up the deep rosewood box, we are surprised to find a record there—no fountain pen, ink, nor a stack of thick, speckled paper, as we'd expected. But leaping from the cover of the blue album, a photograph of the ocean with a huge tail of a whale plunging down into the depths. Across the front in giant letters: "WHALE SONG."

We look at Esther but she just smiles back. After I place the record on the turntable, we sit down. A few minutes, listening intently, Esther sings: unzere planete ist zayre teyre, mir mussen···the whales, she says, the whales are singing in Yiddish! Our planet is very dear, we must take care, we must see how all things interconnect, we must treat all living things gently. The earth, her oceans, are living things. Listen.

IV
Sid

Saturday, after coffee and delicate scones mamie baked early in the morning, and hugs and a gushing good-bye, we make our way back to the airport. On the flight home to New York, André pleads with me, trying not, I can tell, to sound pleading. But a crack in his voice betrays him:

God, this is so hard, all this on and off. I feel so close to you now, and Esther treats me like family. You tell me that we're back together, but you're...well you're pulling away from me while you're pulling me in. It's incredibly confusing.

I'm just out to sea. I'm sorry, you're right, I just need you, now, to keep hold of me.

I'm trying to stay patient, but just so you know, this is not easy for me.

Oui, je le sais bien.

André rests his head on my shoulder and conks out. As he sleeps another plane ride, our first together, to visit dad in Chicago, comes floating back to me. On that trip, when we were just getting to know each other, I'd peppered him with questions: André, tell me all about Guadeloupe. Are the beaches big and white and sandy? Do your feet burn when you walk on them? Does salt water everywhere make everything rusty? What about the tourists? Do they go whale watching? Where are they from? Do you miss it?

He gave me a mischievous look. Honey, I'm from the bush. We rode on the backs of turtles because cars hadn't been invented yet and we slept in hammocks swinging from wild palm trees. Sometimes a coconut would fall down and hit me in the head, just like that. Wham! And then you're wide awake, he'd jested. I rolled my eyes, reached out to stroke his hand, so I figure he knew that I knew he was teasing me. We've lost that lightness. I want it back.

No seriously, we have to go there someday, Sid, I mean, if we...

I would love to. I'd said, kissing his delectable lips.

We hadn't yet managed the voyage to Guadeloupe. Something always got in the way, work, money worries, one of our breakups. He did answer lots of my questions, stacked up like a deck of cards.

Guadeloupe is always warm, he'd told me, the air's laden, heavy but in a good way, like a warm bath. There is salt everywhere but the air doesn't seem salty and your skin stays soft because of all the coconut oil you put on it. The light is incredible—he said I'd go crazy with my camera. It can be hard for outsiders to quite get the general sense of humor—it's kind of like cayenne mixed with mango.

I got a sense of that from your dad—that day we spent together, ambling around the Guggenheim and then having a lavish lunch at Café Mendelssohn, will always remain one of my favorites. Your father is so witty and interesting and your sister...she seems like a force to be reckoned with. Somehow, I don't want to cross her. But tell me more about Guadeloupe please, be my guide, until I can get there, and yes, yes, I must go there, we must go there, we will...!

Stretching out his hand as best he could in the small airplane seats, André pretended to be a tour guide. Stunning trees grace Guadeloupe, he'd said, a little grandly, for comic effect. The gorgeous dancerly palms, the huge cottonwoods wrap around themselves as they go up and one appears like an ant standing next to them. I suppose it would be about like the difference between a human and a blue whale, something like that in terms of scale. At night you hear all sorts of birds talking with each other in strange languages. Sometimes I would lie in bed, he'd said, with an air of cocking an ear, and strain to try to make sense of it and when I listened hard enough they would say insensible things like snearkertoes, sneakertoes, sneakertoes. Animals, I suppose, have vast languages all unto themselves. Swimming is mostly for tourists but sometimes we locals do take a dip. All the food is fresh, in season. In New York, we can eat berries in the middle of winter, but there, only what's growing right nearby is available. Sometimes tourists ask for an avocado in January and the ladies at the market just laugh at them and say something like, 'if you find an avocado, you go ahead and bring it here to me, d'accord?' The school system is very French so I studied most of the time, in college and, anyway, it's a truth universally recognized that literary scholars are always the last ones anyone wanted to dance with...

Bah! That can't possibly be true..tu sais que tu es tellement beau.

Sid, do you really want to know about those other girls? I thought we said we'd leave that a kind of blank spot in the history book, remember? I don't want to know about anyone before me—it makes me feel, well, jealous, n'est-ce pas?

OK, OK you're right. And I think I would get jealous

too. You're so handsome, and smart, I'm sure all the girls were chasing you...your olive skin, your gentle eyes, those big hands, oh yeah, they were. Tell me more about what Université was like? What was your favorite class?

That's an easy one! 19th Century American Literature, of course. I fell in love, very quickly, with the thickness of those descriptions, with their expansive worldviews, with the idea of the quest.

Tell me more about Guadeloupe—it's so weird to me that I've never seen where you're from—you're such a New Yorker now.

I don't know exactly what else to say...you're going to have to make the voyage. My father wants us to come and visit maybe this coming winter? You know, escape the dread of the New York city chill?

Let's try. I'm not entirely sure we can afford it?

Well, yes, true. But, yes, let's try. Father's getting impatient with you, and so is Marguerite.

Just them?

At this I probably shot him a mysterious look.

OK, let me see what else I can tell you. When I was a kid, I loved going to visit dad at the Université and the physics department was full of mysterious machines and wild experiments. Once, when I was about fourteen maybe, sometime after mom…anyway, Marguerite and I met Leon after work and he was feeling playful so he took us behind the veil.

Veil?

As it were. Leon beckoned us into the forbidden zone—

the door with INTERDIT! PHYSIQUE EXPÉRIMENTALE CHERCHEURS SEULEMENT emblazoned on it in no uncertain terms and he showed us the weirdest things: a dollop of milk under a microscope swimming with tiny particles made huge; a two-channel test to determine locality with a polarizer set in opposite directions; all sorts of experimental set ups which Marguerite and I were under strict instructions not to touch. But we looked and looked and gazed in wonder as our father went on and on about quantum entanglement and all sorts of things that make no sense to me, not then, and not now, either.

He must love being a physics professor, in his pocket the keys to the universe. Exploring time. I remember learning once that physicists have no idea why time's arrow always goes solely forwards...sometimes I feel it going backwards, too.

Do you? That must be fun. And impossible, right? But yes, my father loves to experiment with all sorts of things— Aaron explores literary form while Leon explores the forms of the universe through examining with a formidable intensity the tiniest bits of it. I hope our fathers get to meet each other, some day. From what I know of Aaron, thanks to his books, I think they would get along like a house on fire. But I guess I'll need to meet the father first. Do you think he'll approve of me?

I didn't dignify this with an answer; I just kissed his cheek. Then I asked a question I've always regretted.

How come Leon never re-married? All those years... women must've flung themselves at him. Unlike my dad, Leon is so charming and outgoing and talkative.

I can't even believe you asked me that, Sid.

We sat in our narrow airplane seats silently for a while and somehow, although it was an innocent question, rendered, I thought, sweetly, André bristled that I could have suggested it. This must have been the first—and certainly not the last—time André was angry with me. He insisted that Leon would never have considered dating after Charlotte died so suddenly. They were desperately in love, he said, even when they fought, that was bloody obvious. André didn't talk to me for the rest of that years-ago flight; he'd turned his gaze out the window, and I watched over his shoulder as the clouds below formed into animal shapes. He's angry like that again, now, sleeping on my shoulder. Damnit I am so sick of failing, all the time, failing to just let this relationship unfold as it could. I can't keep screwing this up. But I'm having trouble catching hold of how we can go forward from here. So much confusion, so much hurt. But also intensity, desire, love clearer than any I've ever felt. We'll need to remake us. I need to fucking fix this.

André rouses when the flight attendant comes around. We clink cups, and drink hot chocolate to Esther. l'chaim, we say. I kiss him, feel the slight bristle of his unshaved cheek.

Then I turn to him, pretend for a moment that he's not pissed off at me: Is there something transformative that happened to you? Something on the scale of Dorothy's intense transformation at the Hovhaness whale concert—the one Michael told us about?

He looks as though he's considering whether or not to

continue to sulk, but gives in: Well, when Aunt Thérèse...

Oh, she is lovely! So welcoming and warm—when we went to the West Indian Day Parade with her and ate too many saury and dombre—I thought I was going to burst.

Yeah, yeah, you survived. Anyway, she went to University of Michigan Law School before she came back to New York and I was visiting her in October, I guess it must have been 1988, in Ann Arbor. Toni Morrison came to speak.

I blink at him. When I read *Beloved,* I knew she was a total genius. *The Bluest Eye* frightened me beyond belief. I can't believe you got to hear her speak.

Yes, really. I got there early to Rackham Hall and if I hadn't, I wouldn't have gotten in—that two and a half hour speech, well, it changed my life, just like that crazy Hovhaness whale music changed Dorothy. So yes, these hinge points, inflections points, these things that happen and after, nothing is the same.

You've never told me, this, why?

I guess it just didn't come up—I wasn't keeping it from you. Morrison gave an amazing speech, all about the canon and why it's so very white, and what Melville was really saying. In a sense my whole dissertation—my book, I should say, is one long footnote on Morrison. She is, it's safe to say, the greatest living American writer.

Naturellement.

Morrison said something along the lines that Melville basically understood whiteness as ideology, that Melville wrote *Moby-Dick* against the backdrop of fervent U.S. anti-slavery activism and that, by having Ahab forget the whaling mission in order to fulfill his maniacal goal of exterminating the white whale, Melville made the whale itself an allegory for all the problems with whiteness.

Oh wow, that makes total sense. Also, I am pretty sure your whole book is not, my dear, a footnote!

OK, yes, ok, you're right. Not a footnote—just heavily influenced by Morrison and C. L. R. James.

You've talked about him a bunch before but can you shade in more about what his main ideas are and who he is?

Was.

Was.

So, remember? that's basically why I ended up at Columbia, for the archives—and I'm so sad that Maryse Condé, the amazing writer from Guadeloupe, who's just joined the faculty in French, wasn't there when I was a student—she writes, incidentally, about Jews in the Caribbean, among other things. Someday I'd like to learn more about that story, my ancestors' migration from Brazil to Guadeloupe, their going underground, being Jewish to the core but pretending, for centuries that they weren't. I don't know how they could live that way, one face showing a real side, the other showing a fake side. But I guess they didn't have much choice, if they wanted, oh you know, to keep breathing.

André traces the line of my arm with his fingers, reaching across the small seat and I inhale that chemical blend of airplane hot chocolate on his breath makes me want to go down on him, right here, now.

I take a sip of chocolate, turn my mind away from unwanted musings.

Yeah, I've thought about them too, these unknowns in your past...they must have been terrified, all the time, always on the cusp of being found out. I don't know much, either, beyond grandpa. What life was like for them 'in the old country.' Doesn't sound like much fun. But tell me more about C. L. R. I like those initials, like Royal Lewis Carroll, but backwards.

Ha! Well, the C. L. R. James archive has all sorts of things—some 48 boxes of rare stuff. He was from Trinidad and, while stuck unfairly in Ellis Island in 1952 wrote this brilliant reading of *Moby-Dick* that most Melville scholars (not racist, are they?) totally, completely, and utterly ignored. Hopefully they'll wake up to him. He argues that Melville predicted the totalitarian type—the kind we suffered when Hitler was around. So maybe my book-in-the-process-of-its-becoming is a footnote on Morrison *and* James, huh?

No—still not taking the bait, sweetie—you're just to smart (and too cute) to be a footnote writer!

Our flight touches down to the whirring sound of the huge engine slowing to a whimper and we hop in a cab back to my apartment, crowded with those many faces in contrasting hues. We're exhausted with the weight of myriad strange and interlocking clues that seem to lead to scraps without end. After a darkening walk on the East River, we make a simple pasta dinner, open a red wine, and enjoy the lights popping on outside.

Sid, André says, come and sit here, next to me, I want to read you an extraordinary poem by Lucille Clifton:

the earth is a living thing
is a black shambling bear
ruffling its wild back and tossing
mountains into the sea

is a black hawk circling
the burying ground circling the bones
picked clean and discarded

is a fish black blind in the belly of water
is a diamond blind in the black belly of coal

is a black and living thing
is a favorite child
of the universe
feel her rolling her hand
in its kinky hair
feel her brushing it clean

Oooh, that is lovely, I mutter, nestling into his shoulder, taking a small bite, she's taking the idea of blackness as negative and inverting it, as she should, she's turning the earth into solid and liquid at once—the bear and also the fish—the water and also the coal—a living thing, just like the record we found at mamie's…

You know, love, if it doesn't work out for you as a photographer, you can join me as a literary scholar.

Ha, ha. No but seriously, that is a beautiful poem. What made you think of it just now?

Well, it's about the living earth, about things not being what they seem. Your mother, as Esther was telling us, was all about justice, setting things right, and later, all about listening to whales, right? The poem encourages us to see the earth, with all its variegated oceans, with all our possible interconnections.

I look up at him then and he leans down to kiss me, fully.

That night the frost is utterly gone. We get to know each other all over again, excitingly familiar and yet new at once. We simply can't stop touching each other everywhere. André finds every inch of me with his tongue, his hands, I don't even know anymore what's untouched. Nothing.

It's early morning before we fall into a long overdue sleep. I'm sailing, so happy to be really, truly, finally, back together and also, naturally, worried that it won't stick. Again. But this mourning, these crumbs, there's a shift below me, as if I'm riding on the back of a whale.

I dream of the great house. In the dreamscape I'm back in the green room, around my neck the Torah necklace has turned into twisted incandescent green snakes, and on my feet the red shoes stick painfully as if affixed with crazy glue. I try to run through the house looking for a key—a key I had dropped somewhere—a key to nowhere, nothing—but I can't run in those heels so I stagger around, frantically trying to find the key and take the shoes off at once. The shoes carry me to the blue room and there on the walls I am confronted by a giant painting of dolphins frolicking in the sea, rendered in delicate and new blues that I'd never seen before.

I awake in a sweat and scratch at my feet to make sure the shoes are gone, trying to rip the necklace off. I'm lucky I did not break the chain. As I relay the dream to André he holds me, strokes my hair, dries my sweat.

It's OK Sid, there's nothing on your feet, nothing around your neck, just your favorite pendant, you're OK, I'm here.

We make some coffee and then he kisses me, biting my lip slightly, in a way that makes me wish he didn't have to go prepare his classes.

That afternoon, my feet take me, as they often do when I need solace, to The Frick. I had been there a million times and I thought I knew every painting, every sculpture. Wandering through the familiar, comforting, space, a shiny pendant on a small portrait catches my eye, stops me in my tracks. And there, on the canvas, a young girl, no more than fifteen or so, the same age as Sol, a gold chain with a Torah scroll necklace around the thin stem of her translucent neck. As my hand flies to my necklace and I stroke its smooth surface the pendant becomes fever-hot. I pull my darkroom loupe from my pocket to peer at the painting, so close that the alarm pings and the guard comes hurrying over to tell me off.

Miss, you're getting too close to the painting! I whirl, magnifier in hand, unprepared to verbalize or rationalize exactly why I need to be here, in The Frick permanent collection rooms searching for another clue to complete this quixotic trail my much missed father so strangely dumped upon my shoulders, our shoulders.

I'm so sorry! This, you see, my necklace, it matches the

one in the painting and it's the only thing I have from my mother…she's been gone since I was almost seven.

I'm guessing the guard is more accustomed to dealing with irreverent toddlers and their trailing, embarrassed parents than overzealous mourning young artists tripping the security wires in his gallery. Perhaps I strike him as somehow familiar. After all, I've ghosted The Frick since before I could walk, and I recognize him. He lifts one eyebrow, a practiced gesture for one in his line of work, turns abruptly on his thick black-soled heel and goes back to his post, leaving a pointed reminder not to get too close.

But I'm already engrossed in the curious canvas again. I must have, André and I must have, walked by this painting a million times and somehow never seen the necklace. How is that possible? Like the purloined letter in Poe's story it was right in front of us the whole time, unseen. The paint is impeccable: each fiber in the girl's rich green dress shines as if painted yesterday. Her hair swept delicately into a high knot, and her eyes unbounded by space or time, pour their light into mine. The artist captures the play of sun from the window behind her as if it entrusted its feathery white footprints to her skirt. The plaque describes the origin of the painting:

This unusual portrait, painted in 1662 in Turin, depicts the artist's daughter, Solange Luzzatto, on the cusp of womanhood. If you look closely, you might see that she wears a most curious necklace. On the outside it

appears to be a miniscule Torah. But on the inside is inscribed the Talmudic phrase that translates roughly as: 'The one to whom the miracle is happening does not recognize the miracle' (Niddah 31a). The artist, Lev Luzzatto, painted many famous portraits of Italian nobility and became quite a favorite in court circles. No one knows who gave his daughter the necklace or where it is now.

Staring at the painting, I remember that William's press is named Luzzatto, after a painter he admired. And somehow, perhaps it's the necklace, I recall that, on the morning after happening upon the suitcase, I sat in the dust-drenched armchair by the desk where dad liked to read, overwhelmed by all that had to be done, and a light beam from the window, thickened with motes, caught a set of Tefillin in its gaze. While everything except the circle around *Slobgollion* was filthy, the Tefillin appeared strangely, uncharacteristically spotless, perfect. I picked them up, inhaled, and the smell of leather invaded me as I heard the slight rattling of the prayer scroll coiled up inside, a benevolent snake awaiting benediction, as if it, too, were breathing in a slightly raspy breath. André and I puzzled as to why my father, a deeply secular man, would have left these religious objects right in the middle of the hardwood floor. Ever fuzzy on Jewish rituals, André asked me to remind him of the purpose of this odd, antiquated contraption, but I only vaguely remembered from Hebrew school…

something to do with prayer, inside there's a fragment of Exodus, I think, about liberation from bondage and getting into the land of milk and honey. Dad never prayed. I can't imagine why he held onto these relics. But he couldn't let anything, or anyone go.

As I stare at the painting, I so desperately wish I could ask Aaron but it will always now, be too late. I can never ask him anything again, and a titanic scroll of imaginary questions I never posed rushes over me, as a hurried school of herring might fly over the sea. Even though he never answers my questions, I nonetheless irrationally, repeatedly, imagine he is still alive. I'm terrified that he might arise from the lake and return to his apartment, angry and dripping wet, and wonder what happened to all his rare stuff. I visualize telling him:

Dad, they told me you were dead, they told me those were your ashes. They gave me your wallet.

Yes, it's true, I continue my imaginary conversation with Aaron, my lips moving imperceptibly on the bench at the museum, I wasn't able to see you, they cremated you before I got there, but the emergency room doctor said you died of asphyxiation, because of a hernia no one knew brewed in your insides; she told me you left this world in the ambulance on the way to the emergency room. You died alone and for that I am so sorry, dad.

I rest on the thickly cushioned velvet lined bench opposite the painting, my hands slackly at my sides, and stare. And stare. The miracle you don't know...is this the same necklace? Dusk falls and the guard, now quite sympathetic to me, seeing that I'm clearly overcome, ambles over to tell me gently that the museum will close in five minutes. Rousing slightly, rubbing my eyes, holding the cooling pendant, I wander out into the crazy bustle of streets and it seems as though everyone else walks in a great hurry on a different planet and I'm barely operating on molasses-slow time. It's only a few blocks to Greta's house and I need to absorb this new and unresolvable clue.

After I ring and hear the now familiar tinkle of the bell, Greta peers through the peephole and then opens her great door wide to enfold me. Tea, my dear? She asks.

Um, do you have anything stiffer? I'm sorry to barge in on you, Greta, it's just...

I was only reading *Jacob Bloom* again, my dear. I don't have so very many appointments these days. Let's open this lovely Bordeaux—I was saving it for I don't know what occasion, honestly!

As Greta and I nestle on those stiff but comfortable forest green chairs, Greta proudly displays her handwritten invitation to Aaron's memorial. We talk about how to arrange the day, flowers, who will speak, and then we decide to unarrange it. Greta tells me she attended a Quaker memorial service once, in the 1950s, on the Upper West Side, for a friend who helped her family escape, and everyone just sat silently, thinking about the loss, mourning, until someone felt the need to speak. A memory would flash up then, like a fish poking its head above water, silence, and then another memory, another story, another revelation of character. In this way the mourners learned things about

the beloved they may not have known but without hierar-
chy, without speechifying. We decide Aaron would probably like that. And I'm pretty sure André would agree if
he'd been here. Without warning I suddenly find I'm keenly
wishing he were next to me. And Greta hands me an invitation, proudly.

Dear William,
Please join us on Sunday February 18,
1996, for a celebration of the life of Aaron
Zimmerman.
With love, Greta Eltman

These invitations are so delicate, they must have taken
hours, non?

I feel Aaron will be pleased with this, wherever he is.

Yes.

I recount to Greta all about the necklace and she offers
no reassurance.

The necklace...how it ended up in The Frick and also
the only gift you have from your mother...that may need to
remain a lovely mystery. Not everything has an answer, ja?

I gaze down into my wine glass, watching the dark red
swirls, the color shifting as the light flows through the
thick, stained glass window panes. The paperweight? That's
the last thing, apart from that weird manuscript. I take the
heavy object out of my satchel and place it on the coffee
table, next to the Bordeaux. It seems right at home there.

Ja, my dear girl. This is a very special paperweight. It's a
Seguso, made on Murano, just near Venice. Aaron took this

Seguso and figuratively stretched it out, expanded with his vivid imagination into the looted object returned, yes, but too late, to its rightful owner in *The Craked Vase*. But it's not your clue—it's Jacob's.

Jacob?

Jacob Bloom, from the novel. It's his clue, not yours. I know, Sid, you want everything to line up. But when you get to be my age you start to see how life isn't lockstep. It's mess and confusion, and change. Aaron was fascinated by glass. It became a metaphor for him. It looks solid, unchanging, but it's liquid. When they measure the stained glass windows of medieval churches they find that the glass has dripped ever so slowly, thickened at the bottom, imperceptible to the naked eye but true all the same.

That is utterly beautiful. And so sad, as though we can never capture any surety, never find an anchor.

We do. We can. But we must somehow know that there is motion in the stillness. Like Lucy. When I look at her I almost feel I can see her breathing, she is so alive, although so solid, heavy, stone. If this is a clue at all, I think Aaron may be asking you to read his novels properly.

She says this and I internally repeat the phrase inscribed on the necklace:

"The one to whom the miracle is happening does not recognize the miracle." I instinctively place my hand on the small circle between my navel and pubic bone.

V
ANDRÉ

I walk home, up the steps with the familiar creaks, back to my weird space, my dear Glenfiddich waiting for me. My studio is a postage-stamp sized, fourth floor walk-up. Cracking open my door now I step gingerly on the thickly painted green floor. Who knows how that happened? Someone decided it made sense to paint the floor. Expliquez-moi ça. I feel temporary, all the time, and not much into interior decorating. Besides, my place is more like the bed I keep when I'm not with Sid. The bathtub is right in the middle of the kitchen, which has made for some funny scenes when Sid putters around and makes dinner and I take a bath. Once, she accidentally dropped an entire bag of rice into the tub. The rice expanded and burst its confines but it turned out OK because I pulled her in, fully clothed, and we had quite a lot of fun undressing her while wet (her jeans were spray painted onto her) and making love amid the suds, the chopped carrots emitting a sharp smell as they burnt, forgotten on the stove top. The bed, over by the window, folds down from the wall and has to be re-made each day, perpetually renewed, like an ironing board big enough to sleep on.

I pull the bed down, now, on my own as I was in this place for all those years of bachelorhood punctuated by the occasional, brief, girlfriend. Until Sid, no one really grabbed me. Everyone I dated, mostly other Columbia graduate students, was OK but somehow not so interesting, and maybe a bit soggy, like the rice we'd scooped out of the tub. Either she broke it off or I did, but in each case (and it's not like this happened often, I'm talking about three women here), it was as though, after an initial, physical pull, a soft ennui would settle down and we'd sort of run out of stories to tell. Until Sid, I thought maybe there was something wrong with me, maybe I just wasn't cut out to be with some-one. Too nerdy, too immersed in words on the page and the pleasure of pulling them out and forming them into ideas people would think about. Just like Aaron. But then, once Sid and I connected, I knew it wasn't me. It was just that I hadn't yet found the right chemical potion. And now that I've found it, it keeps threatening to dissolve.

Sitting down at the tiny table in the kitchen, I pour myself another whiskey. I should move on, I tell myself for the millionth time, I'm stuck in love with a wavering girl who can't see a good thing when it sits on her lap. I take a big sip. Delicious burning. But I shouldn't move on. I should, must, stay. The night we got home from Québec was stunning. We were so together, are so together. And yet I told her I would stay here tonight. I'm fucking terrified she'll go into one of her glass woman modes. I don't want to rush in, crowd her, so I'm flying solo for one night.

I get out my notebook, put the envelope I'd found

in the attic on the table, flip on the TV, and insert the VHS tape of Aaron's one and only recorded interview, on the David Kepesh show, 30 June, 1995. Aaron sits in a tan suit on a light green armchair opposite Kepesh. They're both white gentlemen of a certain age, both with white hair. But Kepesh looks a lot more vigorous than Aaron:

DK: So, Mr. Zimmerman, thank you so much for joining us, and it's a pleasure to meet you. I think it's safe to say that one of the things readers notice about your work is that your books are so distinct from each other. Some novelists write different versions of the same book all set in New Jersey or so, but you seem...restless. What guides your thinking and how do you come up with such diverse themes?

AZ: Well, you know, the Jack Johnson book grew out of my incessant flânerie, my love for Baudelaire and then Walter Benjamin's concept of the importance of physical and psychical wandering. I spent my childhood, well actually, really my whole life, apart from college (University of Michigan) in Lakeview, in Chicago, and often found myself striding through the Graceland Cemetery there. Each time I did, Jack Johnson's tombstone arrested me. I was always interested in who was coming to visit him and, eventually, years and years later, I read everything I could

about the boxer (it's very convenient, you know, working in a library, I mean).

I traveled to Canada to interview people who knew the pugilist and I became great friends with William Benedict. His father, in turn, was a great friend of Johnson's, towards the end, when the amazing, stunningly talented fighter reflected on all that had passed in his storied life. But I couldn't bear to end my novel—which I won't reveal! as it unfolded historically.

DK: I see. I understand you're working on another novel, this one a whimsical fiction entitled *Slobgollion* about whales who speak Yiddish. How did you come up with such an extravagant idea?

AZ: Extravagant? Well, I'm not sure it's extravagant. Anyway, my wife, Dorothy, she was obsessed with whale communication. She started out as a linguist and then, when she was pregnant with our daughter, Sidney, Sid for short, we heard this stunning Hovhaness composition that was an homage to whale song, and she began researching and learning everything she could about whale communication. Anyway, it's not a novel—I must have mentioned it in an earlier interview—I decided not to publish it.

DK: Why?

AZ: It's too...well, you see, since Dorothy disappeared...

DK: Disappeared?

AZ: No comment.

DK: Ah, I see. Let's move on, shall we? You said your daughter is named Sidney? Isn't that an unusual name for a girl?

AZ: To tell you the truth, Dorothy and I had no idea how confusing it would be to name a girl Sid. We were your quintessential luftmenschen and rarely thought concretely about anything other than our work, social and environmental change, and big ideas. We were in love, if you will, with Sidney Poitier, and we watched and re-watched and quoted the 1967 film about a white girl, Johanna, who brings a handsome and accomplished black doctor home to dinner to announce to her parents their imminent marriage, to seek their blessing. *Guess Who's Coming to Dinner* hit the screens the same year as Loving v. Virginia succeeded in abolishing anti-miscegenation laws across the U.S. We, naturally, were very glad those laws were gone. At an impassioned moment in the film, Johanna's parents, memorably played by Katherine Hepburn and Spencer Tracey, hear a quiet ultimatum from Sidney Poitier who refuses to marry their daughter unless they freely give their unambiguous consent. Johanna's mother pointedly reminds her father, particularly reticent to embrace the doctor, how they raised their daughter, and she says:

"She's twenty three years old and the way she

is, is just exactly the way we brought her up to be. We answered her questions, she listened to our answers. We told her it was wrong to believe that the white people were somehow essentially superior to the black people or the brown or the red or the yellow ones for that matter. People who thought that way were wrong to think that way—sometimes hateful, usually stupid, but always, always wrong. That's what we said. And when we said it, we did not add, 'and don't ever fall in love with a colored man."

Dorothy and I could have had no idea, when we named Sid in 1970, that her name would cause all kinds of confusion, that our daughter would become a photographer who creates stunning, really quite moving and celebratory black and white portraits of black and white couples, or that she would fall in love with a dashing black Jewish Melville scholar from Guadeloupe. Her name now seems like a portent.

DK: Those are, indeed, an amazing number of coincidences. And I see resonances with Sidney Poitier's character also in your novel *The Cracked Vase*, **right?**

AZ: Right. Yes, certainly. Charles in that book is very much based on John, the character Poitier plays in *Guess.*

DK: So, in addition to *The Cracked Vase, The Eagle's Nest* is also about World War II. Can you talk about what it was like to serve in the army then?

AZ: Well, let me be clear, lest viewers get the wrong idea. Apart from in basic training, I never fired a gun. As I made plain in *The Eagle's Nest* (I'm a thinly disguised Isaac), I was put into a job more appropriate for a nerd as I could not have been less well-suited to serve as a soldier. My friend Michael Gruber (clearly the model for Mike) took photographs and I catalogued looted art. So, yes, I have always been fascinated with all that plunder—how the Nazis so brazenly stole from Jewish art collectors and Jewish and other families, how they amassed enormous wealth— the sheer moxie and magnitude of it amazed me—still amazes me, even in my old age. In *The Cracked Vase* I decided to write an updated *Golden Bowl*, set in the 1960s and revolving around a looted object. I changed it from James's original, again, reflecting our fascination with *Guess Who's Coming to Dinner,* and made racism the reason the original couple, deeply in love, could not marry, rather than lack of funds, as in James's version. Perhaps because I leaned on the not insignificant crutch of Henry James, that seems to be my best book.

DK: I think so, too! So, if you've abandoned your Yiddish whales, what are you working on?

AZ: It's just a draft, I haven't gotten much further than the opening. The provisional title is

American Berserk.

DK: Would you mind reading it to us?

AZ:

It was the summer of the floods in Chicago, the lake overspilling, reclaiming the city, the concrete piers buried, the river flowing into skyscrapers, taking out the electricity. The bottom of the Sears Tower was an electrifying, terrifying swimming pool. It was the summer of the riots in L.A. and the ferocity of outrage at lynching in plain sight. It was not a good summer to be a witness to police brutality, unprotected.

It was muggy and close as Nathan locked up Monastery Books at 7:16pm on July 11, 1992, and, his suit sticking to him like a series of clothed barnacles, wiped his forehead with his handkerchief. He was late. Caroline would be annoyed, as usual. Sabrina would be hungry. And Squirrel, the dog, would need to go out.

The scuffling was audible, but just barely. Nathan looked down the alley and saw, framed by two overflowing dumpsters, four white police officers, one man, tall, black, about 50 years old, on the ground. One of the officers pinned him, knee to neck. The scene was strangely still, like a portrait, but gritty, and the officer with his knee on the man's neck looked out towards the street, to check if anyone was watching, and then pressed harder. "I can't breathe," Nathan heard from the gentleman on the ground, "please, let go."

Nathan ducked away, unseen by the officer. He'd never before had a chance to use his Steineck ABC Wristwatch Camera—it was a gift, an extravagant one, from Caroline for their twenty-year anniversary. Sweating, but trying to stay cool, he ambled past the alley, pretended to check the time, and clicked a few photos.

As soon as he arrived home, Caroline jumped on him. Predictable.

"Sabrina's hungry!"

"I know, my love, I am so sorry to be late. Again. I'm working on it." Nathan reached out to her, took her by the waist, and tried to bring her in for a kiss. Caroline pulled back.

"You look...pained. What happened? A shipment of books didn't arrive?"

"No, no it's nothing. I'll take Squirrel now," and he managed a kiss on the cheek.

"Daddy, can I come with you?"

"Yes, pumpkin, come on, it's hot out there, kiddo, you got your sunhat?"

"Yep, ready!" And here Sabrina saluted him, as if she were a soldier and he the general.

Outside they heard sirens. As they turned the corner they could see a crowd growing outside the alley.

"What's happening, daddy?"

"I don't know, sweetheart, let's go through the park, ok? Squirrel wants some grass."

"Do you think he'll chew on it, like a cow, like he usually does?"

"Let's see."

DK: Thanks so much for reading that. Can you tell us whether Nathan turns those cops in?

AZ: No, but I can say that the tensions in the novel focus on Nathan's desire for justice balanced against his need to protect his wife and daughter from possible, and possibly nasty, retribution at the hands of police furious at being betrayed.

DK: Well, Aaron, thank you so much for joining our show and we look forward to talking with you again!

So, Aaron had mentioned *Slobgollion* somewhere? I had not known that. And that must mean that at some point he'd intended to finish it? Make it public? It does feel, as he said in his note, intensely private. Like Sid, I'm now wishing we could do a sort of séance and ask him a million questions. I pour myself another whiskey and start playing the scene over and over of the day we met—what Toni Morrison, in *Jazz* describes as something like a record stuck in a groove, getting deeper the more it turns. I'm stuck, and I just keep turning myself more so. What other strand of some multiverse would I be on now if I'd never been out in the park that day? Would I feel happier? Or more solid? But I can't regret meeting her, or her zany father, not now, not when it feels like we're finally, if precariously back together.

When we met, I was wrapping up grad school and about to be a newly minted visiting lecturer, and Sid had only just landed in New York, a Midwestern, French-speaking transplant. It wasn't proving particularly easy for her to make it as a photographer. Her woman in a flannel suit job at Shlovsky Motion Pictures in midtown was interesting enough and paid the rent enough. But it wasn't exactly Sid's imagined life as a creator of delicately rendered, handsome images. She sported high hopes, and those were usually dashed. But I always believed in her, and she knows it in her bones (or at least I hope). Her day job as an Operations Coordinator entails keeping the company organized, anticipating all that wants doing, and setting everything in motion. She's, if you like, a legal fixer. Each day, as she juggles the circus act of a motley crew of things and people, she visualizes a high profile exhibit opening at a sleek gallery in Chelsea, and a big-name publisher printing in a glossy, coffee table book smelling intoxicatingly of paper processing chemicals as if a mini darkroom came to life, some of the hundreds of portraits of interracial couples she painstakingly produces. But she never does much to realize those dreams, and I often get frustrated with her glacial pacing, her dreaming, so like her father, living as she does in another time, or in many other times, other places. I bring her out, she brings me in. I've never been so attracted to anyone, wanted anyone so badly. I'm training myself—or trying to train myself—to want her less. But something in her just pulls me. And I pull her too. Most of the time. No, I can't give up now, not when it feels like we're on the cusp of something. Not when things seem to be changing.

The moment my life changed, I was in Tompkins Square Park, a few blocks from where I lived then and still live now—we never moved in together, but we'd discussed it a few times, inconclusively. On a bright October afternoon, 1991, we were both out and about. Sid was taking her camera for a tour of her new neighborhood when she encountered one of those faces she just knew she had to capture: mine, apparently. Because I was leaning over to tie my shoe, she first saw me quite upside down.

May I, I mean do you mind if I take your portrait? she'd asked me, bending down so she, too, became Alice-inverted, upside down and squinting as the sun caught her unsunglassed eyes off-guard. More than a little taken aback at this, I looked at her curiously—here was a curvy white-ish woman with long black hair, small black hat, outrageous red converse, asking me for something. Something very personal, like asking a complete stranger if you could sit on their lap. Why me? I quizzed her, a slight smile playing on my lips, there are lots of people in this park, *Il fait beau, n'est-ce pas?*

Ah! she replied, much to my surprise, Vous venez de France? Ma grand-mère, Esther, vient de Montréal, puis elle a déménagé à Québec, mamie, je l'appelle, et donc, moi, je parle Français aussi, mais pas parfaitement... This rather pretty girl, pretty in an unconventional, unexpected sort of a way, toting a big camera spoke French to me with a funny accent, placing too much emphasis on the 'reeealll' at the end of Montréal.

The portrait she took of me that day forever remains my favorite. I sat on the same cold wrought iron bench that had recently propped my leg up as I tied my shoe and she stood in front of me. I smiled up at her and she told me I looked open, relaxed, expectant. Over the years Sid photographed me hundreds of times but because of the tangled nature of our relationship she could never again capture that openness, my broad smile unhindered by any shadow of the rocky times that we were to put each other through.

She said, thanks, simply enough. And then, as if an afterthought:

If you'd like me to send you a print, I can do that. But I would need your address, I mean if that's ok? her fat voice came out reed thin, as if she was asking something inappropriate, which maybe she was, but she also handed me a piece of paper and a chunky stub of a pencil that looked chewed up, like a kid who might munch her nails had gotten to it.

How old are you? I surprised myself by blurting out, remembering too late that mother told me sternly, never, ever to ask a lady her age.

Twenty-one, she replied casually.

I took the paper and wrote out my address, carefully, so that she could read it. I decided to leave it at that and thanked the budding artist for her interest in my apparently fascinating face.

But her eyes, I couldn't help noticing, were a strange serpentine green, tinged with the ocean on a stormy day. And when she fixes you in her gaze you feel not just seen, but X-Rayed. It's a curious sensation, and not entirely pleasant.

About a week after I handed that stubby pencil back to her, an envelope arrived through the mail with a black and white portrait inside. Sid rendered my face grainy on thick, ever so slightly curled at the edges photo stock paper. It smelled freshly printed, with a slight hint of metallic chemicals. As I gazed at myself looking at Sid I realized I was already just a little bit into her, my look so unguarded, and ever so slightly bemused. I stared at myself watching her, superimposed her face on mine: her pale skin like a bleached peach, and, I imagined, with a slight stirring, just as soft; those sea-cut eyes of hers, salty, and a color I'd never seen before, especially not on someone whose hair is as black as mine. I was just about to prop the portrait up on my dresser, make coffee, and head to work, when I noticed a small piece of paper fluttering to the ground at my feet.

Do you want to see *Harbour of Desire* (Mizoguchi) at Film Forum on Friday? Sid.

I swallowed. Hard. Surely this woman is bad news? Right? Younger than me by five years, kind of lost, a cliché, I thought, a struggling artist. No thanks. And yet. And yet those eyes. Her lightly padded creamy form shown off with tight jeans. But those weird rubber bracelets? Like a teenager. I was caught, a worm in a bird's bill, unable to move but wriggling in indecision. And then I was almost late to teach my class.

That little innocent-looking slip of paper caused me copious internal debate. I took quite some sweet time to decide to venture out to see *Harbour of Desire* with that young photographer. I was drawn to her and the tow was so fierce that I caved in and phoned her a few days later; we arranged to meet at Film Forum. As I wandered the city, restless and impatient to see her, I kept thinking I'd made a mistake in calling her but I also had no choice but to follow her lead. It was—is still—a magnetic pull well beyond my powers of resistance, rebellion, or mutiny.

The venerable old cinema on Houston gifts room tumbled upon small, cramped room of incredible films and it's a treat, each time I go there, often alone and weary after a day of teaching but unable to face the stack of papers I should be grading. It was the perfect place for a first date. As Sid and I sat next to each other in the dark I smelled her slight coconut scent and something else, lavender, maybe? or ginger? It's a bouquet that would become so familiar to me over the years and yet one which I could never pin down. Something spicy but also seductive. Vanilla?

After the film we ambled over to the Cedar Tavern, talking about the Mizoguchi masterpiece and I understood by slow degrees that Sid sees fundamentally differently than I do. Just like we read the illustrated rare edition of *The Whale* with totally distinct emphases. A nerdy kid who became a nerdy lecturer, I read the movie for plot, for character, for emotion. I'm also obviously much more of a romantic than Sid. She scanned the resplendent film for the lighting and angles and contrasts, speaking beautifully about the images but the emotions were...well, not quite invisible to her, but just unseen. At the bar, as we settled in over glasses of red wine, conversation turned organically from film to literature. Along with a stream of other writers I mentioned Aaron Zimmerman as a quirky but interesting novelist most of whose books I'd read. I knew her last name was Zimmerman, but I didn't know until just then that Aaron was her father. Sid was moderately surprised to hear about my familiarity with his work—he's not exactly a household name.

I appreciate, she'd said that night, tossing back her hair and setting down her glass after a big sip, your counterintuitive and witty way of describing things. Sometimes you speak almost as though you're composing each phrase as you might when writing that dissertation you'll be submitting for approval.

And you, I replied, speak as though you're composing a photograph or drawing a sketch. You perceive things so acutely visually as if all your senses were joined in those stunning eyes of yours.

At that the blood rushed to my cheeks and I looked down into my wine glass and then beyond to my toes. Clearing my throat and trying (no doubt failing) to sound nonchalant, I talked about Aaron's books and told Sid that *The Cracked Vase* is my favorite by a long shot but that I also like the one about the boxer, and enjoyed the wittiness of the one about Jacob Bloom, which is called, well, *Jacob Bloom.*

Your father, I said, recovering, and thinking expressly boring thoughts in order to stay calm, while trying to say something sparkly to her, managed to import, in *The Cracked Vase,* a Jamesonian sensibility into a poignant story about a looted object. I just wish he'd made some of his characters more open. Most of them seem remarkably solitary for people supposedly intimate with each other.

Yes, yes good point, Sid Replied, I think that may be in part why I haven't read them meticulously— they make me feel lonely. Or, rather, they hold a mirror up to my father's loneliness and that has always made me scared.

Scared?

Laughing a little and touching me gently on the shoulder, Sid replied, What? You can't see me in 40 years, living by myself with nothing but photographs of people for wall paper and forty cats to feed? She shrugged and displayed her hands as if she were holding out two flat plates.

I looked at her then very closely, like a book I was parsing, letting each syllable roll off my tongue through my inner ear, and leaned in close to her delicate ear, with slight peach fuzz, bedecked with a small purple stone. She told me later that, as my warm breath reached her neck a slight shock spread down her spine like a rose, but with thorns intact, trembling to bloom.

No, I said lightly, I can't see that in my handy crystal ball. Not at all.

As the evening of our first date drew to a close, I walked Sid home and bid her farewell at her stoop. No kiss. But I looked as far into her eyes as I could see by the dim halo of the streetlight as she said, that was fun. Do you want to maybe do something on Sunday?

Yes, I do. But I'm a little scared of you, I must say.

Now it was Sid's turn to ask, scared?

Let's leave that in play, for now, ok? It's late and I have work to catch up on in the morning. See you Sunday.

Four years later, I'm alone in my studio, pouring another drink, conjuring that smell of hers, and still scared, still totally drawn to her.

*

I call Sid in the morning but she's heading out to catch a yoga class, and she asks me to meet her at her place after. Along the way I'm thinking that it's no wonder so many aspiring American photographers, Michael Gruber among them, end up in New York. The city offers endless fodder for the lens. As I pass a couple, a black woman holding the arm of a Puerto Rican woman, I think New York is especially ripe for photographers whose subjects are interracial and/or mixed couples. But it was hard for Sid to make the move here, unlike it was for me—I felt like coming here was a sort of homecoming, but Sid was worried about Aaron, about leaving him in Chicago. She'd longed to be out on her own but feared regret would settle thickly on her if she left. Not wanting to leave Aaron lest he fold and slip even more into the ever-widening solitude of his life, Sid selected De Paul University, a short bike ride from their apartment in Lakeview. Majoring in art she painted, took color theory, sculpted, and honed her photographic skills. Once installed in the Big Apple, she called Aaron every night just to check on him and the brevity of their phone calls often amused me. As we readied to go out to dinner Sid might say, one sleeve in her coat, and the other reaching for the phone, hold on one sec, sweetheart, I just need to...

I know, call dad.

Sid would pick up the phone, switch hands so she could get the other coat sleeve on and ask, hi dad how are you doing?

Hi Sid, I'm fine I went to Unabridged today and just started on the new biography of Roosevelt. It's very interesting how he dealt with Jewish immigrants or rather didn't deal with Jewish immigrants. Did you know that right across from Treasure Island a new store just opened up called 'Something New' and they sell household goods—might be a good place to get a gift.

Not that Aaron really procured gifts for anyone other than her. Well, weirdly, we thought he had no friends. But now all these fine people have jumped out of that suitcase. Maybe he did have a reason to go there. These terse phone conversations starkly differed from the long talks Aaron and I habitually enjoyed; sometimes Sid would hand me the phone and I'd talk with Aaron for a bit, so she could fasten her boots.

Sid also phoned Aaron every night each summer of her childhood, as she stayed with Esther. She described it to me as a jarring contrast that as the weather warmed, and school ended, she morphed between the promising but unclean, stuffed, apartment she lived in during the school year and her grandmother's great house. Esther welcomed her so warmly each summer as Sid conjured vividly her lost daughter and conversely Esther reminded Sid of Dorothy. They settled into summers full of rambling rides to the sea and other places, art projects, games, voyages to the attic when it rained. Suspecting Sid's proclivities, Esther loosely left paints and canvases and colored pencils and stiff, thick paper around for Sid to explore. I'd formed an image of the magical house before I'd been there in person and it unfurled differently in reality—Sid had captured the color change details of the rooms perfectly but I thought it would be more symmetrical. Yet the house, and especially the attic exuded a kind of appealing chaos that I had not seen coming. I can't believe Sid never found that envelope, did Esther even know it was there? I still couldn't decide when or if to tell Sid about my well-intentioned theft.

Sid surprised her father by asking for a camera for her birthday that fall after Dorothy disappeared, when seven-year old Sid could barely hold the thing steady. Her pale peach skin under her long straight hair swung out as she walked (Aaron often joked that her hair was more Japanese than Jewish), Sid proceeded to document their apartment in incredible detail. An image she still kept, stilling the swirling dust motes caught in the light, a worm in a bird's bill; a Cezannesque still life of a bowl of fruit, only this one with squishy white and green fuzz marring the rounded edges of the oranges, dark spots forming on the outside of the green apples, you could almost smell the rot when you gazed at the photo; a portrait of Aaron, in his reading chair, *What Maisie Knew* turning into a kaleidoscope of multicolored notations.

As I pass Avenue A and walk through Tompkins Square Park, I'm thinking that this is right where Sid usually begins her Saturday treks in search of photographic subjects; sometimes she'll take the train up to Central Park or over to Brooklyn, always carrying a stack of little printed cards and handing them to couples with interesting faces, mostly interracial couples, the kind of faces she might also want to paint, if that were her medium. Sid is fascinated by how people respond to her as she hands them the card:

If you want to be part of a photo book please come to my studio (700 East 9th Street, Apt. 3B) at 2 PM on Saturday. Wear comfortable clothing, come together and be prepared for an hour-long photo shoot. I am a struggling photographer so I can't pay you for your time but if my collection of photographs gets published you will receive a complimentary copy of the book.

When Sid guessed, she figured around 10% of the couples to whom she handed the small, slightly textured card actually showed up on any Saturday. I always worried about her choice to invite strangers into her home but I never tell her what to do, so I can't figure out why she sometimes feels stifled or unfree, and why she used to use that as an excuse to pause from me. As I mount the steps to her apartment, so stuffed with photos of the couples crowding her out, gazing down on her a tower of images, her walls transmogrified into living things, I wonder if sometimes these anonymous people furnish welcome company on a lonely night, the nights when I'm not there, or if they remind her of her solitude, her fear of being alone like Aaron, and render her hollow, a tin cup capturing a useless penny, the sound echoing. 2D, silent, people she barely knew. I look at the walls with slow eyes, endeavoring to catch each new addition. They look miserable, I think, she's cute but he's greasy⋯what is she doing with him?

When I've been there during the photo-shoots, it's amazing to see how people self- present in so many different ways. Some couples come in and hanker for Sid to take pictures of them making out; some sit primly next to each other, and others arrive with a puffy redness around their eyes—a sure sign that a massive fight about whether or not they should accept this (strange to some, dream to others), invitation ensued as they walked through the sticky East Village streets to her studio/living room.

As I look at her walls I wonder if her book of photographs will be too fat because Sid could never figure out how to edit it, preferring as she does not to leave anybody out. When I'd suggesting editing, she'd said:

But all these people entrust themselves to me, give themselves to me— even if just for an hour or so, and I know they want to hold the book in their hands and find themselves in its thick pages, inhaling the new book smell and enjoying the electric shock of recognition. Also, the shock, perhaps, of misrecognition.

Sid's photos sometimes change people. When we bump into them they would tell us that projecting themselves onto the quilt of all those other faces on her walls altered, if even ever so slightly, how they viewed each other.

About a week after each session, Sid dutifully put

through the mail at our favorite post box, a copy, as she had when we first met, of the most luminous photo from the day. Or rather, she mailed them a mirror image only when they agreed to give her their addresses, but not everybody did. So, some of her models at least had that. But most of them hungered to be printed enjoying the paper company of the other interracial couples that they slyly acknowledged when spotted on the streets. Straight, queer, bi, some still fighting with their families, described epic battles with white parents much less understanding than the ones in *Guess Who's Coming to Dinner?* One couple for example, a black woman and a white man, told us that they had been together for a decade, the woman had never met her in-laws. They refused to come to the wedding, never set their four blue eyes on their grandchildren, their wrinkled shoulders cold to the touch. The woman's black parents, though, embraced their son-in-law, and loved those kids without reservation. Yes, it was 1995 and not 1955, but still.

Waiting for Sid to return from yoga, I pour a glass of water and sit on the sofa, propping my feet up on the scant space of the coffee table, I recall that Sid and I often discussed the vague similarities between the parents in the film, *Guess Who's Coming to Dinner,* important to her because she's named, as Aaron reminded me in that interview, after Sidney Poitier, and Aaron and Dorothy. Like Spencer

Tracey's character, Aaron zealously attended to his wife, but often only in his head, he was so busy writing and re-writing— outwardly he remained much less outgoing than Tracey, more tightly coiled within an inner landscape that others found impossible to navigate. Or at least we'd thought they did. He'd be barren and terse as a moonscape but then sometimes, as he was in the Melville class, green and giving as a mythical garden behind a small, impossible to open door. Dorothy, as far as Sid could remember her, was very like the Katherine Hepburn character, larger than life, bold in her statements, strong, determined, impressive. Sid is refusing to engage with what Michael hinted, what Mr. Oravid said, what the weird manuscript suggests, and I'll just have to wait until she's ready.

And we'd talked over with Michael Gruber all the crazy clues Aaron left, another missed opportunity for him to communicate with her, the unknown well from which the darkroom that cements Sid's art springs.

I lean back, close my eyes, I reminisce, that one day, about a year ago, while we sat basking in the sunshine right here on the red couch and she gently played with my hair, rolling little tufts around in her long fingers, she'd told me that, at about sixteen, she came bounding home from Lakeview High School, burning to tell her father about a project. Plunked in her Buddha pose on the floor at the foot of Aaron's usual chair, where he'd been reading the newspaper, she started to tell him a whole long story about the photography project for which she'd gotten a special press pass to the Cultural Center, and managed to get in to hear Sally Ride, the first American woman to go into space, describe time without gravity. As Sid kept talking and talking, she reached up and put her hand out to touch Aaron's slipper, but the slight buzz coming from his nose told her that he'd dozed off in his chair. All those words fell on ears that could no longer hear. So many missed opportunities between them. The starkness of the bridge between living and dead.

She returns from yoga, looking peaceful but also clearly not wanting to talk. I take a bath as Sid unpacks the breakfast burritos she'd picked up at Benny's on the way home.

When I get out, she's munching a corner of tortilla and reading the rest of *Slobgollion,* so I settle my towel around my waist and read over her shoulder.

VI Slobgollion

"**Y**ou said what?" Aditi boom-sang.

"It...it just came to me, Aditi, please don't be mad," Sol sang tremulously, "There was no way I could talk with him, he was very rude, in a rush, very curt. I was thinking on my feet and I thought this would distract him from harpooning you all."

"It may also lead to World War III!"

If you've never seen a one-hundred foot long blue whale angry, keep it that way.

Sol treaded water, her flippers sticking to her feet despite her agitated kicking, and waited. Marvin's mom swam over very quickly and then braked just before she reached Sol so that she could nuzzle in close to her, her long nose lightly touching Sol's arm. She looked as though she would battle Aditi if the Great Whale threatened Sol in any way.

Taking a deep breath above water, the Great Whale softened a bit, and sang out more gently: "Thank goodness Ishmael has just returned from his mission."

Aditi never failed to surprise Sol, so longing to see her father but now that the moment had come to its crisis she was suddenly scared, and unpredictably not at all sure she wanted to see him. What if he wasn't the same? What if all this time transformed him in ways she didn't like what if?...

"Dad?" For a tiny minute Sol was not positive that the creature swimming rapidly towards her was really him. His gray beard had grown about a foot in the past year and was tangled with seaweed so he looked part human, part merman. But he swam over to her and enfolded her in the most enormous hug she'd ever been encircled by. Even though they were underwater, using flippers like fish, she knew this water-logged fellow was her father. True, the clovey smell wasn't there. And what she could see of his skin was wrinkled like her fingers used to become when she stayed in the pool too long; he seemed to have grown four shades whiter than his previously tan shade, when he'd been digging around among fossils and seashells under a blazing sun; but it was him, she could feel it in her bones. And she knew.

They swam over to their glass rooms, their glass beds slightly cool and damp, the changing light streaking across the translucent walls. Sol felt as though she hadn't taken a breath, not really, not fully, until this moment. She imagined what they would look like from above, a water-logged merman with his arm around a seaweed drenched teenager. The relief mixed with rage.

"Why didn't you tell us where you were? You could have conveyed a message? Nana and I have been panicked this whole year we had no idea. It's not fair, dad! Why?"

"I know, hon, I know you're angry. If I had sent you a message, Barents would have kidnapped you. Or worse."

"Oh."

"But you could have let us know..."

"I know how you feel, or at least I try to. It must have been so hard, this whole year, not to know where I was. I am sorry. Aditi and I discussed this extensively and unfortunately, we could not tell you or Nana. I simply could not take that risk. I've had to balance making you and my poor mother very anxious against keeping you safe. And I elected to keep you both safe. Or at least to try. Airavab left you alone because they knew you had zero idea where I was. So, you see, Sol, I had absolutely no choice."

Sol struggled to absorb what her father told her and she was beginning to understand and maybe even forgive him for going away without warning for an entire year and traumatizing Nana who always seemed tough and put a good face on; but Sol knew that Nana was missing Ishmael and worrying and mourning, all the time. Nana was staying strong for her, so she wouldn't freak out too much. Sol felt a little guilty now that she knew that her father was just fine but there was no way she could tell Nana.

"It's going to be hard for Nana and I to forgive you, dad." But Sol looked at him with wide eyes.

"Sol, honey," Ishmael said, drawing her closer on the glass bed, "there is more I need to tell you. Aditi and Marvin explained to you all about Airavab but there's a part they left out—I think they didn't want to overwhelm you even more."

"More?" Sol asked, unable to comprehend that there could be even more.

"Yes. You know I used to tell you about those beached whales in Iceland, in St. Simon's island off Georgia, in New Zealand, the Canary Islands, the Bahamas, in Australia, all over our precarious planet? Well, there's been lots of speculation among marine biologists as to why. But no one uncovered the real reason, until just very recently. You see the virya contributes to the whales' ability to echolocate."

"Oh! Yes, Marvin did tell me."

"Good, I'm glad he got you started. So, here's more of the story for you, kiddo. Unfortunately, researchers at Airavab rather than marine biologists discovered it. The first time they found it, several whales beached because their sonar was thrown off. You see the mineral is extremely delicate and cannot be extracted without dire consequences for the whales."

"So, wait, hold on. All of those beachings happened because Airavab messed with their virya?"

"Yes. And, of course, Airavab doesn't care that the whales are beaching, in fact, it helps their genocidal goals. But they would like to discover how to extract all the virya so that humans no longer need fossil fuels. Airavab would become the richest corporation in the world if they could take all the virya out of the sea and find a way to reproduce it synthetically. You see, the mineral is so strong you would only need a tiny pinch to run your car for a year, and they are already working on the technology to convert existing gas-fueled automobiles into virya-fueled ones."

"So, if they don't care about the whales, what is stopping them from stealing all the virya?"

"Well, you see, each time they attempt it, whales beach. And then, scientists like me try to figure out why. And we interrupt their devious plans by bringing boats to investigate. At one point, when we collaborated and brought a Navy vessel with us, we thought it was the U.S. Navy's sonar that was throwing the whales off—not a bad guess, but not quite right, either. So, just after I found the virya, Airavab decided to take me out. That's when Aditi asked Marvin to save me, just like he picked you up and brought you here. Airavab realized I would tell the scientific community my findings and that the National Cetological Society would then send out the coast guard to protect the energy source."

"Dad, Aditi said Maisie and I would be able to convince Drake Barents with our bare hands (or paws) using nothing more powerful than rational argument. Not to rain on Aditi's parade, but that seems like a long shot. He's...Dad, he's an asshole."

Ishmael sighed a huge sigh and Sol saw his

breath ruffling his long, flowing, Neptunesque salt and pepper beard speckled with green seaweed. He closed his eyes for a minute as if gathering strength and then, looking right into his frightened daughter's eyes he said:

"When Barents was a boy he had a twin sister, she had long black, curly hair and pale white skin. He loved her more than anything or anyone. One day, his parents took the kids on a fun boat ride along the Mississippi to see the dolphins—he's from New Orleans. Leaning out over the edge of the boat, trying to take a photograph of a beautiful white dolphin, his sister fell in, and well, the current was very strong and they never found her. From that point on he became a bitter, bitter child and then a bitter, destroyed shell of a man. He's fueled with hot vengeance from without and desiccated from within. The memory of his sister grew like a cancer in him and he closed off the world and sought only the destruction of all things water related, especially all cetaceans. Aditi banks on the fact that his steel heart will melt when he sees you, again, so reminiscent of his lost twin, and that you alone can convince him. I sure hope she is right! I also know that Maisie would never let anything happen to you."

"Oh my god. Now I finally get it! All this time the pieces of the puzzle have not added up, why me? I kept asking myself, it didn't really make sense. Let me guess, Barents's poor sister was called Lotus."

"Yep, Lotus. Now, it is very late, you and Maisie better get some rest."

Ishmael kissed her forehead and then went out through the antechamber and swam over into the next glass room. Sol and Maisie witnessed him sitting at his glass desk through the thick walls so he looked like a shadow-father, studious and slow.

Sol drifted into an uneasy sleep and dreamed of a churning boat on the muddy Mississippi, the big, red wheel of the steamer chugging along like a train, the white tips of the water jumping up over the brown. In the dreamscape there were white dolphins, playing, splashing, just like the Yangtze River Dolphins she'd learned about in high school. She fell overboard chasing the dolphins, their clicking language in her ears as she went under and felt the strong magnetic pull of the current.

The next morning, Sol woke up to a very loud, low song and was surprised to see several whales gathered outside her glass house. They seemed agitated as they listened to the song. They were waiting. Sol stretched and hurried to swim out to see what was going on.

Aditi's face appeared, shockingly close to hers, and she sang out:

"Sol, I do apologize for my fury, I've been trying to tease out the implications of what you conveyed so precipitously to Barents, but I feel ready to discuss it more fully now."

"Aditi," Ishmael swam out to be closer to the Great Whale and said: "Please, let's think this through. I agree that Sol should have stuck to the script, she should have asked us if this ruse was a good idea. But let's try to think about what possible positive outcome there might be here. Let's find the gold in it."

Aditi swam up to the surface and took in a giant breath of air before spraying out and then coming back down to face Sol. "Please, my dear girl, continue, tell me what Barents said when you blurted out this fantastical tale."

"Well, actually," Sol replied, feeling a surge of surprising courage, and puffing out her chest, "I was thinking that it was not all that fantastical, given that no one really knows what's inside the famous—or OK more like infamous Area 38 on the Cape Cod National Seashore and the speculations have been much, much weirder—everything from aliens to the movie set of Armstrong's moon landing."

Aditi gazed at Sol, indicating she could go on.

"My outburst certainly got his attention. Barents looked up from the desk again, closed the ledger, stood up and walked over to Maisie and me. Without saying anything he bent down and scritched Maisie behind the ear. At this she sat down, so I knew I was on the right track. Then he twisted to look a little closer at me. That, I must say, was really uncomfortable. I started sweating, which I hoped he couldn't see. Or, worse, smell."

"You remind me very much of someone I used to know," he'd said, dreamily, like he was talking through a long tube from far away, "tell me, please, Lotus, how you acquired this amazing bit of information."

"Well you see, sir, my parents decided to take us on a drive down the coast to the seashore one day, to look at the flowers—it was the week of the bloom, breathtakingly beautiful with all the colors of the rainbow represented—more than the colors of the rainbow, even, it was magical! And Maisie—that's my dog, Maisie—she jumped out of the car all of a sudden and went trotting off—she was chasing a gopher, I think, or something. Anyway, she ran past the big NO TRESPASSING sign, through a hole in the fence, and right into Area 38! So, well, you see, I chased after her, of course, I squeezed in pretty hard to get through that hole in the barbed wire fence, and then Maisie stopped dead in her tracks and sniffed and turned around and I stopped by her and there was this low buzzing...a big machine of some sort, I wondered? Later I read in a newspaper article about how virya emits this low buzzing and so, you know, I put two and two together."

Aditi went up to the surface, took a big breath in, and the humans could see from under the surface a shower of water landing and merging with the colder water below. If whales did yoga (and who is to say they don't?) she would be practicing her calming breathing now.

"Aditi," Ishmael said when the Great Whale returned, "Sol has just magically bought us some more time. Barents is no doubt preparing his corporate army to stealthily invade Area 38; of course he won't find any virya there when he does, and Sol might be in big trouble if she goes back....but for now at least we can breathe a little, right?"

Sol had been thinking fast and she swam over to Aditi and sang out: "Hey, how about this: and, I am so super sorry if I made a colossal mistake—but what if we put just a tiny bit of virya inside Area 38, soon, before Barents gets there; then he'll find it and he'll think I was telling the truth, and then he will trust me, right? And we can go ahead with your plan for the second meeting. What do you think?"

Aditi, who had been doing her inner meditation thing and didn't seem to be listening, shimmied closer to Sol, giving the teenager the distinct impression that if the whale had arms she would have hugged her (and that might have been a bit frightening).

"Sol, yes, you are right! I think we can save this." Aditi pivoted around and addressed Marvin:

"Can you please take a tiny bit of virya to Akira and ask him to break into the heart of Area 38? He'll need to bring Sol with him. They can wrap it in a scarf, so it looks like it was put there by a human—oh, and Marvin, and here Aditi sort of whispered, I think we have a green human scarf, left over, you know?"

Turning her cloudy saucer eye back to Sol, Aditi sang out: "Sol, you will need to go back to the Hancock Tower under some pretense which we will figure out, and only after Barents has found the virya. You and Akira will plant it. The utmost caution will be required."

"Aditi," Sol sang, sweating a little even though she was, naturally, already soaking wet, "Drake is human, all too human, it's not like defusing a bomb—a simple wire that needs to be cut—changing a person's mind is not so easy and he— he's like a person who is constantly being eaten alive by something no one can see but he can feel—as if he had anger cancer. He's not very nice, Aditi, and I really can't understand how Maisie and I can change the course of history by changing his mind...we can't read people's thoughts the way you all can, but we know he's hard inside his core, harder than londsdaleite, which I learned about in school—it's from a meteor or something and was named after a woman scientist who figured out how to use x-rays to examine crystals—anyway, his inner core is rock, rock hard—meteor hard, Aditi, I am scared...."

Sol had not anticipated hot tears just then. In case you have ever cried while talking or rather weirdly singing to a blue whale under water, it is a curious feeling because the warm salt water from your eyes mixes in with the cold salt of the sea and you might feel a little like Alice, drowning in her own tears. Ishmael swam over then and gave his daughter a big hug.

"Aditi, I am going to take Sol back to our glass homes now, she is very tired. Please do remember that she is young, only a teenager, and that this is an awful lot for anyone to take in, much less someone who only a few years ago celebrated her Bat Mitzvah!"

"Yes, Ishmael, quite right. I have been at fault, and I am sorry. I will work with Marvin tonight to gain a clearer picture of the mission. I see that Sol does not believe it will be possible to use rational arguments to sway Barents. And your daughter might well be correct in that assessment. Marvin, come with me."

"Stop by my mom's house on your way home, Sol, she has a special treat for you! Hang in there, kiddo," Marvin said as he followed Aditi first up to the surface for a big breath and stretch and then over to confer with her in hushed tones.

Akira had become instantly fond of Sol and Maisie. He conveyed to Sol that being a double agent meant he had no time for a wife or a child and befriending her offered a bittersweet consolation that also made him long for a child of his own. Sol was attached to Akira, too, and not only because he brought the life-giving peanut butter and dog bones to their little community of water-logged humans living under the sea. Sol appreciated his profound way of listening and describing things—it made sense to her that he was in charge of recording and deciphering whale song and she wondered how much more he could understand than other humans.

But Sol had been utterly terrified, and with good reason, to confront dread-Drake, as she secretly named him. That first meeting was only supposed to introduce "Lotus" to Drake Barents, to get him to be comfortable with her and Maisie, and to convince him to allow them to return, for more quiet conversations that would somehow save the planet. Sometimes, she thought Aditi and the other whales were nuts.

The day Sol and Akira headed to Area 38, was hot, volcano-hot, or so it felt, after being under water. Carrying a miniscule sealed flask of virya, Akira disabled all the security cameras by using a neodymium magnet—one swipe each was all it took. The dobermanns patrolling the area were easy: Maisie taught Sol a special bark which basically translated into "chill out, it's just me, and guess what? I have a treat in my pocket, here you go!"

After giving all the barking, bared-toothed dogs a treat and a pat on the head through the fence, Sol found a small opening in the chain-link and managed to cut a hole in it just big enough to slip through. Akira had thought to bring an extra roll of matching wire with him and managed to seal up the fence so that it looked almost as though the breach never happened, but he left it so they could unhook it on the way out and rehook it after they returned to the safe side of the fence. They left a small, slightly pink, rock just next to the breach point so they could see it on the way out. Once through they were on guard for guards and cameras.

Akira dressed up as an archaeologist and Sol as his assistant. Gazing out at the variegated, sandy horizon that so few people had seen, they were struck by the grandeur of an out of place sand dune that even the mythical lore could not explain. Taking big swigs of water and each grabbing hold of a walking stick, they set out to climb the dune. At the base of a graceful clump of sea grasses, they found some rocks artfully arranged and decided this would be the perfect place to plant the virya. They hadn't packed a shovel as this would have aroused suspicion so they had to make do with their walking sticks to double as their sole implements. They took turns but digging with a stick on a boiling hot day was sweaty work yet they needed to plant the virya far enough down so that Barents would be forced to struggle for it, lest it be too obvious. Finally, Sol's walking stick hit something that felt too soft to be earth. Bending down, they could see that it was a paper scroll tied with a ribbon. Akira put the scroll in his backpack, deposited the virya wrapped in an emerald green scarf, and tried to make everything look untouched. Sol had taken a Polaroid photograph of the rocks before they began digging and they now took a good look at it and did their best to replicate the past.

After all the brittle above sea air, it felt so good to return to the whales, to the cool, the salt, the buoyancy. Sol went right into her room, had a snack, and feel asleep. Akira forgot about the scroll in his backpack, he was so tired from all that digging in the brutal heat. It was his day off from Airavab and so he planned to spend the night in one of the delicious glass rooms—he knew his sleep would be so beautiful, rocked by the sea, held aloft by the salt. Akira often wished he could stay there all the time and his land bed felt so ridiculously barbaric and too immovable, away from the natural slight swing of the glass room. As he was preparing for bed and unpacking his backpack, the dirty scroll tumbled out. Exhausted as he was, yet curious, he spread it out on the small glass table and tried to see what was there. The scroll was strangely, utterly blank and curiously undamaged by having been buried unprotected for however many years.

He figured it must be some sort of permanent paper written on with a kind of indelible ink. Most indelible inks Akira could think of were activated by fire—or rather by heat—you put a lit match next to it and poof, the words appear. There was no way that he could light a fire in an oxygenated room below sea level. Given how intensely dry the sand dunes were, he reasoned that perhaps a drop of water might bring it to life. Putting a little dab on the oddly clean scroll brought out some fine lines, a map, maybe? It was unclear and he was beyond wiped out. He sank into a watery sleep, rocked like a baby by the waves.

Early the next morning, taking out his magnifying glass, he saw that the dabs of water had opened like sea anemones into an ever-widening map. He continued to dab the scroll gently—not daring to flood it, and Akira realized that the scroll was a map of all of Area 38. And that there was, indeed, virya buried all over the place. Oh my god, he thought, oh my god.

He had to show this to everyone right away. Akira sang a rudimentary whale song he had memorized and magnified the sound with a device akin to a microphone but that operated through a conch shell resembling a Shofar. As one sang into it, the sound waves spread out. Soon enough, Aditi swam over to his glass room and placed a giant eye against the walls. "What is it Akira," she sang, "you so rarely sing out to me?" Akira unfurled the scroll and placed it flat against the glass wall so that Aditi could read it.

She looked at it for what seemed an awfully long time before singing out:

"Oh my this is stunning, however if this map is true and if my calculations are correct then the virya that remains on Area 38 will have biodegraded. You see, isotopes of the virya have a short shelf life."

Sol, Ishmael, and Maisie swam out, hair streaming every which way, thoughts struggling to grasp the magnitude of this discovery. Sol was having a very hard time believing that her entirely made-up on the spot idea that there might be virya in Area 38 was creepily true. They all stared at the map and tried to comprehend its full implications.

"Do you think there's any way to save the virya—to reactivate it somehow?," Ishmael sang.

"Ishmael," Aditi sang, "I think there might be. I will need to do some investigating tonight."

Turning to Akira she added, "you are very brave, Sol and Akira, to go to Area 38, in the blazing sun, without any cooling blubber or lovely salty water all around you. I want you to know that we whales are very grateful to you. We understand that you, Akira, have sacrificed the human part of your life to help us. We just want you both to know that we are in your debt."

If whales could bow, well, then Aditi would have bowed to Sol and Akira; she then briskly swam away to conduct her research.

Early the next morning Aditi awoke the humans with an insanely gorgeous but incredibly loud song. "Whale-human ally congress NOW," she boomed. Brushing sleep out of her eyes, Sol opened the glass door so that Ishmael could sit next to her and Maisie as they listened.

"Time is of the essence," Aditi sang, "I do not wish to appear abrupt but it is imperative that we act quickly. Akira has come up with a brilliant plan: he constructed a simulacra of the scroll but with the virya's locations around Area 38 altered—to throw Barents and his henchmen off the scent. Sol and Akira will replace the original scroll with the fake scroll today, hopefully arriving before Barents. Yesterday, when they planted a tiny bit of virya, that will have been enough for Barents's detection machines to pick up so he should be led straight to the scroll. Any questions?"

At this, Ishamel, who'd been listening while stroking his long Neptune beard, said: "Aditi, last night you suggested there might be a way to activate the actual, expired virya that is all over Area 38. How?"

"Good question, Ishmael. Our engineers understand that we can emit ultrasonic pulses to heat up the virya and convert it into an enormously powerful material. Please note: only whales can do this. In other words, even if Barents finds all the actual virya, it will be useless to him without us." At this Aditi smiled. Now, it's hard to imagine a blue whale smiling but she looked...self-satisfied, like the cat who got the canary, is really the only way to describe it.

"If no one has any further questions," Aditi continued, "Sol and Akira, please take all possible precautions. We will await your return most anxiously. We will never forget that we are in your debt."

Before he became a double agent, Akira was a tireless campaigner against illegal whaling who was repeatedly arrested for vandalizing private property while sneaking aboard whaling vessels all over the planet and replacing the steel exploding harpoons with identical ones made of spray-painted bamboo fashioned to look like metal. The whalers had no idea of the subterfuge until they drew abreast of a glorious whale and launched their harpoons only to see them bounce gently off the great surface of the magisterial animals. Akira performed this same trick six times before the whalers connected with each other and filed a complaint. They had to complain to Airavab rather than Interpol because what they were trying to do was highly illegal. Aditi sent Marvin to get Akira just when they became aware that Airavab would disappear him, as they had many other radical environmental activists. He was totally surprised one evening when, sneaking onto a whaling ship, a huge blue emerged from the water and sang, "Akira, time is short, the whalers and their corporate backers are coming for you. We are honored each time you transform a harpoon into a harmless twig. You have protected us, now, please, quickly, get onto my back, we must hurry."

Akira had hopped onto Marvin's back, held firm, and plunged into the ocean, hair flying out behind, seaweed tangled and salty. By the time Sol arrived in the whale universe, Akira had been living part time with the whales for several years, he never wanted to go home, despite the glass pillow. For the past two years, using an assumed identity, he'd been a double agent, pretending to believe in Airavab's goals while all the while supporting the whales.

Now, as they surfaced and headed back to Area 38, Sol was both terrified and excited. She breathed in tentatively not sure how much ordinary air she could take. "I suppose it's like riding a bicycle," she told Akira, with some surprise. He just grinned at her.

After again temporarily disabling the cameras with a magnet, they eventually found the breach-spot in the fence and wiggled through, once again, replacing the wire and situating the pink rock for a hasty exit.

It all seemed very quiet on Area 38. Almost too

quiet. They climbed the dune, found the artfully arranged stones and began digging. They placed the fake scroll right next to the active virya, under the stunning, spindly grasses and descended the dune, down and down back into the salty sea.

Three days later, Aditi again called everyone together: "Whale-human alliance, please, listen."

The whole company gathered around, the humans with their fins, imitating fish, and the whales perked up to listen, just as though they were sitting around a conference table, Aditi sang:

"Sol and Akira deserve an award for bravery. I now need to know if Barents has fallen for our bait and found the fake scroll. If so, his men may already be digging all around Area 38, finding nothing. It may be time to strike up a deal. However, Solange and Maisie, I need you to return as Lotus and, well, Maisie, you told Barents her actual name, did you not?, I need to find out what they know and what they have found."

"Right, no pressure then, Aditi, we got his, right, Maisie? We're like on it," Sol was sweating again, "and we'll go tomorrow morning, OK to the Hancock Tower?"

"Thank you, ziskeit."

At this Ishmael sang out extraordinarily loudly: "Aditi, with all due respect, I don't think it prudent to subject Sol to another terrifying meeting. I request permission to accompany her."

"Permission denied, Ishmael, and with apologies. You know full well, do you not? That you are among the most recognizable Cetologists on the planet—everyone at Airavab would know you in an instant, there is not a guard nor a janitor in the Hancock Tower who would not turn you in to Barents straight away. And that would be the end of you, dear Ishmael. We cannot risk it. Maisie will protect Sol. And I have reason to believe that Barents does not want Solange harmed, she is a doppelgänger for his beloved Lotus and he would never risk another loss."

That night, as Sol and Maisie attempted nearly in vain to sleep, Sol observed with heightened attention all the luminescent fish swim above, below, around, slightly distorted by the thick glass, and she thought and worried about facing Barents again. He had been so rude the last time. And he had stared at her so oddly. So oddly, indeed, that she had felt x-rayed and exceedingly uncomfortable, as though he could see through to her ribs. The thought made her spine prickle as if she were lying on a cactus. She knew she needed to return to the Tower of Dread, but right then she just wanted to be a teenager again. It wasn't really all that great, she mused as she drifted off to sleep, this saving the planet thing.

Early the next morning, as Sol and Maisie hopped onto Marvin's back for the journey to the shore, it felt familiar, even though they had only done it once, the trek up to the Hancock Tower. Each detail had imprinted itself into Sol's impressionable mind, as a daguerreotype would.

At the entrance this time the guard didn't seem surprised to see them. Sol gathered all her courage and held her shoulders high announcing, in her loudest voice:

"Lotus Nistaraka to see Mr. Barents, please."

"Do you have an appointment, Miss Nistaraka?"

"No, but I think he'll want to speak with us—with me, I mean."

"Wait here."

After a few minutes the guard returned and ushered them into the elevator. When the door opened Barents was there, all right. But this time they had his full attention straight away.

"Ah, Lotus, Maisie, do come in. Please, sit down. Would you take some tea?"

What's with all this weird formality and kindness, Sol wondered? what gives?

"Um, no, thank you. We don't need any tea. I'm just wondering, sir, if you found the virya I mentioned when we came here before?"

"Well, I need some tea. Please, do sit down, let's get to know each other, shall we?" And he crossed one leg over the other.

Maisie was already sitting so Sol took a seat on an entirely white settee with white furry pillows.

When she touched them, they were so soft and she realized with a slight chill of horror in the marrow of her spine that these must have been constructed from Artic fox fur. Her stomach performed a wild back flip.

"You see," Barents said, taking a sip of tea from a white porcelain tea cup on a white porcelain saucer, "as it happens we did find a tiny amount of virya. Next to it a map—a map that supposedly led us to all the virya we could dream of! You see, little 'Lotus,' here he formed scare quotes, "we know about the marine biologist!"

"The marine biologist?"

"Ah, you don't know, then? Well, please get comfortable as I tell you a little story."

All this stuff about tea and comfort was weird, to say the least. Sol looked at Maisie but the dog was still sitting still so she figured she would lean as far away from that revolting real fur and listen as Barents, glorying in holding their full attention, continued:

"A very beautiful marine biologist once lived in Area 38, the only resident from before it became Area 38, back when there were a few sparse homes there. She lived in a cozy little cabin, and the U.S. government let her stay there as long as she took an oath of silence and solemnly promised never to tell anyone all of what she knows about what goes on in Area 38. In fact, they wouldn't let her leave, lest she spill the beans.

She kept her promise. She never uttered what she knew to a single, solitary soul. Fiery red hair, pale white skin freckled with light brown dots. Her strong features reflected her fierce determination but also her delicate sensitivities; she was magical just to look at, like one of those Viking goddesses you might have learned about in school. She was fearless.

Being a whale lover, it was naturally heavenly for her to live in such close proximity to the whales. But she felt her wings clipped and she longed for her family, with whom, naturally, she could not communicate.

In her isolation she took notes—you see, she knew she shouldn't but she made a map of all the virya they'd been hiding there and then she buried the precious map where she surmised no one would ever find it. She was an extremely, extremely good woman who would never break a promise. But this silence extracted a great cost to her since she had not been able to talk to anyone for so long about all of the energies that swirled around in her head, hidden deep within Area 38. Eventually, she decided the moment was ripe and she must bury her map. She took a shovel, some snacks, a water bottle and a walking stick. Making her way up a particularly tall dune, she paused at the base of a beautiful collection of grasses. She rolled the map into a scroll and tied it with a yellow ribbon and placed it gently into the ground and covered it up first with sand and then with artfully arranged big rocks. She made her way carefully back down, her knees aching all the way, back to her little home on the edge of the sea."

As Barents kept talking, Sol became more and more nervous. Why did he use air quotes around Lotus? And how could he possibly describe just what she and Akira had seen and done? And how could it be so similar to this mysterious marine biologist?

Then Sol and Maisie heard an ominous click.

The door to the office, and the sliding door over the elevator both locked as if by themselves. Maisie barked and then rolled over. Sol ran to the door and tried to open it—but it held firm, stronger than a Kryptonite bike lock.

"Solange Amaral," Sol now heard Barents booming, "daughter of Ishmael Amaral, most wanted man by all of Airavab, how dare you use my sister's name? Did you honestly think I was some sort of sentimental fool?" His face now went from flint to butter. "I admit, when you and that mutt of yours first came here my heart did catch a little—you do resemble her, I must say, but then when we executed a modicum of digging, and I could not believe the gall! The—what would your people call it—oh yes, the moxie! And then planting that fake scroll? You and the whales have no idea with whom you are dealing!" The veins on his neck bulged an uncanny blue.

Maisie barked now, piercingly, and Sol knew Maisie was communicating with the whales, she knew they would come and save her. Somehow, right?

"But, but," Sol stammered, "how did you know the scroll was fake?"

Barents appeared to Sol as though he enjoyed this cat and mouse game immensely; he took a deep breath, sat back down, poured himself yet more tea, added milk from the pitcher and sugar with a tiny spoon, swirled it all around, took a sip, and then said:

"Well, let me count the ways!" And here he held up each finger.

"First, a scroll that has been buried in the dry sand for many years would, naturally, show no sign of salt water, correct?"

Sol nodded, lamely.

"We subjected the fake scroll to a brief lab analysis it showed significant salt water and, strangely, traces of peanut butter. That part we cannot quite understand but the saline residue was a dead giveaway."

Good, Sol thought. He doesn't know about the peanut butter. Hopefully that means my father is still safe, hopefully he does not know Akira is a double agent. Or his real name. And maybe he doesn't know about our luminescent, emerald, floating glass world in the vast blue ocean.

"Second, once we began digging, based on the map, we found nothing, absolutely nothing! What you people would call bubkes."

Here Barents came around from his desk again and pushed a little button.

"You have heard the ominous sound of the door locking, Solange Amaral, and you will have surmised that the elevator can only be opened by me. You will also have observed that we are 60 stories above your beloved sea-level. There is, in short, no escape. I will inform The National Cetological Association, and they will then certainly reveal the location of your father. I will inform them that you are being held prisoner until he releases the original scroll with the complete and accurate details of the location of all that virya! I will also demand that your father issue a statement saying he was completely incorrect to anthropomorphize whales by making up communicative and intelligent capacities well beyond their simple animal natures!"

As he spoke he turned red and his voice raised into a high pitch while a slight bubble of spittle formed on the left side of his thin lips.

Maisie stopped barking and stayed very, very still, one cashmere soft ear cocked up just ever so slightly, her back stiff as a londsdaleite meteor.

They waited.

Then a low rumbling, like distant car tires, spread into a cacophonous noise which grew steadily louder and louder. Barents waited for the effects of that little button, ignoring Sol and Masie while gazing out of his epically tall window. A tiny trickle of water slid down the top corner of the walls. Right above the window, water dripped down the glass in ever fatter streams. Barents, a drop of water having landed on his nose, jerkily exclaimed:

"Oh, they must be cleaning the windows, how odd, I thought they just cleaned them yesterday."

He turned back to the room to face them just as another gush of water—this one more like a geyser than a trickle—came shooting out of the little sink in the corner. As Sol was splashed, she tasted salt on her lips.

One fish and then another landed each on one side of Barents' white suit leaving orange marks there like double fish-shaped insignias.

"What the devil is going on here?" Barents bellowed, pushing that little button with all his strength, so hard that he might well have broken it.

Maisie, meanwhile, grabbed hold of the bottom of Sol's jeans with her teeth and pulled her towards the elevator.

Sol pushed the call knob with everything she had in her small frame. Barents furiously punched numbers into his huge phone and worried the button under his desk ceaselessly. Steam practically shot out of his ears.

The bolted doors to the elevator gaped open rapidly emitting a huge metallic clang, but instead of an elevator, an immense water slide filled the shaft. Sol pulled Maisie hastily to her chest and they jumped on and slid all the way down and down and down the elevator shaft, like juice tumbling out of a container. As they descended they observed all the workings of the little box that had carried them up to Barents's terrifying office. Cords of braided steel swinging loosely like strands of hair. Rails with rusted undersides welded into place to hold the great tower for an eternity. Rebar in vast shades of brown and grey.

Then the slide popped out a window and landed on Clarendon Street. They blinked in the bright sun. A piece of the slide disconnected from the rest and formed a shrunken dingy for Sol and Maisie as the powerful current floated them straight into the Charles River and then into Boston Harbor. Maisie was all wet and she shook the water off in one big wiggle. The boat bobbed up and down and Sol wiped a mountain of sticky water and golden fur off her relieved face.

They floated around for about two minutes before a flat spot appeared for a beat as if an enormous oval steel tray floated just under the water's surface. What they thought was water became the slick back of a giant whale. They jumped onto Marvin's back, noticing that his black whale eyes were bright and they saw another whale emerging out of the sea; when she got closer they grasped that she carried a passenger too.

Ishmael leaped off the whale's back and landed mid-hug with one arm around Sol and another lifting Maisie clear off of Marvin's back. The dog's wet paws made happy circles in the air. Sol felt as though her father might break all her bones he hugged her so hard, his beard caught on the string of her sweatshirt and it felt like he would never let her go.

"Dad, dad it's ok, we're ok, Maisie is ok. Really. Can you please tell us what just happened?"

Ishmael unmistakably struggled to let go of Sol, so Marvin intervened and sang out:

"Ishmael, I fully understand you do not want to release Solange. But, well, here's the thing. We're in the middle of Boston Harbor, having just caused a major flood in the Hancock Tower. I can hear the human sirens now. We need to go back to our world exactly now because otherwise people will begin photographing us and we try, whenever possible, not to be noticed unless we want to be."

Ishmael reluctantly let go of his daughter.

As soon as they arrived in the emerald glass world that had become a temporary home, Akira and the whales flapped their fins impatiently and looked most anxious. Aditi transported into full whale-yoga meditation mode. Her eyes closed and she floated and breathed as if she were afraid to open them, lest she not see Sol. Akira swam over to her and sang out: "Aditi, it's ok, you can open your eyes—they are here, they are safe, Aditi, hello? Can you hear me?"

After a brisk swim up to the surface and a large release through her blowhole her great eyes opened and Aditi swam to them. As her enormous body came right up to Sol, she felt a slight chill down her spine. Aditi's blue skin, speckled here and there with the odd barnacle, was about a foot from her face. Curious. Even though Sol had been living with the whales for some time, it was taking a while to acclimatize to these sorts of vast scalar differences. Aditi swam straight up to her and Sol reached out to embrace her as best she could.

"Aditi," she sang, "I know you were super worried—I can see that. Maisie and I are just absolutely fine. Barents, I am not so sure. Can someone please explain to me how you managed to get a giant water slide into an elevator shaft...not to mention how you filled the Hancock Tower with salt water?"

"I am quite overcome, verklempt," Aditi sang, "and I could not have anticipated such forceful maternal feelings toward this human child. Akira, can you please explain to Solange and Maisie how we hatched our little plan?"

As they squeezed into Sol's glass room, Akira explained that they gained access to the blueprints to the Hancock Tower so they could see exactly where the drainpipes and the water supply tanks were housed. They connected with discreet environmental activists who managed to get an aircraft escape slide corporation to create an extra, extra, extra, long inflatable slide. Then, when the Airavab offices were closed, Akira snuck into the building, disabled the security cameras, and, with the help of the environmental activists, schlepped in the rolled-up slide, and installed it on the inside of the elevator shaft so as not to impede the elevator's normal functions. Later, a mechanical engineer hooked the slide up to the air supply and tinkered with the water supply to the building, allowing the whales access to the out-take pipes, which, naturally could be reversed.

"So you see, sweet pea, Akira concluded, it was a bit complicated but we did it!"

The following morning, a Friday, Akira appeared to go to work as usual. He had conveniently called in sick the day of the flood. His office was also on the 60th floor, not too far from Barents's.

Akira found Barents on the first floor, naturally, since the whales had made the elevators non-operational.

"Mr. Barents," Akira said as nonchalantly as he could, "what happened?"

"Akira, it's good to see you. As you can see, there

was a flood of biblical proportions. Frankly, we do not fully understand what happened. But it has something to do with that dangerous child, Solange Amaral. She seems to have escaped, somehow, during the flood. This escape is most inconvenient to me. You see, my trusted Akira, I was planning to kidnap her, in order to control her idealistic nutty-crunchy-we're-all-interconnected-whale-loving-President-of-the-National-Cetological-Society father."

"Oh, were you? Well I am most sorry that she escaped, then."

"Never mind. We have, excuse the pun, bigger fish to fry. We must return to Area 38 and find all the virya hidden there. We are going to have the most successful alternative energy company on the planet!"

"Yes, very good, Mr. Barents, that sounds like a wonderful idea. I'm planning to hike up to my office and see if I'm able to save any of my files or records of whale sounds. Please let me know if there is anything else I can do to help you."

"Thank you, no, I am all set for now. We are arranging the expedition to Area 38, so, yes, please do see if you can conserve any of your invaluable research."

Meanwhile, Ishmael and Aditi worked incredibly hard to figure out the finer details of virya isotope regeneration. Careful sonar emissions could alter the number of electrons to re-activate the virya. Only whales could emit the correct volume of sonar emissions, so Aditi remained incredibly cool about the whole thing. She knew there was no way Barents and his team of scientists, no matter how clever, could make use of the virya without her and a ton of other whales. Barents, of course, had no way of knowing the virya had expired or that reactivating it required collaboration with his arch enemies.

The plan was that Ishmael and Sol, in disguise, naturally, would return to Area 38 and try to bring home as much virya as they could get. That way, Aditi's experiments with re-activating it, underwater, in the emerald world would proceed apace. They hoped to get there before Barents and figured he would be a bit distracted trying to dry out and clean up the Hancock Tower.

Sol and Ishmael, this time bringing Maisie with them, as Aditi suggested, set out together the next morning for Area 38.

It again felt almost too quiet on Area 38. They walked along, following the accurate map, and managing to collect at least some of the virya. It was hot. Ishmael, in particular, struggled with the strong sun after so very long in the cool, cool water, and Sol worried he might be getting slightly sunburnt. They brought titanium containers to hold the virya safely, and they filled two of them. This was the first father-daughter mission they had embarked on, together, and they each felt tender with worry for the other. Sol's anger at her father's disappearance was melting into the excitement of virya gathering and whale, oh and planet, saving. Her heart beat like a multitude of locusts.

And then, quite suddenly, they heard a rustling that could not be coming from grasses and then they saw them: not Barents himself but a team of men in the unmistakable white on white on white outfits of Airavab. There was nowhere to hide, the dunes offered a modicum of cover, but the men spotted them and began running up the dune. Ishmael got into position with his walking stick now doubling as a weapon but Sol had other ideas.

Just as the men, huffing from running up in the heat, reached them Sol unlocked her long tangle of hair from the comical mask and wig she was wearing and stretched out as if she were about to do some yoga. The men had no idea what to do—they had seen Ishmael in fight mode and they were ready to strike...and then? While they were flabbergasted and pondering, Maisie trotted right up behind them and, throwing one end of a rope to Sol, began circling the totally unprepared Airavab team so that they all collapsed in on themselves and were completely tied up together, like floppy dolls.

"Way to go, Maisie!," Sol shouted.

As they turned to face the tied team, Ishmael, not seeming in the least bit frightened, rang out in a clear voice: "We will not harm you. Please tell Drake Barents that we would like to work together. You see, he may not be aware, indeed, is not aware, that the virya in Area 38 is inert. Only whales can activate it. Barents has not exactly ingratiated himself with them, but he is going to need to change his tune if he wants to get his greedy hands on this virya! Go ahead, you may use your extra special walkie talkies to tell him."

Ishmael signaled to Sol and she let go and Maisie unhooked her jaws to release the Airavab team who all scurried off to the Hancock Tower, their tails, as it were, between their legs. Maisie followed them.

Ishmael high-fived Sol and then picked her clear off the sandy ground and spun her around before they swam down into their emerald world to tell Aditi and Akira the good news.

Aditi hummed a low song and seemed to shimmy a little when Ishmael and Sol regaled her with the story of their adventure. Sol wanted to be happy, but she was exceedingly worried about Maisie. The whale-human alliance needed to know what Barents was up to so Aditi asked Maisie to spy on him, but Sol thought this was much too dangerous. The great whale calculated that a dog could slip through more easily than the humans and, even standing tall on all fours, was below the level of the security cameras in the tower. But no one could have anticipated what Maisie knew—and would bark out to the community under the sea later.

Trotting softly behind his chagrined crew, Maisie entered the Hancock Tower. Barents appeared to be struggling to digest the fact that he was powerless to activate the virya. When the crew returned, Barents snappily asked one of them to bring some of the records his research team had made of whale song down to him as he sat brooding over the best path to the whales' ruin. He didn't want to hear what had happened in Area 38, he knew what he needed to know. Maisie, unseen by Barents, watched and listened as he rested one of the records on the turntable and heard the thump thump thump of the machine rotating before a lilting whale song came singing out. When Barents had heard these sounds before, he dismissed them abruptly as mere sounds. But this time he picked the needle up and pulled it back an inch or so, listening again. Then he repeated the gesture and listened again. Maisie thought that maybe he finally began to hear a pattern that he had not detected before; she guessed that he started to think that maybe there is more intelligence than he allowed earlier.

Barents picked up his phone and dialed. "Bring me the grandmother," he said, and slammed the phone down, causing a small crack to open on the edge of the plastic casing.

Masie snuck out of the tower to alert the others that Barents was taking Nana.

Now, Nana had traveled all around the world, painting, watching. She'd had her camera stolen by a smelly man fishing through her belongings while he thought she slept on an overnight train, she'd ridden helmetless on a motor scooter clutching for dear life onto the ribcage of a man she barely knew. She'd raised four children. Almost nothing could scare her.

But she'd been scared.

The team of men in white arrived at the house on stilts on the elbow of Cape Cod with the angry Atlantic roaring at its base as quickly as they could after Barents' fury-laced phone call.

They climbed around the aquarium and up the stairs and picked the lock into the house where Nana was now alone, with no idea where her family had gone.

One reached around and clamped a sweaty palm over her mouth just as she was reaching up to add a layer of luminous aquamarine to a painting. The other simply picked her up and carried her into the waiting car. They injected her with something that put her instantly into a vast dreamscape full of the flora and fauna of nearly a century of memories.

Then they locked her in Barents's former office, now empty but dry.

They gave her bottled water and matzo with peanut butter.

Fans were still running to dry out the flooded

tower, but the fish were gone, the saltiness cleansed, and the whole had become a compact hive of activity. Everything returned to an eye-squinting, sunglass-wearing brilliant white.

When his minions escorted Nana out of the freight elevator (the regular one being still out of commission), Barents, now having recovered somewhat his smug equilibrium, and wearing a dazzling white, unstained suit, extended a hand to Nana and gestured for her to take a seat.

"Tea?" he offered, by way of greeting.

"Yes, thank you," Nana replied tentatively, not wanting to accept this hospitality but also dying for a cup of tea. She perched gingerly on the slightly damp white chair and wondered, as Maisie and Sol had, why the tea and kindness?

"So, you are the mother of Ishmael Amaral. Quite a thorn—a harpoon sized thorn in my side I must say."

"I am most proud of my son. In fact, I demand you tell me what you have done with him and with Sol."

"You don't know, do you?"

"Of course not."

"Clearly, I was wrong. I have been wrong before, it is nothing so terribly shocking."

"Where are they?"

"I have no idea. That granddaughter of yours, with her mutt, no less, somehow managed to flood my entire tower. And then they escaped. It is possible I have underestimated the whales."

"Oh, have you?"

"I listened to some of the recordings my research team made of whale sounds. I must admit, I was wrong, yet again. Upon closer reflection I did detect patterns in the sounds and I could imagine that these patterns do form something like a language. I have also been given to understand, via your irritating son, that I require the whales to activate the virya we captured from Area 38. He is quite right, it is inert."

"Listen, mister, you've taken me from my home, you've kidnapped my family, I have no earthly idea what you're talking about. And why the hell would the whales want to help you, of all people? You are not making sense."

"Well, as you can imagine, I no longer, as of two days ago, harbor genocidal intentions against the Leviathans. In fact, my virya factories cannot function without the whales. I am quite powerless, you see."

"I really do not get you, or your wild plans. I want my son and my granddaughter. I am tired, my bones ache, I demand to be taken home."

"Ah, that. Well, you'll have to wait, Mrs. Amaral. But why the whales will want to help me—that is relatively simple. These gigantic creatures and I are on a sort of metaphorical see-saw, if you will, where it appears from the outside that all the weight is on their side and they win. And yet, another branch of the research department has been conducting some fairly extensive studies into the transformations of the earth's delicate climate. It appears that the whales, well, indeed, all living things, are being threatened quite severely by global over-reliance on fossil fuels."

"I still don't quite—" Nana sat forward on the settee.

"Please, do get comfortable, take some more tea, be quiet and, if you ever want to see your family again, let me finish. Now, where was I? Ah, yes. It may appear initially, from the outside, that, if the whales and I were balancing on a see-saw, the advantage would be all theirs. They would win hands down, any sort of weight competition, naturally. But seen from another angle, there is a bit more of a mutual dependence at work. Quite a powerful need for collaborative action. So powerful, in fact, that the see-saw, if you will, would be flat. The whales would like the humans to stop the dangerous warming of the oceans, correct?"

Nana leaned back, defeated. "Yes, of course. Their lives, and ours, are threatened by global ocean warming. It's in the papers every day."

"And we have failed to fully grasp how essential whales are to the health of the oceans, we have failed to consider, certainly during the great whaling era, but now, too, how much carbon they absorb, how, if we let them simply live and circulate freely, they essentially help us, organically, to keep the oceans healthy, correct?"

"Naturally," Nana said, mechanically, still not grasping where Barents was going with all this.

"So, they would benefit a great deal, of course, if we suddenly stopped using fossil fuels and polluting the planet. Therefore, it would be in the whales' best interest to make me one of the richest men on the planet! It's actually quite funny in its utter, Machiavellian perfection!"

Barents made a kissing gesture by putting his index finger and middle finger right next to each other, pressing against his white thumb and pale lips.

"So," Barents continued, warming even more to his topic as he slurped up some tea, "Airavab has already begun construction of multiple mechanisms to turn ordinary fossil run cars into virya-cars—we are exploring the best title for these converts, viryamobiles? We are not yet sure. At any rate, we can also engage this same technology to, within about a decade, convert most of the world's factories into virya run, zero-carbon emitting, exceedingly efficient spaces of production. If my calculations are correct, the planet, so close to the tipping point beyond which there is no return, will begin to tip back, ever so slightly. The oceans will cool, the po-

lar ice caps will not melt, the whales will be fruitful
and multiply. The beachings will stop. And I will be
fabulously, insanely, utterly beyond all counting,
rich. Mouahaha!"

As she caught sight of Ishmael, Sol, and Maisie
storming the tower to save her, all Nana heard then
was laughter, an intense, deep laughter echoing
all around the tower. A laughter like the ending of
an I.L. Peretz story in Yiddish about a simple man
who does not ask for much. Eventually, the angels
tell him he can ask for anything at all and when
he says he just wants a hot roll with melty butter
every day they laugh and laugh and laugh and do
not stop laughing.

VII
ANDRÉ

It's not really about my mother, is it? Sid says, in the now darkening evening. We're still on the sofa, limbs stiff, necks aching. I stand up and stretch, roll my neck around, a crunch. At some point I'd replaced my towel with sweatpants.

It's as though, she says, still slumped on the sofa, dad started out wanting to write about her and couldn't. All these clues, this manuscript, they lead back to him, not really to her. Maybe that's why he left it a fragment? My mother slips in, as though she'd been living in the glass universe, or a cabin by the sea, Aaron gets close, plants her green scarf like a seed, and then pulls back. We're never going to know, are we, André? Never.

For some reason, my love, all I can think of is Derrida: "une lettre," il dit, "peut toujours ne pas arriver à destination, et que donc jamais elle n'y arrive. Et c'est bien ainsi, ce n'est pas un malheur, c'est la vie, la vie vivante, battue, la tragédie, par la vie encore survivante."

Yes, I suppose so, Sid replies slowly, that's sort of like it's the journey not the end goal, or as Mr. Oravid was saying, the labyrinth, yes?

We move to the table, I get out a bottle of wine, the muscle movement of evicting the cork feels good after so much stillness. But I'm tired, she goes on, of my father's endless turns, all the Melville, he's also been sort of baked and scorched by losing my mother.

She picks up my *Moby-Dick* as if to chuck it across the room and I pull her arm down and bite her neck playfully. She breathes in, reflecting.

Because of Aaron's deep well of loneliness, she says wistfully, she had been determined to stay close, becoming her father's sole spindly thread to the living. She feels guilty, she says, now, but after college staying with Aaron and his books and his dust weighed her down, as if she wore a paper jacket made heavy with the white pages of his manuscripts, so many of them, like the one we've just read, unfinished. Almost, it seems, unsculpted. Aaron's favorite pen, she says, taking a sip, was one of those kidly multi clickers with the option of a different color in each click so when Aaron read he scribed and clicked, a palimpsest of multicolored comments thickening the margins on each rereading; his books appeared almost Talmudic, Aaron arguing with himself over the years like Rabbis duking it out over the centuries.

After dinner we climb the loft. Sid begins to play with me but I just can't. That envelope I'd stolen feels like a betrayal. It's the letter that never arrived at its destination and I am utterly terrified to tell her that I've stolen it from her grandmother.

I'm so sleepy, I say, turning on my side as Sid spoons me.

She's soon fast asleep and I lie awake. I don't

know what to do with the envelope. It feels as though it has a book inside, perhaps? I'm dying to open it but I figure I had better leave it to Sid. But? Should I? Why would Esther not have opened this? I can only imagine that it must have arrived and seemed inconsequential and maybe impossible to open. Maybe she was saving it for Dorothy, it's addressed to her, after all. I need to make a decision and the longer I wait the worse it feels. Like a ticking below the floorboards. The envelope drives a wedge between Sid and I just when we could be closer. I push the thought away.

Shifting slightly and trying not to wake Sid, I recall that the final time we saw Aaron, two months before he died, he was⋯ "robust" would be putting it too strongly, but he certainly seemed very much alive in September when he flew to New York to visit us. I knew my students would love meeting him and he was clearly touched that I'd asked him to be the class visitor. Sid abruptly broke up with me that evening, after class. No explanation. Or none that made sense to me. But the day before, when everything was normal, we'd picnicked in Tompkins Square Park under a magnolia tree with slight brown edges forming on the leaves, some of which fell onto our multicolored blanket. I asked Aaron about his novel-in-progress, *American Berserk*, but he was strangely elusive, offering us only a scant smile he simply said, You'll see.

With other books he delighted in describing the plot arcs to us, coming alive as he chronicled the worlds he built from thin air, and I so enjoyed hearing about and reading his eclectic, slightly odd, definitely unique novels. It was a great treat to learn the backstories of some of his zany ideas. After the picnic, Aaron pulled out of his worn leather briefcase, a copy of the bible. Inside, a handwritten inscription drawn in a careful, full figured almost calligraphic script rendered in fountain pen:

Given to Aaron Zimmerman on 2 January, 1935 on the occasion of his Bar Mitzvah, Temple Sholom, Chicago. The Bible had become unstuck, the binding, shriveled up and dry like ash. As ever helpless with practical things, he asked Sid to bind it. She solemnly promised, as if she were swearing on the bible itself; but in the busy scurry of her New York life she never managed to take it to a book bindery and Aaron died alone in the ambulance before she could return the bound Bar Mitzvah bible to him. The bible stays unbound on her little black table by her door in the kitchen and now it's all too late. Maybe we should have bound the bible after all, I muse, maybe Aaron wanted it for a particular reason that he never told us? Now we either have to preserve it unbound or finally bind it but which would be the more fitting memorial we don't know. I think keeping it unbound would be more Aaron, but Sid continues to weigh the question, and the bible waits for her.

In the morning I resolve to tell her about the envelope.

But then I don't. We've finally reached this beautiful spot and I worry that she'll drop me if I tell her. Why the fuck did I not tell her and Esther the moment I found it?

I head up to CUNY to teach and she hops on the train to Shlovsky.

After class I'm determined to work on my "Aaron biography" as I've come to think of it. Aaron's inventive re-writing of Henry James's *The Golden Bowl* remains my favorite of all of his novels, and I figure I'll start the project there, and not chronologically.

In *The Cracked Vase,* I write in my head on the train, in place of a delicate, if flawed glass bowl as the central metaphor, Aaron's novel swirls around a strange object looted from a Jewish family in Vienna. Set in the 1960s, but replicating James's ingenious structure where each of the main characters takes charge of his or her own section, Aaron's novel alternates perspectives between a young woman who falls in love with a man she cannot marry, the gentleman in question, and his father-in-law. In James's novel, Charlotte (and perhaps I liked Aaron's book so much in part because the original character shared my mother's name) can never marry the Prince despite her dazzling beauty because, poor as a church mouse, she's too powerless to capture one of those lost European aristocrats in need of American cash, aka, the Prince.

Aaron maps these class and cash clashes onto intractable American racial issues: Susie's white parents cruelly withhold their approval of her marriage to Charles (loosely modeled on Sidney Poitier's character in *Guess Who's Coming to Dinner* and, like him, an accomplished black doctor). Before Charles's marriage to Susie's friend Amber, the former lovers go shopping for a gift. In a dusty antique shop they find a vase—or at least it looks at first like a vase but because it is so very thin, they are never sure. The grace of the object renders them breathless but they decide to dig deeper. As the novel spools out they discover the true provenance of the glass and they seek out the original owner only to discover her two days after her funeral. The strange vase had been a gift from her lover, made from glass blown outside Venice, and looted when both were deported to concentration camps. She survived but he was murdered in the camps, so the original owner longed for this valued gift, only to have it returned too late. Aaron's rewriting makes space for James, keeps the Jamesian structure, but also turns that chronicle into love and loss in the dual contexts of the Holocaust and interracial love before Loving v. Virginia. He sensitively interconnected these things in a way that left readers pensive, musing, and forging ties across difficult stories. This novel seems to me more vital than his others, boasting a huge heart, and chockablock with satisfying meat on the characters. Aaron was right, as he'd said in his Kepesh interview, that it was his best book. Even still, of *The Cracked Vase*, *The New York Times*'s Filipa Vertigenoux said it was "delicate, a stunning homage to and updating of James but slightly emotionally cold."

On Sunday we take the train out to BAM, to catch a dance matinee. On the subway, Sid leans her head on my shoulder. André, she mumbles lazily, do you think we should have tried to do a memorial? Now I feel crummy that we didn't, that we're leaving it to Greta.

Sid, we weren't 'we' then···you forget what a shmuck you are, sometimes, you know?

We're rocking slightly with the kinetic slides of the train, but Sid sits fully up, her shoulders pushing back into the hard, grey plastic seat, her x-ray eyes drill into me. Totally, a shmuck. But you? You're a mensch. Honestly, sometimes I get so livid with myself when I act like such an idiot! I love you. And you don't deserve all my shit. You've taken care of me through this whole crazy search. You've been next to me for everything and I just want us to stay together now, ok? Is it too late? No more roller coaster. I am done with all that. Done, done, done!

On the last "done" her voice rises emphatically and some of the other passengers look our way, they're sleepy, she's interrupting their naps, but they want to make sure she is ok. New Yorkers are cranky, but caring. Sid takes my hand, puts her head back on my shoulder, and sleeps like a baby all the way to Brooklyn.

I look around at everyone as the lights change skin tones to off hues of umbers and green and feel just slightly hollow; Sid isn't entirely giving me a chance to agree or disagree. One voice inside my head offers futile mutiny. The other voice pops champagne corks and parties. It's Sid's world and I'm so happy to live in it; but then I wonder if it will always be like this, if the search for Dorothy will forever take over our lives or if, like Greta had to do after the war, we can rebuild somehow, forge our own lives, move on to something just ours not always panting after these threadbare crumbs from the past. I check myself, remembering my in-class revelation about those eyes full of lingering images, and remind myself that she's just been through an awful lot, and it's pretty strange, as though we've jumped into that suitcase, and clear through the bottom of it into that fragmentary text about whales. Like it expanded into the size of a tank, and we're swimming around, all the clues multicolored fish. And I've lied to her, which now makes me feel worse.

When Sid and I finally land back at my place after the dance my neglected mailbox is overstuffed. Each time I start staying at Sid's again, it fills up like this, like a bloated corpse. We hike up the four flights to my pad and I fling the mail on the table, so bone tired. Sid drinks a glass of water and then fairly crawls to pull down the bed, falling into a deep sleep as my mind wanders back to *Slobgollion*. The answer in Aaron's novel is just too weird to be true. Like a Rolodex clicking through my head I review the suitcase items: the shoe, the paperweight, the matchbook, the photograph, the sculpture, the blue gloves. What was Aaron playing at? He knew we'd chase everything, he knew we'd follow his letter, the mesmeric charm all hope of Dorothy holds for Sid, he knew I'd be a sucker for all his tantalizing inklings. He scripted me.

Morning. I am barely awake, just coming to consciousness and dreaming of a huge cup of coffee when Sid bursts through the door, all energized from yoga and tells me, André I learned how to breathe!

Coffee.

She putters to the kitchen side of my studio, puts the kettle on. Folding her cute ass on the edge of the bed, she instructs me to lie back down...and rests her head on my rib cage. I casually reach for her nipple, softly touching her, circling, but she puts my hand back on my abdomen. Which leaves me⋯hanging.

Imagine your ribs opening up like windows⋯ I try to concentrate yet I'm both aroused and inwardly laughing at the absurdity of the metaphor.

But, I gamely close my eyes and breathe in and out and then I do actually feel my ribs opening up like windows one rib at a time from the very bottom rib tucked in and almost lost, a small scrap of bone hidden beneath the larger mass of lung tissue the next rib bigger and broader. I'd never been able to visualize—or physically feel—so clearly the scalar change in my ribs. As my breath travels to the next rib this one splintered by a chaotic fall as a child down the stairs, my breath gets closer to my heart. Climbing the ladder of ribs, I picture glass French doors opening onto a garden and smell the peonies coming in adding perfume to my full ribs. When I describe all of this to Sid she looks very pleased, like a cat who's gotten the canary.

Learning how to really breathe, Sid says, is like learning how to swim, well, sort of, not how I learned to swim—but it's a way of becoming hyper aware. I feel I can concentrate much better in the darkroom if I'm breathing properly, you know?

Coffee.

Sid pours steaming water over the glass carafe and the tiny space fills with the earthy smell as I casually flip through the letters we picked up from the overfull mailbox. A letter from The University of Chicago catches my eye, the envelope is slightly creamy in thick paper only used by private schools. I have to read it twice before I fully grasp its contents:

Dear Professor Azevedo,

We were very impressed with your application and we are delighted to inform you that we invite you to an on campus interview and visit. This will entail an interview with the search committee, teaching a class, and meeting with graduate and undergraduate students. After that you will give a job talk at 5pm and then dinner with faculty at the Reynolds Club. Please phone the department secretary, Ms. Zelig, at your earliest convenience to arrange your visit.

We look forward to meeting you in person.

Sincerely,

Gerhard Stein

Professor and Chair

English Department

Sid, honey, bring the coffee over here—I need to show you something!

After she reads the letter she hugs me harder than I thought she could with those small but surprisingly strong chaturanga arms of hers.

I phone Ms. Zelig and she assures me she will arrange everything for my campus visit, to take place in the winter quarter. I'm not exactly used to the red carpet treatment, being a contracted lecturer isn't what you might call cushy, so I'm pleasantly surprised that someone else will take care of all the details. I'm nervous about this campus visit, naturally, having never done such an august thing before, but also strangely calm. One of the faculty in English, a Professor Ahem, works on 19th and 20th century American literature and even reviewed one of Aaron's novels, so I figure we'll have a lot to talk about. Chicago, or at least the parts of it I know, Lakeview and downtown, is so familiar from all those visits to Aaron and he took us to the fabulous Rare Book Room of course, so Hyde Park doesn't feel like Mars, and I'm trusting I'll have an hour to stop in there, to read. I hope I won't be one of those deer-in-the-headlights lost applicants, but I'm too superstitious for any moxie. I reread Ahem's review, so I can talk with her about it.

Jacob Bloom
By Aaron Zimmerman
Godolphin Press, $13.95
Review by Gloria Ahem

Aaron Zimmerman has once again shown that he is the Zelig of contemporary writers. I heard through the grapevine that he is even working on a novel about whales who speak Yiddish—this, I should add is an unsubstantiated rumor so I don't mean to jump ahead of myself, but just to signal that Zimmerman seems endlessly pliable, and endlessly curious.

Jacob Bloom tells the story of a youth who sneaks out of his home in London in 1888 and becomes a kind of child-vigilante super hero who saves random people in need during the nocturnal mayhem of Jack the Ripper era London. The child always returns before his unsuspecting parents wake up, find him sleeping peacefully, and rouse him for school. Eventually, his parents' lives intersect with his nighttime adventures when he saves one of their good friends from Jack the Ripper himself.

Bloom is an adventurous young lad with a strongly developed superego. One day everything in Bloom's life changes: as he walks through the dense fog thickened streets of Sherlock Holmes-era London he encounters a strange object. It's a heavy glass paperweight that he finds inexplicably balanced on the railing of London Bridge. So, naturally, instead of taking the object to the police or to a private detective he decides to sniff around much the way his hero, Holmes, would have done. Bloom enters a slightly menacing, low-ceilinged pub and, taking the paperweight out of his school satchel, shows the rare thing to the barman near the bridge where he found it. Holding the heavy object in his beer -soaked palm, the barman's eyes register a glimmer of recognition. And yet he sets the rounded, oddly egg-shaped glass down on the bar and shakes his head saying, "sorry lad, I've got no bloody idea what this thing is. Good day." Bloom, though, captured that one moment of hesitation in the barman's eyes. Later, defying his parents as he does nightly, Bloom sneaks out and, lying in wait for the barman at the end of his shift, follows the man through the gnarled streets.

Without giving away too much of the plot I can say that the paperweight, embedded within it a fascinating key, was the first clue in a series of juicy hints that ultimately led Bloom to solve the mystery of Jack the Ripper and to save a beautiful young girl from his clutches.

As he did in *In Love with Great Black Hope*, Zimmerman here gives history an optimistic twist. Along the route, Zimmerman, true to his day job in the Rare Book Room at the University of Chicago (and, full disclosure, I should add that I am a Professor at the University of Chicago who has a passing acquaintance with Zimmerman), includes many fascinating historical details about Jewish London in the 1880s. For example, one of the clues takes Bloom into the Machzike Hadath synagogue on Brick Lane. Incidentally, during World War II, the synagogue provided refuge for children saved by the Kindertransport. But staying true to the setting of 19th century London, Zimmerman only includes details up until the close of the novel in 1898 when Bloom, now a young man, marries the delicate maiden he had saved years earlier.

Only a slight, dry cough saves the novel from a whiff of cheesiness that might have marred its otherwise fast-paced narrative. Zimmerman is well aware that his nod to Joyce (in the name of the main character, naturally) chronologically falls after *Ulysses* and yet of course Jacob Bloom is set some 50 years earlier. But Zimmerman, ever inter-textually masterful, knows how to weave in myriad literary references without the reader (or without this reader, I'll just say) feeling bludgeoned or feeling the need to reach for the encyclopedia.

Second full disclosure: reviewers of literature are likely to be as lit nerdy as the authors we review and thus less likely to mind ferreting out all of these references. Indeed, in a particularly well-wrought scene, Bloom, searching for a clue on the banks of the Thames, accidentally falls in and gets sucked away by the current. As the youth feels his life slipping away from him, and as he cuts his hands quite badly on a menacing, jagged rock, he is ultimately saved by a young girl who throws him an elegant emerald green silk sash; I enjoyed Zimmerman's ever-clever re-writing of the scene from book five of Homer's Odyssey (and thus looping back to *Ulysses*).

As is typical in Zimmerman novels, Jacob Bloom boasts quite complex framing. The opening chapter is narrated by Bloom himself and then the chapters alternate between Bloom as a young boy at the time of the main events and as an old man with grandchildren on his knee to whom he tells different interlocking versions of the same stories that the young Bloom has already told us. Most of the time this complex narration offers satisfying meta reflections on truth and lying in literature. But Zimmerman might have simplified in some moments, and let us know what actually happened. I doubt I am alone in awaiting eagerly those zaftig whales and whatever adventures Zimmerman might take us on next.

That evening, over pizza, Sid's all curious and light, like a weight's been lifted. She asks me about my classes, my book, the upcoming campus visit. We go over plans for the memorial and I studiously avoid discussing my theft. After dinner, we head to *Film Forum* to catch *In a Lonely Place* with Humphrey Bogart and the luminous Gloria Grahame. Bogart plays a hot-tempered screenwriter whose work has gone cold, hackneyed, but who is surrounded by a cohort of ageing Hollywood agents, actors, and producers who put up with him nonetheless. One evening, Bogie gazes across the courtyard at his new neighbor, who happens to be standing there, looking at him while wearing, naturellement, a resplendent, pale, negligee. Expliquz-moi **ça**. It's Gloria, of course. They begin a romance based on passion and typing and yet the shadow of a murder hangs over them. Grahame's character remains unsure until the very end whether Bogie killed a girl or not.

As we walk back to Sid's place with the sounds and images from the film ticking through our heads, we discuss the slightly odd movie. As was the case on our first date, she's all about the angles and the shadows and the light, and I'm all about the romance. But Sid does say: Oh, I so wish they could have stayed together! If only that police commissioner had phoned them just one day earlier!

So, you are getting a bit romantic, eh?

At this Sid cuffs me gently. Then she kisses me fully on the lips. I inhale that indescribable spicy smell that always clings to her, and always makes me want so much more of her.

*

The minute I return to New York from Chicago, Sid wants to hear every detail of my campus visit, she refuses to wait until we know the outcome. We're on the red sofa, the evening sky brings all the colors of the city into the living room. She has her head in my lap, my hands like seaweed threaded through her hair.

So, what were the students like? How are they different from CUNY students?

Well, I only had one class so I don't exactly claim to be an expert. The U of C students, well, yes, they did seem⋯different than your average CUNY undergraduate and very organized. I have to say, they asked excellent questions! But so do my students.

I bet they loved your class. Did you only talk about Melville or did you manage to bring in other writers?

Thanks, hon, for that vote of confidence. So, yes, I did talk about Melville—hello, it was the Melville class. But I talked about Melville's relevance now, about Morrison and C. L. R. James's take on race and whiteness in the great whale novel, about the implications of species decline as we are starting to see more and more species going extinct. No one knows, for example, exactly how many blue whales are left. So, you know, I balanced—or tried to balance anyway, close readings with stuff they might see in a newspaper.

And the dean? How was he? Or she?

He. Very dean-ly. A middle aged white guy who wore a navy blue suit with gold buttons and a gold watch. He was a scientist of some kind, I think. But a very generous fellow, gave me a hearty hand-shake, that sort of thing. He'd read some Melville and Henry James—he said his favorite was 'Bartle-by'—so we chatted a bit about preferences. It was a pretty pro forma meeting—he held my CV in front of him, put on thick glasses to read it, and raised his eyebrows at the appropriate moments as he pulled the glasses off to glance from CV back to me and asked questions about my work, my plans, and so on. I think it went well? Hard to tell.

I'm sure you were perfect. And what about dinner? That was likely the most important test, right? And were there any sexy professors to flirt with?

Uh, no. Luckily dinner was fantastic. Three American Literature scholars nerding it out over pasta and red wine, what could possibly go wrong? No, seriously, we talked books, we compared New York to Chicago, we compared the Met to the Art Institute, you know, that sort of thing. But it was a lovely dinner, I felt they were rooting for me, encouraging me.

Of course they were! Fingers crossed, I won't say more now, I'm too superstitious. Speaking of Melville, I don't think you ever told me how you gave dad the name of the weird fragment of a novel? I miss him, you know? It's weird because I really couldn't have predicted how very much I would miss him, how much I would think about him. And how could I know that once he went, mom would rush in...memories of her would appear out of thin air···or rather out of his suitcase. Dad, well, dad was so stubbornly reticent and I think I'll always be furious that we've been pushed to the chase. But then again, I wouldn't unlearn anything we've gleaned. Knowledge, as your dad might say, can only be enhanced, not subtracted.

I feel it too, with Aaron, and with my mom, the small things that make them up, after···

I am so profoundly sorry I never met her. Marguerite, is she like her? And Thérèse she is so very like her, non?

Very much so.

We breathe in silence for a few minutes, in the wave of losses. Sid sits up, puts her feet on the coffee table. A photograph falls to the floor, we sip our wine.

But you asked about the title of Aaron's manuscript? Do you remember on one of our trips to Chicago, I can't actually remember exactly when, maybe after we'd been together for about a year? We were visiting Aaron and staying on Aldine—I think you had gone out to the lake to take some photos and I asked Aaron to tell me more about what he was writing—at that time it did not have a name. Given the cetological subject I picked up his copy of *Moby-Dick* and read out to him Melville's remarkable description of a 'singular' substance that resonated for me with the novel's message about whales' interconnectivity.

And here, of course, I reach over to the bookshelf for my multicolored, underlined copy. Melville portrays a moment of hands interconnecting during the gruesome process of whaling: "There is another substance," he says, "and a very singular one, which turns up in the course of this business, but which I feel it to be very puzzling adequately to describe. It is called slobgollion; an appellation original with the whalemen, and even so is the nature of the substance." Aaron loved the name and adopted it right away. He hadn't remembered that particular nugget from Melville's novel.

You've really influenced him, huh? Are you going to write that literary biography of Aaron or what?

Maybe. Let me see what happens with University of Chicago, first. Everything is on hold but also moving, gaining fragments. How did Virginia Woolf put it in *To The Lighthouse?* "life, from being made up of little separate incidents which one lived one by one, became curled and whole like a wave which bore one up with it and threw one down with it, there, with a dash on the beach"? Something like that.

*

For Aaron's memorial, my father and sister voyage from the warmth of Guadeloupe to the chill of New York, Esther and William travel together from Québec via plane, Michael Gruber takes the subway, Mr. Oravid and Henry walk across the park, Paolo Gemina hops into a cab, and Sid and I, leaving very early in the morning, decide to walk the length of the city. This is part of our memorial to Aaron, whose long strides took him all over Chicago, all over New York, all over. It's possible we wouldn't have been able to match pace with him had he been walking in step with us, but we try, as if we were chasing his ghost uptown. It's a crisp morning. Sid's camera, naturally, is slung over her neck, bouncing slightly as we go. We opt to cross 9th Street, west, to Fifth Avenue so that Greta's house is a straight shot up. Sunday morning is a sleepy time in the city that never sleeps, especially on a day this cold, so we walk without being surrounded by the usual sense of rush and busy that so characterizes this city I have grown to love, but also suspect I have to leave. On the corner of 18th and Fifth, right in front of one of the hugest bookstores in the city, we bump into two familiar faces: a couple I recognize from Sid's wall but could not name. They stop with their matching *It's a pleasure to serve you* blue and white coffee cups emitting a hot, inviting steam as I imagine it warms their hands and say, Hello! Then, after quite a long, but sweet look at me, one of the women says, Ah, I see now why you chose us as subjects, and she winks at her girlfriend.

Yes, I suppose so, Sid replies with a chuckle, this is my boyfriend, André.

So nice to meet you, André. (Awkward handshake, balancing coffee cups). Sidney, do let us know when the book comes out! And thank you for the portrait, it's our absolute fave. Ciao, have a good walk.

Boyfriend? I ask Sid as the happy couple continues on south and we head further north.

Well, Sid says, taking my arm as a lady might, you got another idea?

We could fix that, you know, that 'boyfriend' thing.

Oui.

When we arrive at Greta's, Esther and William are already there. My father and sister stayed with aunt Thérèse in Brooklyn and they arrive a few minutes later followed by the rest of the guests. Greta arranged flowers everywhere—she chose gladioli because they fit into very long vases and she figured Aaron would appreciate the nod to *The Cracked Vase.* He was indifferent to flowers but I agree, he would have appreciated that allusion. As we all sit down in Greta's gracious living room, facing each other, a somber silence fills the air. Bruno settles down first at Sid's feet and then in the warmth of her lap, and she gently strokes his back. We each hear the others breathing and I remember Sid's lessons in feeling your ribs open like windows. I close my eyes and breathe. The first to break the silence is my father.

Greta, he says, thank you for this lovely gesture. I am still, will always be, mourning my dear wife, Charlotte, and all spaces of mourning bring her back to me again and again. Aaron and I met only once, when I came to visit Sid and André. I will say, as a physicist, I am quite used to dealing with, shall I say, socially awkward people? André had prepared me, bien sûre, for his...oddities, so I knew what to expect. But I was not quite prepared for his raw intelligence. We got to talking physics and he managed in his rusty but passable French to convey to me that he grasped a surprising number of the big ideas—the math, well that was not his strong suit. But I will never forget that conversation with him. He said something very profound, punctuating his points capaciously with his long arms, about the interconnecting parts of the micro and the macro universes and he somehow understood (perhaps more intuitively than rationally) the resonances between particles and black holes. Sid, my dear girl, he was a remarkable man, remarkable.

We sit silently again, the sound of our breath like waves gliding into shore, Greta gets up to refresh some tea cups and I gesture for her to sit down, and then I pour out more tea. My sister is the next to break the silence.

Papa, that was beautiful. As you know, I never got the chance to meet your father, Sid, and for that I am so sorry. I do know from my brother that he was larger than life, expansive with André's students, and that new things keep unfolding about him as you two followed all the clues he placed with such characteristically bizarre care in that curious suitcase. I've come to think of Aaron in the abstract as a sort of puzzle master. He crafted so many pieces and left you two to fit them together. That you did, mostly, is amazing. In a sense we are all, here, now, that puzzle formed into a myriad, breathing, living whole.

Marguerite closes her eyes then and I understand that she is praying. Sid looks at her with so much love, reaches out her hand to hold Marguerite's, and in that instant she and my sister become family.

Paolo issues a quiet cough and then says hesitantly: Hello, thank you for inviting me. Sid and André, they came to find me about the shoe, the one red shoe I made many years ago. I never had the chance to meet Aaron—or maybe I did, and sadly don't remember him among so many visitors to my loft—this Aaron who we remember today, I hope his memory always gives blessings, but I know that his daughter loved him very much and loved her mama, too, bellissime scarpe per una bellissima donna. It was definitely a molto speciale evening when Sid and André found me at Fanelli's and I only discovered much later that there was a note inside the secret drawer! I made those little secret spaces... everybody she has secrets, si? But Aaron, found the secret space and put inside it a note for his daughter.

Paolo dabs at his eye with his handkerchief.

Mr. Oravid and Henry whisper to each other and then Mr. Oravid speaks out in a clear voice: Sid, the day you came to see me at the museum was a day I had anticipated for a very long while. The truth, they say, is stranger than fiction. It was of course your father who sent me to look out for you. I am not sure what he thought I could do to protect you but he needed a sort of proxy, I think, someone who could focus more and who was in New York while he was in Chicago.

We all stay silent, Sid not able to say anything, I can tell from her face as she looks at me before closing her eyes gently, patting Bruno.

Michael Gruber is the next to speak:

More than forty years ago now, Aaron and I touched down in Berchtesgaden. It was late April, 1945 and very, very cold as we parachuted through the mountains. Aaron was not particularly easy going, even then. You had to work to get him to talk, to pry him out of his endless inner fictional universes. It's hard to mutter under your breath and dream in a novelist landscape when you're jumping from an airplane, though. If you forget to pull your parachute, well, that's that. So in a sense the war forced Aaron, for a few years at least, into the present. He had trouble, a lot of trouble, we all did, facing head on the realities we uncovered by May of '45. Layer upon layer of revelation—we knew it was bad, but we did not know it was that bad; so many people murdered, the insanity of the Nazi looting machine, and for what reason? Aaron and I were helping out, cataloguing, photographing, trying to make sense of the amassing and amassing of other people's treasures, treasures like those of your family, Greta, and thousands upon thousands of others. They had no right. It moved Aaron to the core, the injustice of it all and that boy he made up in *The Eagle's Nest,* he was a sort of metaphor for corrupted innocence. Aaron never gave up trying to depict things that mattered. But, I wanted to share with you my favorite photograph of my friend. I took copious photos of him over the years but here is my favorite. I like to think it captures a moment of pure presence.

Michael passes around a photograph, black and white. A bright sunny day. Three people on a boat, and behind, in the ocean, a slight spray, perhaps a breath out from a whale. Aaron stands firmly, his legs broad to brace him as the boat sways, Dorothy holds his arm interlinking his, nestled in her other arm, very close to her heart, a baby swaddled in a blanket, fast asleep.

*

A few months later, two letters arrive, one to each of our apartments, on the same day. Sid's is from William, and mine is from the Dean of the Division of the Humanities at the University of Chicago. We find Sid's first, since we're staying on 9th.

Dear Sid,

First, please thank Greta for such a meaningful memorial. I think I can speak for all of us when I say that it felt miraculous for the shards of Aaron's various friendships to be united into a whole. I was immensely moved.

But I am writing now on a business matter. I have a colleague who curates a gallery in the West Loop, in Chicago. He very much wants his space to be cutting edge and photography focused. When he asked me for young artists to recommend, I naturally thought of you. If you decide to display some of your work there, and if it goes well, Luzzatto Press would be delighted to publish the book. We just need to gauge audience reaction first. If the prints sell, the book will sell. I am sorry I cannot give you something more definite now. But I am hopeful that everyone will love your stunning work. Thank you so much for bringing me to your atelier after the memorial. When I beheld all those faces on your walls and stacked on the tables I saw exactly what André meant—the portraits are not about race. They are about love.

Please let me know as soon as you can so I can tell my colleague at the Enderby Gallery.

With Love, William

Sid, congratulations this is wonderful!!!

———-.

Why are you so pale, what's wrong, this is amazing news. The West Loop is becoming an incredibly happening place for artists these days···why aren't you happy? Expliquez-moi ça.

———-.

Honey?

People will see them—they, oh I don't know how to say this. I've been living with them for so long now, they line my walls, they look at me, I look at them, we talk. It would feel like putting my bras on display in a museum or something. And, and, how to choose who gets to go to Chicago? They won't all fit!

Sweetie, just practice your breathing and think for a minute, ok? This is really a good thing, you've wanted an exhibit and a photobook for so long. And, well, it's not just for you. All those people, they're waiting, they also long for the book—they tell you that, patiently, when we see them, but it would make them happy, and, let's face it, you have not exactly tried? N'est-ce pas? Sid looks pretty shocked. Sometimes I can't figure her out at all. I make us a pot of coffee and then she goes off to Shlovsky like a sleepwalker while I take the train up to 20th Century Literature. That day I teach a class on *The Golden Bowl* and mention *The Cracked Vase.* To my surprise, one of the students had read it and discussed the weirdness of reading the two novels in the wrong order, as it were. He wishes he'd read the James first and then the Zimmerman, but actually, he concludes, it's kind of cool to read them backwards—he could import all the clues Aaron planted back into the original.

After work I pick up Chinese-Cuban takeout and meet Sid at my place. As we sit at the table by the tub with our garlic bean curd and broccoli, the letter stares at me, and I stare at it, too frightened to open it; Sid carefully undoes the clasp of the envelope, as if she were unlocking a delicate writing desk, glances at it, smiles that cat smile of hers, and hands it to me.

Dear Professor Azevedo,

I am delighted to offer you, on behalf of Gerhard Stein, Professor and Chair, English Department, the search committee, and the entire English faculty, the position of Assistant Professor of English.

Your appointment will begin on July 15, 1996 and we expect you to be in residency in Chicago by that date.

Please contact Ms. Zelig to complete all necessary paperwork on time.

We were very impressed with your campus visit, your scholarship and teaching and we look forward to a long and fruitful partnership.

Sincerely,

Arthur Verver

Dean of the Division of the Humanities

André, are you ok? You look like you might faint! Getting you some whiskey, hang on!

I take, as a nineteenth century heroine might inhale smelling salts, a small sip of the whiskey Sid hands me, sit down shakily, and look up at her. What are the chances? On the same day, two letters? Chicago squared? Aaron, hey Aaron, did you have anything to do with this?

(Crickets.)

Feeling emboldened by the grog, I tell Sid: honestly, I need you to trust me, now, and for what is to come. I found a package in Esther's attic, an envelope. I···well, I stole it, actually. And I think we should open it on Aldine, not a minute before.

Sid's reaction surprises me. I thought she would

be furious, I thought she would storm out, I was terrified she'd cause another breach. But instead: I can't handle anything else right now, anything other than this current of news taking us back to Chicago. Yes, yes, let's open it there.

She says this unnaturally calmly.

We talk a lot about legacies and circles and inheritances in the weeks that follow. We're hyper aware, as if we're looking at a photo with enhanced, vibrant color, that we're going back to Sid's grandparents' home and we feel sure Aaron would be exultant that we're moving in with him, as it were. I hope he doesn't feel crowded out with us there.

*

May, and this is the spring I will always think of as sweet and salty. Slowly, hesitantly, sprigs start to flower. My classes at CUNY wrap up and my chair is delighted for me, she says, and sorry that English cannot muster a tenure line position to counter University of Chicago's offer. Sid informs Shlovsky's CEO that we're moving to Chicago and he surprises her by reaching out to a friend in the business and securing an interview for her at a sister company in the Loop. Getting Sid to peel those images off her wall and send them to the West Loop gallery is a bit of a process involving calls to both Esther and William who then phone Sid and, after a series of long conversations, eventually convince her. Stubborn, I would say. By mid–June we pack everything up from both of our apartments into the moving van and drive out to Chicago.

Unlocking those crusty locks to Aldine, we step inside its familiar walls, like putting on a good old coat you haven't worn for a while and didn't know you missed. Sure, we need to clean, and paint, and move stuff around, and throw more stuff away. That little "maid's room" with its cacophonous myriad of forgotten things has yet to be tackled. Despite what wasn't exactly the sort of happy nostalgia you'd want to hang onto, the apartment became almost a person in its own right. Aaron's parents lived there at his birth in 1922 and even though it possessed a complex legacy, the beloved space emitted grandeur, gave you a feeling of a time when ladies wore dresses and people (or at least well to do white folks) "dressed for dinner," wore gloves, and sallied out to the Green Mill for some fine jazz. The apartment featured a foyer with carefully preserved molding, worn but sturdy hard wood floors, a gracious living room, Sid's grandfather's piano still waiting for some Chopin. During Aaron's childhood, his parents slept in the bigger bedroom and he puttered around and scribbled in multiple notebooks in the smaller room, with a view to the west, gazing out at the city and its stunning sunsets, covering the buildings as the windows caught the fading light and reflected its dying embers back to him.

After Aaron's parents passed away, he lived here with his bride. The newlyweds took over his parent's former room, and then eventually little Sid settled comfortably into his old room, the generations rolling along like familiar patterns on a colorful quilt. There's something so right about the place. We open all the windows to let in the warm summer air. I can breathe freely here, and Sid somehow seems to know this will be where we'll anchor. She takes a deep breath and reaches out to enfold me.

We're finally ready to face the envelope addressed to Dorothy I'd found in the attic. Sid can't know it now, but she'll forgive my trespass. I'd confessed just before we moved back to Chicago, and while she was pissed, she also understood all my reasons. And I hadn't after all cracked the seal.

Sid takes the envelope and sets it down on the table, sitting heavily and clearly gathering all her strength to open it.

Inside, an old notebook with a note neatly paperclipped to the cover:

Dear Mrs. Zimmerman,

Thank you so much for researching at the New Bedford Historical Society. We found this notebook at your table and we wondered why you never returned to retrieve it?

Sincerely,

Camelia Colbert

Librarian

Sid opens the book, her mother's neat handwriting, a faint scent of rose:

VIII
DOROTHY

Diary of Dorothy d'Espinosa
(Private and confidential. If lost, please return to 64, rue de
Dakar, Québec)

28 June 1958

I love Aaron because of, not in spite of, his awkward-
ness. He's so much more sensitive, so different from the
clean-cut, sweet-smelling, nearly hairless boys I'd met at
the University of Chicago. After I started dating Aaron
those boys felt like cardboard cut-outs, silhouettes, nothing
but surface. Although Dale Brownstreet is a bit relentless,
I trust he'll give up at some point. Of course, Aaron's older
than me, lost…and somehow his lostness makes me feel,
if not found then at least home. Aaron's becoming a moveable home for me, a home in exile—a boat floating and yet
with its anchor ready to hand. But, this feeling grew slowly
and has only recently taken root. On our first date we each
confessed that we didn't frequent the temple, and we each
confessed that we returned solely to catch a glimpse of the
other—I think he especially shielded his ulterior motives
from me. Sometimes I feel Aaron is moody like a girl, but
I should probably have more generous thoughts although I
never know which version of Aaron I'm going to get when
he picks me up in his sea blue Chevy Bel Air. I might be
lucky and the super attentive, very present Aaron would
hop out of the car and, as if he were on a Shakespearean
stage, hold the door open for me, brush my skirt in and

close the door, gently. Or, on a bad evening, I might get the strangely apprehensive, completely distant beau, caught in the teeth of some novel he was struggling to write.

1 June 1960

Dear reader, I married him. It was a lovely ceremony, clean and simple as I'd wanted it. I am moving into the family apartment on Aldine, and am a little nervous about taking up the expected position of wife and mother. What I really want to do is continue studying cetaceans. I have to go now, more soon.

6 December 1968

Well, I certainly did not mean to stay silent for almost a decade! I've been so caught up in my studies, and in making sure Aaron has everything he needs. I've been reading about the Yangtze River Dolphin. Fascinating! In China, they are called 'baiji,' which means 'white dolphin.' There were thousands of them in the river and they talked to each other with this clicking sound, a language of their own. But now there might only be hundreds left—no one knows how many but they were here 20 million years or so ago.

The dolphins are white, unusually white, they catch the light as they swim, and a multitude of colors reflects on their skins. They looked a bit like swimming paintings. Because the Yangtze is full of silt and also pollution, they couldn't see very well. But they were expert navigators who got around using sonar. They were enormously clever and, if we are ever able to have a child, I cannot wait to tell him or her all about them.

When Aaron and I flew up to Québec again a few weeks ago, I mentioned the baiji to maman, and she replied in the dreamy voice she gets when she remembers a voyage from ages past, "they were very peaceful, and very graceful, and playful too. You could take a boat out on the Yangtze River and you'd see them catching fish and prancing around. I think I may even have a photo of them somewhere."

I love to visit maman and sit on the little bench in her familiar bedroom that she's kitted out like a lady in a manor. A small but plush bed rests on one side, on the other a tiny roll top desk, at which she sits and writes long letters to friends all over the world, people she met as she traveled with my father to his conferences. Next to the desk sits a dressing table with a mirror and one of those big, heavy hairbrushes flecked with strands of long white hair.

Maman reached into the bottom drawer of the roll top desk and pulled out a red leather folder, about a hundred years old, or so it looked. She flipped through the pages until she found the dolphins.

"Es! Kens-tu gloybn az nokh ale di yorn ikh gefunen zey! There!" she said triumphantly, "can you believe that, after all these years, I found them!"

I looked at the page and saw several black and white photographs of dolphins at play. It was hard to look at the images without color so I closed my eyes and began to paint in the colors, the white dolphins shining in the sun, the brown water streaming all around them, a yellow fish caught in the bill of one of the hungry baiji, I could see it all so clearly in my mind's eye and right then I knew I had to do everything I could to stop the blue whales from going extinct, stop them going the way of the talkative baiji.

11 June 1970

Aaron and I went to the most incredible concert you can imagine. None other than the stunning New York Philharmonic invited Alan Hovhaness to create a piece incorporating whale song. Aaron, in his typically sweet and always unexpected way, got tickets for us. He placed a little speckled envelope by the coffee pot before he left for the Rare Book Room. Inside a note said: "Bon Voyage." From this I concluded that I needed to check in the suitcase he hides in plain sight in the closet, his little Purloined Letter joke, I suppose. Inside, I found a pair of gloves: delicate, blue gloves. Rolled up, one in each hand, like little cigarettes: the tickets! Aaron is perpetually full of clues and tricks. It's one of the many things I love about him—not that I would not like to change a lot of aspects of his personality. Anyway, to the concert I wore my loose bag of a bright green maternity dress, a long strand of pearls, and naturally the new gloves—even though it was quite warm.

The sound of the orchestra tuning is always one of the most mesmerizing; they can hear every little discord—despite the multitude of sounds, often conflicting, all around. I reached for Aaron's hand—he took it, but as usual, I could tell from his face that he was thinking about a book he'd just begun imagining, *The Life Raft*. The rest of the audience, including me, was utterly transported as the human music played so very, very beautifully and the whales sang out in between the strings. I've always nourished a special affinity for these gentle giants, but I could not have anticipated being so changed. I felt as though I could hear everything the whales sang, as if they were speaking just to me. The baby—we are going to call her (I just have this feeling she's a girl) Sidney—kicked like crazy during the concert and I wondered if she, too, could understand. As if the whales spoke a language. As if they were reaching out to us.

The music swelled and sank like the sea and whale songs rose and fell with the orchestra, the musical lines were dancing and dancing with the giant animals. I kept thinking I could hear familiar words...they would leap out at me and then fade...*alevai*..and then at one point...*gilgul*...and I thought maybe *edlelkeit*...how could that be? During the intermission, I tried to tell Aaron. But he sloughed it off as the ravings of a tired pregnant lady. I do wish he could be reached more often. I never doubt that he loves me—that's obvious from the way he looks at me with his slightly sad brown eyes. But, I confess, I want more from him, more expressions of love.

I loved it so when Aaron and I went whale watching, off the coast of St. Lawrence, and sometimes, there, too, I would feel almost as though the enormous creatures were speaking. I've always wished I could live in a glass room, under the sea, so I could just watch them swim, listen to their orchestras. I would feel, then, a sort of grace, I imagine, that it's hard to find above the surface of the water. I do think Aaron understood this, when I explained it again.

13 April 1972

Sid's having a hard time sleeping, poor goose. She must be teething. I dabbed a little gin on her gums and she finally went down. When I check on her in the night sometimes she's made a mess of her sheets—like there was a wrestling match in the crib. I wonder what she dreams? She started kicking like crazy at the transformative Hovhaness concert, and she's not stopped moving since then! I wonder what she thinks of her mother's obsession with whales? I can tell I'm driving Aaron bonkers listening to whale song records over and over again, scribbling in my small black notebook, and Sid's heard them too.

"I'm trying to type!" Aaron bellows from the other room.

"Sorry dear, volume going down, carry on, so sorry!"

I'm trying to interpret sound patterns and ferret out their meanings, and this requires listening to whale records over and over again. Sid sort of dances to them—or rather she sways a little on her tiny (still a bit wobbly) legs. She's insanely adorable. (I know, I'm kvelling, I'll stop now.)

It's so exciting how very many human and whale musical collaborations are developing. Judy Collins incorporates whale song and musicians perform for whales who jump out of the water, at the Vancouver Aquarium for instance, and seem to be dancing to the music. Before I began this research, most of what I knew about whales came from *Moby-Dick*. It's a fine source, I have to say, and it manifests a great deal of tension between whales only for whaling and whales as creatures in their own right with significantly powerful attributes. But, unless I'm forgetting something, I don't think even Melville ever connected whale song with human music, especially, I think, the cello.

Maman encouraged me when I selected cello as a girl and listened with patient satisfaction as my awful, raucous squeaks slowly morphed into melodious, deep sounds. I was ecstatic when I graduated from the three-quarter to the full-sized cello, a gift from my parents when I turned 13 and a consolation prize when I couldn't have a Bar Mitzvah like all the boys.

"It's not fair," I remember howling, no doubt stomping my foot, "my Hebrew is way better than Heschie's!"

"The world hasn't yet caught up with you my darling," maman cooed, trying to sooth me. "It will. Eventually."

As soon as I graduated to the big cello I felt the vibrations of the strings into my bones, even my inner bones, into my organs, all the way through. It was as if the whole instrument took me over. I loved to play with my eyes closed, just to listen to where the sound landed and feel it washing over me, an ocean of low notes. There was a lot of music, which never made sense to me, written for the high end of the cello. That's for the violins, I always thought, and I would search for something else to practice.

I think it must be that childhood spent playing the cello that changed my ears so I could hear the whales sing to me, talk to me.

3 September 1973

A rare treat today! And much needed after a very trying week. Sid started her preschool at Temple Sholom—and it's been very rough on both of us. On the first day she cried, and I cried. I tried not to let her see my tears but she did. After a few awful, puffy-eyed drop-offs we've both grudgingly gotten used to it and I think it's good for her to play with other kids. And it's good for me to be able to dig deeper into my research. But I feel as though my arm has been cut off. As my treat, my consolation prize, I accompanied Aaron to the Rare Book Room today and so enjoyed perusing nineteenth century cetological marvels, something I hadn't been able to do until Sid started preschool. I miss her so much, but I'm trying to treasure my freedom. I found out today that even Henry William Dewhurst, in his 1834 book, *The Natural History of the Order of Cetacea,* already knew that whales could communicate. Dewhurst noticed that in areas where heavy whaling took place, the whales tended to vacate and find spaces less accessible to the harpooners. From this he concluded, "that whales possessed the power in the species to transmit the results of experience from one generation to another."

I cannot quite understand why all the scientists after him seemed to refuse to know this, as if they'd signed some sort of idiot pact. I think, actually, they did know but they didn't know how to interpret that knowledge and their worldview didn't allow them to see the full truth about how developed whales have become. Dewhurst also noted that, "with all its enormous physical strength, the whale is singularly gentle and harmless...the creature is possessed of considerable sagacity."

5 October 1974

The more I learn, the more amazed I grow. Whales have been on the planet for millions of years, before those dinosaurs Sid is already learning about. But I will teach her all about whales, she needs to know that they developed echolocation and communicated with each other across all the oceans of the world. And yet our newspapers are full of articles expressing surprise at how smart they are. Ridiculous.

Scientists and speculators have been stumped as to why the early 20th century harpoon fanatics were so intent on destroying the blue whales. It often happened that they would manage to kill one of them—not an easy task—only to gasp as their beautiful, giant, corpses sank to the bottom of the sea, taking the harpooner's precious oil with them. All those fires, those outrageous hurricanes, the melting polar ice caps, whales have the power to help us…if only we'd learn to listen.

And yet, for so long, whale oil provided the light to brighten the dark and dismal nights of the pre-electric world. It was the crucial liquid that made vast machines run, cleansed people—whale soap was all the rage—fed people—whale margarine was unbelievably popular—not to mention whale meat. For centuries we tried to destroy the very creatures we need most.

The oceans warm as humans excessively use fossil fuels and other planetary pollutants. But whales, if left alone! would allow crucial nutrients to move through the world's oceans, they absorb enormous amounts of carbon, in short, we need them for a healthy planet and meanwhile, during the horrid era of mammoth whaling, harpooners invented exploding harpoons to kill them, even blue whale mothers, swollen with child, were murdered in this way. It was unspeakably violent, so unprovoked, and so utterly shocking. And now, yes, it's true, whales are generally venerated. But the scholarship on whales is, well, hilarious really. It's 96% speculation and intensely vague. We struggle to categorize them, to measure them, to weigh them, to calculate their trajectories, to count them, to chase them, even if, now, mostly but not entirely, to subject them to the scientific gaze rather than to the harpoon. But we have not yet really tried to understand them. To just listen to them.

5 December 1974

The search for the mysteries of the whales, I've concluded, is like looking for the keys to the universe. Everything comes back to them. Cetologists have found whale fossils in the Atacama Desert, in Chile, and from these giant bones have discovered a huge amount they had not previously known. I'm afraid I drive Aaron bonkers with my constant irritation while reading the newspapers; I find article after article expressing surprise at the intense intelligence of sea creatures:

"Manta Ray Invites Diver to Help Remove Fish Hooks" read one headline, as if anyone should be surprised that the Manta Ray recognized the diver and figured out that his small prehensile hands could get rid of those excruciating hooks! "Whales Seem to Communicate Via Sonic Waves" was another favorite of mine to bash, as if that were news.

I often scrunch up the paper and throw it on the table with just enough emphasis to create tiny ripples in my coffee. Honestly, I want to say to the editors of those newspapers, of course whales communicate! They have a complex language millennia old that we could understand if only we designated resources to research it instead of looking for ever more fossil fuels with which to destroy our delicate planet and its mighty oceans!

Whales talk to each other using songs and other sounds, and they travel great distances, further, really, than we can even imagine. The magisterial big blues were almost exterminated during the melancholy times of whaling, and many scientists are not quite sure why these terrible things happened. It seemed like a driven genocidal urge, almost intentional. Before the whaling companies figured out how to add unspeakably violent torture devices such as grenades and gigantic hooks to the harpoons, many blues were killed and their enormous, peaceful bodies sank to the bottom of the sea without reason and without the whalers even taking their flesh for margarine and oil. It was senseless, senseless, irrational, and so intensely destructive!

Many cetologists who have found out all they can about whale fossils, have now switched the direction of their research and begun spending more and more time off dry land, away from fossils, in the ocean, in a wet suit, with a tank on, breathing underwater as if they sported gills.

3 August 1975

The cello, I think, helped me understand how low tones connect with whale song. I've begun posting elaborate charts and graphs up along the walls, and I'm afraid it's driving Aaron a bit crazy.

The lowest note on the cello, I told him today, is 65.4 hz—whale song generally swims between ten and forty hz, so, much lower. But, I asked him, perhaps a trifle too impatiently, just stop typing for one second and come and look at this, please?

At my pleading, Aaron rose up from the typewriter and shuffled over to peer at my drawings: look at this chart, I said, while a divergence persists between the frequencies, notice the rotation here—there is a definite musical pattern in the whale song, just like on the cello—do you see...But by then Aaron had wandered back to the typewriter so he hadn't necessarily heard me. Or at least it seemed to me as though he had not or could not hear.

But my research is finally being noticed. I was able to publish an article in *Science* and from this, a reporter from a radio station contacted me. I was so excited to share the transcript with Aaron and when Sid heard the broadcast she jumped up and down and clapped her hands and pointed to the radio.

Dorothy Zimmerman interviewed by Jenni Frankel, Fort Point, San Francisco, Pacifica Radio

Jenni: Here we are on a glorious, strangely sunny San Francisco day—remember what Mark Twain said (or maybe didn't say), "The coldest winter I ever spent was a summer in San Francisco?"—out at Fort Point in the beautiful shadow of the Golden Gate Bridge. My guest today is Dorothy Zimmerman, whale communication expert. We're talking about humpback whales and why they might have returned to the Bay Area. But first, a little background. Dorothy, can you tell us why you became obsessed—is that the right word?—with these charismatic mammals?

Dorothy: Jenni, thank you so much for inviting me to be part of the program. I am from Québec and, when I was about seven my family took a trip up to see the whales—we were on a little dinghy with a cetologist who was a colleague of my father's. I remember being quite shocked—I had heard of whales, of course, Jonah and all that, we'd learned about him in school, but the size and the grace... and yes, quite right, "Obsession" is the word I would use. But really the major change for me was seeing, when I was pregnant with our daughter, the Hovhaness shockingly beautiful piece performed by the New York Philharmonic of *And God Created Whales.* From that moment on I knew I wanted to study these animals even more intensely and I've tried to learn all I can. But one thing we humans always forget is that what we know about whales is either a) wrong or b) totally incomplete. There is so much more to learn!

And I firmly believe they are more complex and advanced than we can even guess.

Jenni: In what ways do you think they are advanced?

Dorothy: So many ways! Humpbacks, for example—and, by the way, we might just see one from here—your listeners might be able to hear them singing. I've been to Fort Point this time of year a couple of other times with my binoculars just to watch them, or, more germanely, to hear them; anyway, humpbacks hunt together, as a group. They make these air bubbles—we call it bubble-netting because the bubbles attract the fish—when I saw them hunt this way they were catching herring. Then the humpbacks form a circle and one of them sings a song that acts like a magnet to draw the herring in and then they all enjoy a hearty dinner. So, we humans see this and often express amazement that the whales have organized methods of hunting. The joke, I feel is on us. If whales could read what we say about them in our scientific articles they would laugh! Of course, they might say with emphasis, we have a society, a culture, a civilization that is, oh you know, around 50 million years old—give or take.

Jenni: Wow, I had no idea they hunted like that—I thought whales just filtered krill? And I had no idea they were so old.

Dorothy: Yes, certainly, some whales, blue whales, for example, do filter krill through their giant mouths using a filtration system called baleen. Think of an enormous comb. Basically, baleen whales let a huge amount of water, some of it containing small animals, filter through the baleen and what gets caught there becomes their nutrition. It has always fascinated me, the scale of this operation: here, the largest animals on our planet survive by eating some of the smallest. There is something neat about that. And perhaps also a bit strange.

Jenni: Yes, strange indeed! Now, Dorothy, can you please tell us why—or why you think—the humpbacks have been appearing here in the Bay Area lately?

Dorothy: I truthfully believe the humpbacks have been here all along. They just have not been trying to be seen, or maybe even trying to communicate with us, until relatively recently. Standing right here one day I saw a humpback breach up and as she did, she sang. It was a beautiful, moving song—it would have made Itzhak Perlman weep—I felt, and honestly, I know this sounds hokey, but I felt that she was singing to me, to us, she was trying to tell me something. I have been trying to figure out what they are all singing to us.

Jenni: So, Dorothy, let me get this straight: you think the whales are talking to the humans and we don't understand them?

Dorothy: Yes, certainly, I do.

4 August 1977

Maman told me years ago that the d'Espinosa family legend stretched all the way back to Portuguese settlers who arrived in New Bedford in the 1800s, then eventually made their way, through a distant cousin, to Montréal. Maman is with Aaron in Chicago, helping to look after Sid, while I'm here at the New Bedford Historical Society. I've begun to suspect that our ancestors might have been part of the whaling trade in some way, and so I feel guilty, and dirty. But now I've dug up the unfortunate discovery that confirmed my worse fears. I knew that my great grandfather was a crypto-Jew who left Portugal and arrived via the portal of Ellis Island, and then onto New Bedford, to join his brother who ran a shop there. What maman and I couldn't know was what sort of shop or really anything else about the family. I thought there might only be small, dusty, narrow, grains of truth that might be found in the archive, not this huge leviathan weight of fear knotting my stomach, making breathing hard.

The Historical Society is a tiny house on Water Street encircled by a permanent bevvy of seagulls; the white paint on the outside looks very much like it needs a new, glossy, coat and the stairs creak as you go up. The inside feels uncannily bigger than the outside and, naturally, chock full of books and papers and records—so full with so much stuff that they installed a storage trailer at the back.

Hello, I said to the clerk sitting at the old wooden desk, *I am looking for information on my family, last name d'Espinosa.*

Well, the clerk with the tweed skirt (despite the elevated heat of the day) replied, *what sort of information?*

I don't know much about them, you see, and I would like to know more. Specifically, I research whales and their amazing communicative capacities and, well, I am slightly worried that one of my d'Espinosa ancestors was a whaler.

And?

I beg your pardon?

And, I mean if your ancestor had been a whaler, then what? New Bedford was chock full of whalers a hundred years ago— you couldn't so much as swing a cat without hitting a whaler, so chances are good.

Well, then I would have even more reason to save the whales, to right a wrong.

With a skeptical look in my direction, the clerk turned to the card-file cabinet and looked up d'Espinosa.

Please take a seat at table twelve. I will bring you what we have.

As I breathed a sigh of relief I also inhaled ancient dust that made me cough and sneeze and long for the open ocean. I was planning on taking a whale watching boat from the harbor that afternoon, and as I waited I wondered why I wanted this knowledge, why I wasn't on a boat already. I looked up at the worn thick timber that held the roof over head for the last one hundred and fifty years or so and wondered briefly where the great trees that were felled to make this little house had come from. Here by the sea? Or brought over from somewhere else in New England? I mused whether this house, before it became the historical society, belonged to a whaler, or was fueled by whale lamps? Did the inhabitants wear whale corsets? Did they shield themselves from the rain with umbrellas made from whalebones and wash themselves with whale soap? I will need to tell Sid about this horrible era of whale-product reliance, when she is old enough.

A small cough from the clerk interrupted my thoughts; she returned with a cart on which were piled three big brown boxes, labeled d'Espinosa 1, 2, 3.

Here you are. Good luck.

And with that she turned on her heel and returned to her perch at the front desk. She sat down, looked down her nose through her small rectangular reading glasses and picked up her place in *Portrait of a Lady*.

What a load of boring papers, I thought, at first. Penned receipts for dresses bought at the local shop, scraps of paper with words in Ladino that I could not read, announcements of weddings and Bar Mitzvahs.

And then, after about two hours of perusing the boxes, just when I was about to give up, I found the unwelcome evidence. The wrong evidence, exactly what I did not want to find.

D'Espinosa Brothers' Whaling Outfitters. Corner of Fair and Bolton Streets

Stop on by and pick up everything you need to go a whalin'!

There were other ads too, like this one: **D'Espinosa Brothers': Looking for a new hat? Pheasant Plumage is a Very Popular Trimming in Paris!**

Or this one: **D'Espinosa Brothers': Loose a button, come on in and get your Cortelli Silk right here! Spermaceti candles galore!**

I set the advertisements down in front of me and stared out the small, glazed window. It was a general store, they stocked everything from giant harpoons to delicate needles. So, they, my ancestors, were not spearing the charismatic animals I've dedicated my life to comprehending. But they supplied the materials to do that, seemingly without qualm. They were more than witnesses, they were more than innocent bystanders, they were enablers implicated in the gruesome history of one of the worst genocides the planet has known.

To add insult to injury, I found out that our family brought the "recipe" for spermaceti candles from Portugal to New Bedford. These candles are crafted from material inside the heads of sperm whales, for the wealthy who liked their special bright, long burn so they could read late into the night.

I thanked the librarian for her help, even though she was a bit snippy.

Did you find anything interesting? she queried.

Yes, thank you, I did. My great- grandfather and great-great uncle had a store around here, D'Espinosa Brothers' and they sold whaling gear. Excuse me, please, I feel a little ill, and I am going to walk over and see where it was.

I felt I needed air to erase the stain of this unwelcome discovery. I am planning to walk down Water Street, past the Spouter Inn, then turn left on Second, to Bolton to the former site of D'Espinosa Brothers' Whaling Outfitters, which, looking at the map, would now be at Kaplan Square, which I remember held a memorial to a soldier at the center. I am going to phone Aaron on the way and say hello to Sid—she's no doubt being spoiled rotten by my mother. God, I miss her. Then I will wander out to the harbor, where hopefully a captain will let me commandeer a small dinghy so that I can float out to sea and listen to the whales singing to me.

IX Yahrzeit

Sid's glowing. She gets that shiny skin and, after a few weeks of nausea, ginger ale and saltines, she's fine. Bigger by the minute, and yet, somehow calmer than I've ever seen her. And the effect is gorgeous, her skin so sensitive to my touch. I had not allowed myself to metabolize fully how agitated and unsettled it was making me, the annual contract, the uncertainty with me and Sid. The endless unknown of Dorothy. I know, Nietzsche, you're right, there are no guarantees. No real anchors. Just stories, myths. But still, I want to enjoy this surety, so stop rocking the boat. Thanks.

William's friend does an incredible job mounting Sid's photos. He seems to intuit where all the portraits should go and the effect, when you walk into the Enderby Gallery, is breathtaking. The gallery feels like the start of something exciting, perched as it is in a growing row of pop ups in the West Loop. There's a small stack of Xeroxed notices awaiting anyone who enters, if they sell like fresh seaweed, as I anticipate they will, I'll pen my introduction to Sid's antiracist photos, Luzzatto edition.

*

In our living room in the sun, as I place my ear up to Sid's bellybutton and her warm skin heats mine, I can feel you kicking and I imagine that you're swimming around in there, wishing for more space.

You are going to be a force to be reckoned with, I guess, the way you kick at your mama. We're naming you Almondine, combining the L in my mother's name with the A and D of your maternal grandparents. It will be up to you to fashion your path, I suppose. Oh the places we're going to take you! First to Guadeloupe to meet your grandfather and auntie Marguerite, then to Québec to Esther's great house (and of course we'll show you off to William), and then to New York, all around the East Village, to the darkroom, and to see Michael Gruber in the West Village and Greta uptown, we'll take you to Paolo's museum in a loft in Soho, we'll take you to great-Auntie Thérèse in Brooklyn, we'll hold hands below the Great Whale on the ceiling of the Natural History Museum. And when, fut-fut-phoo as Esther or Greta would say, it's time for your Bat Mitzvah here at Temple Sholom, then, and only then, us unbelievers will give you the unbound Hebrew bible gifted to your grandfather. And with it, the Tefillin and the tiny Torah pendant on a gold chain. You'll already be wearing the three gold bangles my mother wore until her last day, when she gave them to me to give to you.

We light candles thrice a year now, one for my mother, one for Aaron, and the final one for Dorothy. Sid was able to mourn, finally, after the diary.

On Aaron's yahrzeit we stroll over to the lake and gaze out at the water. Sid's belly leads the way. We bring a thick, multicolored blanket made up of *little parti-colored squares and triangles*—it's nearly November in Chicago. A light snow falls as Sid burrows into me for warmth and we huddle under the quilt on the empty shore. A bubble floats to the surface and the face of a large fish flashes up, looks right at us, and swims away, tail swishing.

Rare Stuff
Discussion Questions

1) What do the clues in the suitcase each represent?

2) Why do you think Sid keeps breaking up with André?

3) What do Sid and André learn about Aaron as they are looking for Dorothy?

4) How do you think Sid's personality was changed by having grown up with this mystery hanging over her?

5) What do you think of Sid's photography project? Have you seen a photography collection like hers?

6) What did you expect Aaron's manuscript, *Slobgollion*, to be like and how was it the same or different than your expectations?

7) How important are the settings in this novel? Did you have a strong sense of place as you were reading?

8) What did you think of the novel's multiple narrators, multiple voices?

9) If you've ever mourned anyone, does the way that Aaron keeps popping into Sid's head resonate with you?

10) If you had to pick based on the "book reviews" within the novel, which of Aaron Zimmerman's books would you most like to read?

I did not write this book alone. From the very beginning, when I started hand-writing the whale sections in a notebook, my daughter Anya was my constant interlocutor. At bus stops in Chicago, at the café at the Art Institute, in our own backyard in Champaign, over dinner, we talked and talked and I asked her for suggestions. Many of the most innovative ideas, including the plaque inside the whale's mouth at the Museum of Natural History and the water slide down all sixty stories of the Hancock Tower, came from her wonderful imagination. She also, very kindly, read an early draft of the whole book and offered suggestions. As Aditi said to Akira and Sol: I am in debt. My daughter Mel, to whom I am also in debt, helped me shape Sol's voice and not only took the photographs in the book but accompanied me to the wonderful Rare Book & Manuscript Library at the University of Illinois to insert into an antique typewriter a "cover page" of Aaron Zimmerman's manuscript, *Slobgollion*. Mel also spent untold hours generously creating my website. My step-son Orestes read the beginning and offered much-needed encouragement. My husband, Philip Phillips, read the whole manuscript in early draft form and gave me many invaluable suggestions for revision. A theoretical physicist, he was the unofficial consultant for all the fantastically impossible worlds herein, anchoring my ratios and isotopes. He has a keen eye and a beautiful, big, heart. Love.

This book would not have been possible without a University of Illinois LAS Study in a Second Discipline Fellowship. I am extremely grateful to Janice Harrington, then head of Creative Writing, and Rob Rushing, Bob Markley, and Martin Camargo for making it possible for me to receive this fabulous opportunity to work on this novel for a year under the tutelage of Creative

Writing faculty David Wright Faladé, Alex Shakar, and Ted Sanders, all brilliant writers, readers, and commentators. David has been a key player in helping me understand the nuts and bolts of writing and publishing; he helped me think through timing and the process of publication and carefully read many sections of this book. His sage and sometimes difficult suggestions have improved my writing immeasurably; I cannot wait to read *Black Cloud Rising*. Alex offered feedback on an excerpt that got me thinking quite differently about André, and then worked with me during an independent study on this book and my next novel, *Vandervelde Downs*. Ted is an insightful, careful reader who always found ways to make the writing more present. His incredibly sage suggestions have helped me immeasurably on this and the next novel. Rick Powers offered a warm and encouraging response when I told him the good news that I had been granted a fellowship to study creative writing; his brilliant novels continue to inspire and engage me. Amy Hassinger and I had lunch and she talked me through the process as did Patricia Hruby; Patricia generously read the synopsis and then gave me a beautiful gift: her book, *Loving v. Virginia* which I highly recommend.

All members of two fiction workshops I had the honor of participating in are owed much gratitude and appreciation for their incisive comments: Azlan Smith, Chris Vanjonack, Erin Hoffman, Maddy Furlong, Elizabeth Boyle, Vi Aldunate, Drew Jennings, Eric Schumacher. I would also like to thank Corinna da Fonseca-Wollheim and, again Azlan, who introduced Corinna and me and we three formed an auxiliary workshop that proved enormously generative. I thank Jodee Stanley for inviting me to be part of the *Ninth Letter* team during my fellowship year. Thank you all endlessly.

The editors at Spuyten Duyvil, especially Aurelia, t thilleman and Heather, have been so intensely wonderful! They seemed to "get" this book in ways that made me stop for breath with joy.

Brenda Thompson has been an absolute delight to work with. She understood what I was trying to do intuitively and has catalyzed this book's launch into the world with grace, good humor, diligence, and dedication. Thank you!

I am immensely grateful to Caroline Szylowicz, Curator and Kolb-Proust Librarian, for her gracious and generous help securing Carl Sandburg's typewriter for its photo shoot (it appears here as Aaron's typewriter). The index card for the typewriter stored in the Rare Book & Manuscript library reads: "Champlain, Helene. Typewriter on which Sandburg typed articles which later were compiled into the book HOMEFRONT MEMO in Miss Champlain's apartment." More generally the library at the University of Illinois has furnished an ocean's worth of interesting books, some rare, and offered much-appreciated help over the years, and I am so grateful to be able to access its collections.

It was over a lovely lunch that my friend Rob Rushing suggested that the whales speak Yiddish; I said something to him along these lines: "the whales are trying to communicate but they can't get through," at which point, without missing a beat, Rob said, "they're speaking Yiddish, of course!" Of course. And so they are. Thank you, Rob, for that wonderfully quirky insight, and for sending images for the amazing cover design. Early on I texted Jamie Jones, a brilliant Melville scholar and fantastic writer, to ask her for a good Melvillian word to title the inner novel; a few minutes later, a new word arrived in my phone: Slobgollion. Jamie was an early champion of the project and gave me such warm encouragement when I was just starting that I remain forever grateful to her; she read the entire manuscript and wrote a gorgeous response, full of helpful suggestions. I still keep her letter on my desktop and flip it open often for encouragement. Jamie also helped me name the villain, Drake Barents. Her husband, Eric Calderwood, my colleague and friend, read the whole book and supplied enormously generous, helpful and thoughtful feedback in a multi-page single-spaced document. My friend and fellow creative writer, Jim Hansen, and I have been exchanging writing and we decided early on, taking a cue from *Casablanca,* that it was the continuation of a beautiful friendship: Jim's careful readings and feedback have improved my book immeasurably and, along with Renée Trilling's cheerful encouragement, has been most welcome. My writing group, Lilya Kaganovsky, Anke Pinkert, and Justine Murison, offered extremely keen and helpful feedback on early sections of the novel and on the synopsis. Lilya texted me a video of the amazing Hovhaness concert that Dorothy, pregnant with Sid, becomes enraptured by in the summer of 1970. This glowing writing group has been a source of much appreciated sustenance for many years, and I hope we'll continue to be friends and writing helpers for a long time to come.

Martin Srajek helped me create the the conditions of possibility necessary to catalyze this book, and for that and many other things, I am truly grateful.

Several friends, family members, and colleagues offered invaluable encouragement, some just in passing, some much more substantial. But, making a very late career switch from academic writing to fiction was accompanied by the need for loads of support. I have been so lucky in my friendships, and in my colleagues at Illinois and elsewhere, some for many years, and others much more recently. Everyone here encouraged or supported me in ways big and small—but ways that matter to me and I am full of gratitude. Thank you (alphabetical by first name): A.B. Huber, Adam Sutcliffe and Nadia Valman, Allison Thrush and Art Chang, Allyson Purpura, Amy Powell, Ania Loomba and Suvir Kaul, Antoinette Burton, Audrey Petty and Maurice Raab, Ayelet Ben-Yishai and Ofer Shorr, Ayelet Tsabari, Beth Benedix, Bruce Rosenstock, Carol Inskeep, Catharine Gray, Cathy

Prendergast and John Tubbs, Caitlin Lewis, Cecile Steinberg, Chris Freeburg, Chris Lee, Cynthia Oliver and Jason Finkelman, Dana Rabin, Dara Goldman, David Brauner, Deb Grant, Debarti Sanyal, Deke Weaver and Jennifer Allen, Frederick Hunter, Gillen Wood and Nancy Castro, Harriet Murav, Hina Nazar and Gian Castartelli, Holly and Carmella Phillips, Jean-Philippe Mathy, Janice Weintraub, Jenny Mercer, Jesse Ribot, Jessica Greenberg and Marc Doussard, Jordana Mendelson, Judith Butler, Julia Harrington, Kim Curtis and John Randolph, Krin Gabbard, Lara Weitzman, Laura Levitt, Liz Lassner and Robin Cohen, Marianne Hirsch and Leo Spitzer, Manuel Rota and Nora Stoppino, Maria Gillombardo, Melissa Stein, Mia Spiro, Michael Rothberg and Yasemin Yildiz, Mikhal Dekel, Nafissa Thompson-Spires and Derrick Spires, Nancy Blake, Nancy Kricorian, Paul Lewis and Ali Muckersie, Pauly Pagenhart and Jennifer Boesing, Peter Balakian, Rebecca Mercer and Stephen Holland, Ruby Namdar, Ruth, David, Leah, and Rebecca Reynolds, Sayed Kashua, Stef Craps, Stephanie and Jeremy Mays, Steven Zipperstein, Yasmin Mohsenzadeh.

My mother Ann and step-father, Marty, have been exceedingly generous and have always encouraged my writing and for this I am infinitely grateful. My mother is a wonder and a fabulous, energetic writer—an inspiration.

This novel is dedicated to my father, Ralph Kaplan. May his memory be for a blessing.

Author royalties for the print edition will be donated to the Whale and Dolphin Conservation. If you are able, I hope you might consider donating to help protect these magical animals who help protect our oceans and air: https://us.whales.org

Bibliography

Borges, Jorge Luis. "Funes, His Memory." 1942 ("Funes el memorioso"). *Collected Fictions of Jorge Luis Borges.* Trans. Andrew Hurley. New York: Penguin Press, 1999.

Bortolotti, Dan. *Wild Blue: A Natural History of the World's Largest Animal.* Thomas Allen Publishers, 2009.

Clifton, Lucille. "the earth is a living thing." https://poets.org/poem/earth-living-thing

Derrida, Jacques. *La carte postale, de Socrate à Freud et au-delà.* Paris : Flammarion, 1980. Trans. Alan Bass. *The Post Card : From Socrates to Freud and Beyond.* Chicago & London : University of Chicago Press, 1987.

Dewhurst, Henry William. *The Natural History of the Order of Cetacea, and the Oceanic Inhabitants of the Arctic Regions.* Published by the author, 1834.

Eliot, T.S. "The Love Song of Alfred J. Prufrock." 1915. *The Waste Land and Other Poems.* New York: Harvest Books, 1934.

Higgins, Brian and Hershel Parker, eds. *Herman Melville: The Contemporary Reviews.* Cambridge: Cambridge University Press, 1995.

hooks, bell. "Choosing the Margin as a Space of Radical Openness." *Framework: The Journal of Cinema and Media,* No. 36 (1989): pp. 15-23.

Gabel, Kurt, *The Making of a Paratrooper.* University Press of Kansas, 2015.

Farrar, Judy and Cynthia Yoken, *Historical Tour of Jewish New Bedford.* University Library and the Center for Jewish Culture, University of Massachusetts, Dartmouth, 2005.

Faulkner, William. *Requiem for a Nun.* New York: Random House, 1950.

James, C. L. R. 1952. *Mariners, Renegades, and Castaways: The Story of Herman Melville and the World we Live in.* Hanover, NH: Dartmouth College Press, 2001.

Kramer, Stanley, dir. *Guess Who's Coming to Dinner.* 1967, Columbia Pictures.

Melville, Herman. 1851. *Moby-Dick*. New York: Barnes & Noble Books, 1993.

Morrison, Toni. "Unspeakable Things Unspoken: The Afro-American Presence in American Literature." The Tanner Lectures on Human Values. Delivered at The University of Michigan, October 7, 1988.

—, *Jazz*. New York: Penguin, 1993.

Nietzsche, Friedrich. "Truth and Falsity in an Ultramoral Sense," *The Philosophy of Nietzsche*. Edited by Geoffrey Clive. New York: Signet Classics, 1965.

Peretz, I. L. "Bontshe shvayg" ("Bontsche the Silent") 1894. Trans. Hillel Halkin. *The I.L. Peretz Reader,* ed. and introduced by Ruth R. Wisse. New Haven: Yale University Press, 2002. Pp. 146-152.

Pound, Ezra. "In a Station of the Metro." 1913. *The Selected Poems of Ezra Pound*. New York: New Directions, 1956.

Pyenson, Nick, *Spying on Whales: The Past, Present, and Future of the Earth's Most Awesome Creatures*. New York: Viking, 2018.

Woolf, Virginia. 1927. *To the Lighthouse*. New York: Harcourt Brace Jovanovich, 1955.

Citations from the above editions as follows:

Herman Melville, *Moby-Dick*:
"But not yet have we solved the incantation of this whiteness…" (Chapter 42, p. 164).

"The chief mate of the Pequod was Starbuck, a native of Nantucket…" (Chapter 26, p. 94).

"The White Whale swam before him…" (Chapter 41, p. 154).

"Gnawed within and scorched without, with the infixed, unrelenting fangs…" (Chapter 41, p. 156).

"There is another substance..." (Chapter 94, p. 352)

"little parti-colored squares and triangles" (Chapter 4, p. 21).

All citations from reviews of *Moby-Dick* are in Higgins and Parker, eds. *John Bull* 25 October 1851, *Literary Gazette* [London] 6 December 1851, p. 393; p. 357; *Evening Traveller* 15 November 1851, p. 374-75; *Weekly News and Chronicle* 29 November 1851, p. 389.

Virginia Woolf, *To the Lighthouse*:
"life, from being made up of little separate incidents..." (p. 73).

bell hooks, "Choosing,"
"Then home is no longer just one place..." (p. 19)

Friedrich Nietzsche:
"What therefore is truth? A mobile army of metaphors, metonymies, anthropomorphisms: in short a sum of human relations which became poetically and rhetorically intensified, metamorphosed, adorned...truths are illusions of which one has forgotten that they *are* illusions" (p. 508).

William Faulkner, *Requiem for a Nun*
"The past is never dead. It's not even past."
Act 1, Scene III, p. 92

T.S. Eliot, "The Love Song of Alfred J. Prufrock,"
Aaron's epigraph to *Slobgollion*:
"I have seen them riding seaward..." (p. 9)

Maimie quotes Eliot: "And time yet for a hundred indecisions/
And for a hundred visions and revisions" (p.4)

Lucille Clifton, "the earth is a living thing"
gratefully reprinted with permission from BOA Editions

André is thinking of this, from Toni Morrison, *Jazz*:
"That the past was an abused record with no choice but to repeat itself at the crack and no power on earth could lift the arm that held the needle" (p. 220).

Jacques Derrida:
"une lettre..." (p. 39).
Alan Bass' translation : " that a letter can always not arrive at its destination, and that therefore it never arrives. And this is really how it is, it is not a misfortune, that's life, living life, beaten down, tragedy, by the still surviving life" (p. 33-34).

Dorothy quotes Dewhurst, from the edtion in the University of Illinois Rare Book & Manuscript Library:
"that whales possessed..." (p. 83).
"with all its enormous physical strength..." (p. 82).

Caroline McKinzie

Brett Ashley Kaplan Directs the Initiative in Holocaust, Genocide, Memory Studies at the University of Illinois where she is a professor of Comparative and World Literature and Director of Graduate Studies. She publishes in Haaretz, The Conversation, Salon.com (picked up from Conversation), Asitoughttobemagazine, AJS Perspectives, Contemporary Literature, Edge Effects, and The Jewish Review of Books. She has been interviewed on NPR, the AJS Podcast, and The 21st, and is the author of *Unwanted Beauty, Landscapes of Holocaust Postmemory*, and *Jewish Anxiety and the Novels of Philip Roth*. She's the editor of the forthcoming *Critical Memory Studies: New Approaches,* and co-editor (with Sara Feldman and Anthony Russell) of the volume in progress, *Blewish: Contemporary Black-Jewish Voices.* She's at work on a second novel, *Vandervelde Downs,* about the recovery of Nazi-looted objects found in a Vietnamese Refugee Center in provincial England. Please see brettashleykaplan.com for more information.

Printed in Great Britain
by Amazon

28572180R00202